IN PREHISTORY, a girl picks up a charred stick
and makes the first written signs.

TENS OF CENTURIES LATER, the treacherous waters
of Golden Beck take Anna, whom people call a witch.

AT THE BEGINNING OF THE TWENTIETH CENTURY,
in the halls of a Long Island hospital, a mad poet watches
the ocean and knows the horrors it hides.

AND THERE IN THE FAR FUTURE, an astronaut faces
his destiny on the first spaceship sent from Earth
to colonize another world.

ALSO BY MARCUS SEDGWICK:

The GHOSTS of HEAVEN

MARCUS SEDGWICK

SQUARE
FISH

ROARING BROOK PRESS
NEW YORK

SQUARE
FISH

An imprint of Macmillan Publishing Group, LLC
175 Fifth Avenue
New York, NY 10010
fiercereads.com

Square Fish books may be purchased for business or promotional use.
For information on bulk purchases, please contact the Macmillan Corporate
and Premium Sales Department at (800) 221-7945 x5442 or by e-mail at
specialmarkets@macmillan.com.

Sedgwick, Marcus.
    Ghosts of heaven / Marcus Sedgwick.
        pages cm
    "First published in the United Kingdom in 2014 by Orion Children's Books, London."
    Summary: Four linked stories of discovery and survival begin with a Paleolithic-era
girl who makes the first written signs, continue with Anna, who people call a witch,
then a mad twentieth-century poet who watches the ocean knowing the horrors it hides,
and concluding with an astronaut on the first spaceship from Earth sent to colonize
another world.
    ISBN 978-1-62672-125-8 (hardback) — ISBN 978-1-62672-126-5 (e-book) —
ISBN 978-1-250-07367-9 (trade paperback) [1. Space and time—Fiction.   2. Science
fiction]   I. Title.
    PZ7.S4484Gho 2015
    [Fic]—dc23
                                                                        2014040471

Originally published in the United States by Roaring Brook Press
First Square Fish Edition: 2016
Book designed by Elizabeth Clark
Square Fish logo designed by Filomena Tuosto

1   3   5   7   9   10   8   6   4   2

AR: 6.1 / LEXILE: 920L

Und die nie der Sonne lachten,
Unterm Mond auf Dornen wachten.

spiral (noun) from Latin *spira*, and Greek *speira*, "a coil." from Proto Indo-European *sper*, "to turn, to twist."

1. A spiral line, course, or object. **2.** A two-dimensional curve, the locus of a point whose distance from a fixed point varies according to some rule as the radius vector revolves. **3.** A continuous rise or fall, as of prices, for example. **4.** A helix (nontechnical use).

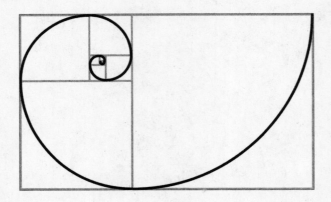

helix (noun) from Latin *helix* "spiral."

from Greek *helix* related to *eilein*, "to turn, twist, roll."

from Proto Indo-European *wel-ik-*, from root *wel-* "to turn, revolve."

1. A screw-shaped coil. **2.** A curve on a developable surface, especially a right circular cylinder that becomes a straight line when unrolled into a plane.

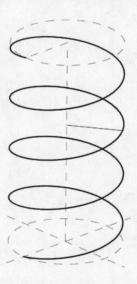

INTRODUCTION

GENERATIONS OF STARS LIVED AND DIED.

Around 4,600 million years ago, the death of one of these stars, in a supernova, causes a shockwave to hit a vast molecular cloud, or nebula, made of dust and gas. Words cannot describe how large this nebula is. Only numbers can; it would take a particle of light sixty-five years to cross it.

The shockwave triggers a reaction in the nebula; the dust particles within it are drawn together and as they collide and stick together, so their gravitational attraction causes more and more material to coalesce, so that now a small part of the cloud starts to collapse and spin. Over the course of the next 100,000 years, the competing forces of gravity, pressure, magnetism, and rotation creates the beginnings of the Solar System; the vast majority of matter forms at the center of this spinning disc, the Sun. Around it revolves a mess of gas and dust that will, as tens of millions of years pass, form the planets.

The Solar System at this time is cluttered and chaotic; an overcrowded maelstrom of rocky planets, gas giants, moons, and asteroids all hurtling through clouds of dust and gas left over from the Sun's formation. Collisions are inevitable, and they occur.

About 4,500 million years ago, a giant body the size of Mars hits the newly forming Earth. Known as Theia, it slews into the proto-planet at an oblique angle; most of its matter fuses with the Earth. Its iron core sinks to join with the iron core of Earth; but a significant amount of the crusts of both planets is flung back into space where it becomes our Moon.

The impact of Theia proves critical to our existence.

The Solar System is bathed in electromagnetic radiation given off by the Sun, deadly to most forms of life—certainly to human beings, but the iron core of Earth is larger than it would have otherwise been, large enough to remain hot and liquid. The warm liquid rises and falls in strong convection currents within the Earth's core, which, together with the Earth's high rotational speed, gives the planet a powerful magnetic field. It is this magnetic field that repels the great majority of the radiation, sending the charged particles back out into space, or spiralling down the lines of magnetism to the poles of the Earth, where they collide with the atmosphere, causing the Northern Lights, and their southern counterpart.

The impact of Theia also causes a wobble in the Earth's rotation—it is this wobble that gives us our seasons; spring to summer to autumn to winter; and yet it is also the continuing presence of the Moon after the collision that stabilizes the Earth's motion. Without which the variation in temperature between our seasons would be much greater, lurching between extremes of hot and cold that could make our life here impossible.

A period of relative peace arrives, but then around 500 million years later, the gravitational effects of Jupiter and Saturn not only move Neptune and Pluto farther out into space, but also start to influence the uncountable number of asteroids in orbit. Many are pushed out into deep space, but some are propelled into the inner Solar System, colliding with the Earth and the Moon.

As the Earth is struck again and again, the temperature of our planet's surface rises high enough to melt rock, turning our home into a deadly hell. Yet the Late Heavy Bombardment, as it is known, dies away relatively rapidly. In its wake comes a steady trickle of impacts with icy comets and asteroids. These deliver water to Earth from the outer, colder regions of the Solar System; water that will form the oceans. And they also deliver something else; organic compounds, from which the development of life itself is possible.

The Late Heavy Bombardment would have almost certainly eradicated any life on Earth that existed at the time; and yet, the earliest forms of life we have discovered, simple cells without a nucleus, known as "prokaryotes," date to immediately after the end of the impacts.

Impacts of objects from space still occur.

It is believed that the time of the dinosaurs ended in a mass extinction around sixty-five million years ago, the result of a collision with an asteroid. Even in the life of our own species, events such as the Tunguska explosion of 1908, or the Chelyabinsk meteor strike of 2013, show that the danger is not over; collision with an asteroid large enough would throw enough dust into the atmosphere to block out the Sun for many years, causing vegetation, and those animals that depend on it, to die out. Of all the species of life that have ever existed, it is estimated that 99.9 percent are now extinct.

Yet somewhere in the time since the dinosaurs were destroyed, the mammals that somehow survived evolved, eventually leading to the arrival on Earth, some 4,598 million years after its formation, of mankind.

We cling to the surface of our planet; we live, for the most part, in a tiny layer of breathable gases wrapped around a ball of rock that flies through space, revolving around the Sun. But our path through space is not circular, because the Sun itself is traveling; heading away from the galactic center as the Universe expands. So the shape that we describe as we fly through space is not a line, nor even a circle; as the Earth revolves around the Sun, which itself moves out through space, we form quite another shape altogether; the three-dimensional spiral known as a "helix."

There are four quarters to this story; they can be read in any order and the story will work. The four quarters are assembled here in just one of twenty-four possible combinations; this order makes one kind of sense, but the reader should feel free to choose a different order, and a different sense, if desired.

Marcus Sedgwick
Hadstock
May 2014

QUARTER
ONE

WHISPERS IN THE DARK

I

She is the one who goes on,
when others remain behind.
The one who walks into darkness,
when others cling to the light.
She is the one who will step alone into the cave,
with fire in her hand,
and with fire in her head.

She walks with the people,
climbs up beside the waterfall.
Up, as the water thunders down.
Up, through the cool green leaves,
the summer's light lilting
through the leaves and the air.

They have come so far,
and ache with the pain
of their feet and their backs,
but they cannot stop,
because the beasts do not stop.

From where they climb,
they cannot see the beasts with their eyes,
but they know they are there.
In their mind, they see the deer:
their hooves, their hair, their hearts.
The antlers on the harts,
among the hinds who have the young.
They take the long path into the valley,
moving slowly, day by day,
while the people climb the waterfall
to meet them
with arrows and spears.

II

Just once, she slips,
her cold foot wet on green moss rock,
and close to the spray,
the water wets her neck.
Her face close to the drop,
her gaze falls on the frond of a fern.
A young plant, pushing its way out from rocks,
the tip curled tight.
Curled in,
in close-coiled secrecy
round and round, tighter and tighter,

smaller and smaller,
forever, it seems.
She stares, forever, it seems,
then a hand holds hers,
and pulls her to her feet.

The waterfall thunders;
and they are deaf.
Muted by its power,
they climb in silence
to the year's final camp,
in the trees, under the cliff,
under the high caves,
the high hanging dark
where magic will be made.

Where magic must be made.

Her thoughts are deep in the caves,
though her body is with the people,
at the leaf-fall camp.

Through the trees; the great lake.
The lake that spills itself down the waterfall.

The great lake: that will be crossed
to meet the beasts at dawn.

They are silent, for the most part.
They speak with their hands
as much as with their tongues.
A gesture; *do this.*
Do that, go there; the pointing hand.
Come. Sit. Faces talk as much as mouths.
Besides. They know what to do.
All of them. The old and the young,
each works hard.
Man and woman, boy and girl.
Only the very young do nothing;
and there are no very old.

She, who has been bleeding for two summers,
will soon give more young to the people.
It has not happened yet,
though she has been with some of the men,
and some of the boys have tried,
it has not happened yet.
She knows it will,
just as the deer they hunt have come to mate,
out there on the plains beyond the lake,
so the people too make new.

The one who will go to the caves walks,
and speaks

to the one who will lead the hunt.
The one who will lead the hunt approaches her.
He looks at her and tells her *food,*
and food it is she goes to find,
while others make fire, and others
fetch wood and others sharpen spears,
and others put huts together from the skeletons of old ones
and others find the boats they left before.

A few of the people set out from camp, foraging.
She leaves them to go their way,
while she goes hers. Leaf-fall is here,
yet the evening is warm.
She leaves her furs behind
and walks naked with the moist green air on her skin.
Through the trees of the wood, which stretches along the whole
    lake shore,
beneath the cliffs, beneath the caves,
beneath the high, hanging caves.

She has a basket, folded from reeds,
and she fills it with what she can find.
There are nuts, which will be good on the fire.
Berries. She finds a root she knows,
and then she lifts
the spiraling fronds of ferns, and finds snails.
Large snails. Good eating.
She places them in her basket,
one by one.

One hovers in the air on her fingertips,
as she traces its shell with her eyes,
round and round, tighter and tighter,
smaller and smaller.
Forever.

Or so it seems.

The snail tries to slip up her fingers, to escape her grasp,
and she puts it in the basket.
Time to eat.
At the camp, the fire is fierce,
And they have returned.

Some have left their furs,
others stay in theirs.
She feels the cold as the sun dips from the trees,
and slips her fur over her back.

They eat.
There is dried meat.
Fish from the great lake.
There are berries and the nuts she found,
which toast on the rocks by the fire.

When the eating is done,
the telling begins, and the one who does the telling
tells of the hunt that will come.
And then he tells

the old tells of the beasts,
and the tell of the fight between the Sun and the Moon.
He tells the tell of the journey to the caves,
and the one who will make the journey stares into the flames,
and *he* sees darkness.

But she doesn't listen to the stories.
She holds the shell of one of her snails,
its body in her belly, its back in her hands.
And by firelight she stares at it.

There is something about the shell,
the shape of the shell.
Like the shape of the uncurling,
unfurling ferns.
It is speaking to her,
she's sure, but she doesn't know what it says,
because it speaks in a language she doesn't know.

She picks up a stick,
a small dry stick, and puts its end in the dust at her feet.
She moves the end of the stick, and a mark is made in the
    dust.
A short, curved line.
Her eyes are fixed on the shell;
on its colors, on its curving line,
the slight white line in the center of the curving body,
    wrapping in,
wrapping in.

Tighter and tighter, round and round, smaller and smaller.
Or, looked at another way;
out and out, larger and larger.
A shape like that could go on forever,
or so it seems,
and still it speaks to her,
and still she doesn't know what it says.
But she knows she has seen it,
when her eyes were shut.

She shifts her foot and the line in the dust is gone.

IV

As the firelight dies, they make ready.

There will be no sleep.
Spears are resharpened, hardened in the fire ash.
Spear throwers checked; here, a new one is made.
Pitch and cord bind stone to shafts,
a splinter of flint with fresh-cut edge:
an arrow.

Gut is pulled across a new bow's back,
it takes strong shoulders to bend it,
but then, the people are strong.

And the strongest will cross the water,
the night-dark water, with half-moon
light to light their way, across the great lake
to the plains. Where, at dawn, the deer will be
waiting, unaware that they are waiting to die.

And then there he is: the one who will go to the caves.
He is old. Almost the oldest of them all.
So it will be his last time in the caves,
and he must take another,
who will become
what he has been.

It is his choice. The one who goes to the cave.
It is his choice to choose the new, and she,
She wants it to be her.

She thinks she knows what he does.
She knows why he does it,
that is something they all know;
the magic made as the hunt begins.
From the high cave mouth,
the plains are across the great lake,
From the high cave mouth,
the beasts can be seen.
And as the hunt begins,
the one who goes to the cave
must enter the dark, and make the magic on the walls.
The magic that makes the arrow fly farther,

the spear thrust deeper.
and the beasts die, quicker.

And she wants it to be her,
she knows it should be her, so she waits
while she should be working, and
watching him, watching him,
hoping he will turn to her.
Come to her and say,
You! Girl!
Come!
Come with me to the high, dark cave,
and I will show you how to make the magic.

She waits, the stick in her hand,
the small dry stick, and now she makes another mark in the
   dust.
A hump, a long curve, a flick at the front for antlers.
A beast, a deer: a stag.
In three lines.
She has seen what he does,
how he draws the shapes in the sand,
when no one is looking, how he does it
again and again, till the line is good and the beast is real.

There is a sound behind her and the one who will lead the hunt
   is there.
He sees what she's done, and kicks at the sand.
He lifts his fist and she hides her head,

but he does not strike.
He does not need to, for she knows it is wrong.
The marks are not for the sand,
the marks are for the dark,
and only he who goes to the cave should make magic.

The one who will lead the hunt is angry,
but he has more to do than punish girls
who are not yet giving children.
He leaves, and in his place comes the one who does the telling.
The one who does the telling points at the dust,
where her lines lay.
He nods.
She smiles.

He sits beside her.
He tells her a tell,
a strong old tell,
about the making of magic and how it is done,
and must be done well, up there, high up there in the
    hanging dark.
How the magic is made to make them fall when the arrow strikes.
For now it's the time for hunting.
At dawn, on the plain.

She listens.
She listens and she understands.
She understands the tell, but she knows
why the one who does the telling has that name,

and that his name means *weaver of words;*
weaver of words,
sentinel of speech,
retreating in awe at the world,
speaking with the divine.
Speaking with the blinding saving light-divine-magic in the dark.

That is what his name means.
He puts the stick back in her hands,
pushes the end onto the dust by the firelight.
Make, he says.
So, with one eye on he who leads the hunt,
she makes.

V

It is time to go.
The leaf-fall night is nearly done,
and the lake must be crossed,
and the cliffs must be climbed, before the dawn of the sun.

He who leads the hunt points at he who goes to the cave.
Choose, he says.
So she stands with the others
as the one who goes to the cave looks

from face to face, trying to see, trying to find something.
He walks slowly round the fire, almost gone now,
and he stops by a boy, then moves on.
He stops and looks hard into the eyes of a girl,
a girl who is not her . . .
moves on and he *is* in front of her.
He looks into her eyes.

Her heart beats hard.
She opens her mouth.
She wants to say,
"Take me with you . . .
take me to the high, dark caves
and I will make magic like you."

He takes one last look,
then turns away, and goes back to the boy.
His hand touches his shoulder,
and the one who goes to the cave has made his choice.

Her head hangs, and her heart is angry, and then,
· the one who goes to the cave comes back,
shoves her shoulder so she stoops before him.
He reaches to the fire's edge and takes burned wood.
Puts it in her hand.
Carry, he says, and she knows she has been chosen.
Chosen, not to make magic, not to go into the caves,
not to go into the dark and make magic.

She has been chosen to carry.
There will be paint. And reeds.
And torches for fire. And a bow for protection from beasts.
And she will carry, while they climb free.

VI

Those who will cross the water have left,
leaving her, the boy, and the one who goes to the cave.

They don't seem to notice her.
They have forgotten she exists,
now that she is ready, with a basket.
And in the basket:
reeds, hollow,
the rock that burns to red,
charcoal from the fire ash,
the things to make fire.
He who leads the hunt
has given her a bow,
with more than one arrow,
long feathered shafts,
which she will use before the dark is done.

VII

At the water's edge, the great lake waits,
lapping lazily against the shore,
against the shins of the people as they climb aboard the
  canoes.
These boats are old,
but they have made this journey many times,
and the people believe in their boats.

They push out.
Climb aboard.
Four to a canoe.
One in front to see.
Two in the middle to paddle,
one to carry the weapons that they will need to kill the beasts.

The half-moon light
guides their way.
The night air is wet and cool,
and they shiver from the air on their skin.
Their furs lie on the ground, far behind them;
wet fur is heavy and colder than nothing at all,
but they shiver as the air strokes their skin.
Soon, the two who paddle will be warm
from their work,
while the others
will feel the cold all the way to the far shore.
The far shore; half a night away.

Paddles dip, silently,
unseen,
each stroke leaves twin spirals
spinning in the water behind.

In, push, out.
Twin spinning spirals in the night-dark water.

VIII

She watches.
The one who goes to the cave pulls off his fur.
He points at the boy, who does the same.

They turn and look at her, just once.
He who goes to the caves gestures now,
and her furs fall to the ground.

He who goes to the caves nods, grunts, satisfied.
He points to the things she will carry, turns,
and walks into the night forest,
under the cliffs, that hang high above them
and the people,
and the boats and the beasts,
and the lake,
and everything.

He who goes to the cave leads the way,
with the blue-gray light by which to see,
but he knows the way because he has made it his own.
It has become his.
Till now, when he hands it on to the boy he has chosen.
The boy's mind is full of fear,
the old man's mind feels only the years.

As she walks behind, the basket digs
into her bare skin.
The bow is slung across her shoulders,
the arrows in her hand.
The torches sit,
unlit, in the basket on her back.
Grasses whip against her legs, but her feet are tough.
And in the unseen green by her feet,
nesting and alarmed,
a snake coils, ready to strike.
Its body pulls in on itself, around and around,
and it tenses, holds.
But they pass and it uncoils,
curling around its eggs once more.

So she doesn't see the snake,
and yet, she's thinking.
She's thinking about the mark she made
in the fireside sand.
Something is trying to speak to her.
But it goes as soon as it tries to appear in her thoughts.

Then she's thinking about something else.
Three things:
the fronds of ferns,
the shell of the snail, and then,
a falcon.
She saw the bird on the walk before the waterfall.
Saw it stooping from the sky
Saw how it dropped, not in a line,
but in the shape of the shell,
the form of the fern tip.
Round and down,
round and down, far below to the ground.

The falcon, the ferns, the shell.
They are all trying to tell her something,
but she does not know what it is.
She cannot know what it is. Not yet.

IX

The cave.

The cave has waited for almost all of time,
waited for the people to come and make their marks.
The cave has waited since the rocks were young,
just after the face of the world cooled,

when the volcanoes grew still,
when the cliffs were pushed up to the sky.

It was a long wait,
during which,
nothing lived.
Stars burned out in the heavens while it waited,
until finally some tiny filament found a way to copy itself.
Some long strand, of twisting complexity,
which made itself anew, and then there were two.

Ages ached through the heaving dark,
and burning light, as the filaments grew,
slowly organized, preparing for the invasion,
the eruption, of life.

And then the cave waited no more,
as ferns grew at its feet, spread, and changed,
and then there were plants, primal and bare
the first flowers and brutal trees
that reached into the air
with the energy of the young,
with the infectious power of the young information inside them,
and the cave was no longer alone.

Then came the beasts, the first small creatures,
things that crawled without eyes,
things that slithered,
things that heard by smell

and saw with sound,
things with hard shells,
things without bones.

Next there were legs,
fur and teeth, fangs
and horns and now, at last,
the people,
come to the high hanging cave
to make marks in the dark.

For lifetimes of men,
they have come to the cave,
and as the hunters hurl their spears,
they draw the beasts on the wall.

But before they can draw the beasts,
before they can draw a horse or deer or bull,
they must announce themselves to the dark,
with the print of their hand at the mouth of the cave.

It is their way; each and every one who has gone to the caves
has left the outline of their hand on the wall.
Ochre blown through a reed,
red powder blown over the hand held against the rock,
and the negative print of the hand is made.
Then, each one who goes to the cave
must make it *his* mark and his alone,
with some sign inside the outline:

two dots, perhaps; three lines.
Crossed lines.
Forking lines.
Five dots.
Each one different, and he who goes to the cave now
has made his mark over forty times, so old is he.
Forty times the same mark: two lines.
Two lines.
Two lines he will make again,
on this, his final trip.
It is two lines he has in his mind,
as he walks with the boy,
and the girl who bleeds but who does not give children.

X

Through the wet, dark forest
she walks,
behind the boy, behind the one who goes to the caves,
who leads the way by owl light;
that half shine of the moon, which will operate on them tonight.

The basket is hurting her back.
She stops for a moment
while the ferns wind around her feet,
and lifts the weight from her.

Waits.
Then walks on after the boy and the man
while the ferns cry out after her
saying, understand us! Know us! Be us!

She doesn't hear them,
because her eyes are on the back of the boy
who is to become what she wants to be.

She sees
his weak arms,
his skinny legs,
and knows his bad eyes need him to keep close to the old man
    ahead.

She hurries, closes the gap
and almost slams into the boy.

The face of the cliff:
the way leads up into the dark
He who goes to the cave doesn't stop,
doesn't look
as he whispers one word: *climb.*

So they climb.

Through trailing plants, they make their way
hand over hand, toehold by toehold.
In the mind of he who goes to the cave

is a single thought; dawn is close.
As they reach the height of the tallest tree,
a breeze hits them, fresh dawn air,
and he doesn't need to look over his shoulder,
to see that the light is coming soon.
They need to hurry.
He increases the pace of his climb,
and the boy is left behind,
and behind him, lower down,
she knows why she was brought to carry,
because the boy is not strong enough to
climb with the basket on his back.

As she comes to the treetops,
she can see handholds ahead of her,
and yet the boy is holding her up.

She calls to him, gently,
worried he might fail and fall back to the forest floor.
He doesn't reply, but he moves on,
and so, slowly, they lift their way up the rock wall,
which runs with water and young green moss.

Her back is hurting, and her arms ache
as she pulls herself higher,
one reach at a time.

She looks up.
He who goes to the cave has gone from sight,

and with relief she knows the climb is nearly done.
Three more reaches and the boy goes, too,
slips from sight onto the shelf.

Three more reaches, and her hand waves into air,
her wrist is grabbed by the old man,
and he pulls her onto the shelf.
Crawls to safety, next to the boy,
who lies panting beside her.

She rolls onto her back,
sits up, and her eyes widen.

There is the world before her,
the whole world
wide and far below her.
The forest through which they walked,
the lake, and the plains beyond.
The far hills still too dim to see,
but the lake sits like a slab of black.

XI

Hurry, says the old man, and they get to their feet.
He leads the way along the shelf,
wide enough not to fear falling,

uneven enough to make the going slow,
but he will not go slowly, because the sun won't wait for them.

The boy is lagging,
and her feet are dragging;
the way has been long and the man
though old, is strong.
He has surprised them both
with this strength, and they hurry to keep up,
through the skinny trees that dare to grow on the cliff side.

Then, they are at the cave.
He who makes the marks stops,
and for the first time,
he looks at her.
Fire, he says, and with beautiful relief
she slips the basket from her back.

Fire.
She has brought two torches,
each a haft of good, strong wood,
wound around at the end with
resin-soaked hair.
She bends to work fast,
taking the fire-sticks;
spinning one on the other
by means of a bow,
a miniature version of the thing on her back,
but with a looser string.

A string that winds around the stick,
so that by working the bow the stick spins.

She's done it a thousand times before.
Spinning the first stick
in the hole she's made on the flat of the second,
till smoke comes, and then flame.
A thousand times, and yet,
it's only now that she sees something.
She sees how the string of the bow winds round the spinning
     stick,
and suddenly she thinks of the snail,
and the falcon, and the fronds of the ferns.

He who goes to the cave shouts at her.
She sees she has made a flame and not even known it,
because her eyes are full of the string of the bow.
From the spinning, fire has come
and she touches the end of the torch to the flame.
Hands it to the old man.
Who turns and goes to the cave.

Come, he shouts over his shoulder,
and the boy follows.
She watches them go, then
she slides the basket back onto her back,
and she follows, too, clambering
over rocks and through brush
into the mouth of the cave,

desperate to see what she has always wanted to see,
so desperate she doesn't heed the warning
that her nose is giving her:
the faintest hint of a smell.

XII

There! Just inside the mouth:
Hands! Dozens of them.
Red hands in negative.
The ancestors of the people,
each hand made by the one who goes to the cave,
made before he goes to work.

The old man beckons to the boy,
points at her, but before she can get the reeds and the red,
the darkness erupts with a roar.

It happens so fast.
So fast, that at first
she doesn't know what it is.
A shape flies at them.
Before the shape lands, the boy is dead.
His head hangs by a cord from his shoulders,
stripped by a giant paw.
A cave lion.

It lands as the boy's body
pumps blood across the cave mouth.

The lion roars.
She stands. Frozen.
Her eyes on the boy,
and she remembers how he came from the belly
of the woman that *she* came from.

In another eye blink, the beast turns,
ready to run at them.
It does, but the old man is quicker
than the dead boy and leaps to one side.
Not fast enough,
the lion catches him with a claw,
and he collapses on the rocks, screaming.

He writhes on the floor.
Blood pouring from between his fingers,
pushing from long wounds in his side.

She scrambles from the cave.

The lion sees her and leaves the old man
to his pain.
It takes two steps, and she turns in time
to see it leap.
But she is fast and her fingers have fitted
an arrow to her bow string.

As the lion leaps, she pulls back the string,
wildly, without aim, the arrow flies, and
it is luck that takes it to its target.

The lion doesn't know it.
The arrow sticks from its mouth,
and has penetrated its brain,
but it rushes at her, knocking her down.

She falls to the ground, and there is no pain,
only the time in which to save herself.
She pulls another arrow from the basket
as the lion turns and stumbles toward her.

It closes its jaws,
the arrow is broken.
The shaft clags on its mouth, stuck in its teeth
but it makes another leap.

She fumbles to fit the second arrow,
and this time she is not fast enough.
The beast is on her, but with a wild pain brain
controlling its body, it paws at her without control,
and so it is
that without control,
the beast and the girl
tumble away over the edge of the shelf,
the shelf of the cliff,
into the dark

waiting
green.

XIII

On the lake,
the paddles dip.

The boats draw near to the shore.
It has been a long night
but now dawn is coming,
and he who leads the hunt calls softly,
across the water,
to the boats behind.

Paddles dip faster,
eager now to be done with the water,
eager to be at the beasts,
to see them run, to hear them stampede,
to watch them fall under the spears.

He who leads the hunt leaps silently,
landing in the shallow water by the shore,
and as he pulls the prow of the boat onto the shingle,
he looks up at the high cliff,
where the sun will soon strike,

and he hopes that he who goes to the cave
is working hard
in the powerful darkness,
making the magic that must be made.

XIV

She hangs.
Just over the lip of the cliff,
strap-strangled,
suspended by the cords of the basket,
caught on a branch of a high-clinging tree.

She twists, wrestles, fights,
her arms pulled above her head by the cords,
and all she does is make
everything in the basket tumble
to the forest below.

Somewhere down there lies the lion,
its body broken across a rock on the forest floor,
the end of an arrow stuck in the roof of its mouth.

She hangs in the air,
and light begins to seep across the valley.
As she twists,

the black lake turns gray, then silver.
Then orange, and sunlight finds her face.

She hangs.

XV

Thoughts are in her head;
thoughts that collide.
She feels as if she is spinning.
The boy is dead,
his head taken and his blood spilled.
The old man's blood flowed, too.
And the lion's is leaking onto leaves below.
But not hers.
Not yet,
though she knows it will if she falls,
and that she will be eaten by birds if she does not.

Her strength is leaving her.
She twists, looking at the cliff,
looking up, looking down,
and she knows that is her chance:
to climb down the tree that saved her.
But she needs to be free of the branch.

She hangs for a moment more and thinks,
and then she sees
that with one heave,
she could lift herself out of the strap.
She waits.
Then she pulls, pulls hard,
lifts herself up;
her foot has found a branch,
she pushes, and slides her shoulders
out of the cord.

The tree sways.
Her head sways with it.
and she looks down at the drop and wants to be sick.

She waits,
and then hand over hand, one branch at a time,
she begins to descend the trunk
as the light grows harder with every passing beat of her heart.

The softness of dawn is leaving.
Down she climbs,
and as she goes, the way becomes harder.
The branches are bigger, but farther apart.
But now that she knows she is not going to die,
she moves faster and finally jumps to the forest floor
where she lands by the lion,
who is still, but still warm.

Heat comes from its body,
and flies are already dancing on its wounds.
She looks at it,
and sees the blood on the claw
that took the head from the boy
who came from the same belly as her.

She turns.
Blood runs from cuts on her back.
The inside of her thigh is badly bruised,
the skin of her breasts is grazed.
The trees are sparse on this shelf of the cliff.
A narrow shelf, like the wider one above.
It runs away to nothing to her left,
to her right, it slopes up and widens out.

With fewer trees, she can see across the whole valley.
And though she is lower than before,
she sees the sun striking the plains.
She sees tiny black dots:
boats touching the shore.
The people have landed.

And there is no magic.

XVI

The softness of dawn is leaving
as she panics.
No magic!
No hunt can prosper without magic.

She looks up at the cliff,
down which she half fell, half climbed.
There is no way back.
But maybe the slope on which she stands
finds its way back to the higher shelf.
Maybe the old man is dead,
and the boy is dead,
but she can make the magic
if only she can find the cave again.

She scrabbles in the scrubby grass at her feet,
hunting.
She pushes plants aside and grows desperate,
and then she finds them:
the things from the basket.
The red ochre wrapped in leaves,
the reeds,
the second torch,
the fire sticks and bow.
Charcoal.

She gathers them together,
makes a bundle, which she binds with summer-dried grass
and hurries up the slope,
hoping to make her way to the cave.

Fern fronds and snail shells crush under her feet,
as she steps,
one eye on the path ahead,
one eye on the sunlit valley.

She must find the cave, and make magic soon;
she knows what to do, but she must find the cave first.
And then,
as the shelf narrows, then turns a twist
as it runs round the cliff face,
she comes to a corner, and her heart leaps.

A cave.
Not *the* cave, but another.
which, just like their own, looks across the water.

She looks ahead:
the shelf shows no sign of meeting the higher one.
It starts to lead down the cliff.
But here is a cave,
from which she can see the people
on the plain.
She can see long grass where the dawn deer will be grazing.
And here, here is a cave.

Something calls to her from inside.
Deep in the dark.
Something waits for her.
Come! it says.
Come, and understand.

She bends, and makes fire.

XVII

As she crosses the threshold,
a thought.
She must make the mark.
She must make the red hand on the wall.
The red hand, to make her part of the cave,
or the magic will not work.

She leans the torch against a rock,
and by its glow, she chooses a smooth face
on which to work.
And she works quickly.
A freshly sharpened flint knife takes the ends off a reed.
It is dry and hollow, and she pushes its end into the red.
The red ochre.

She places her hand against the smooth rock wall,
presses hard.
Then, the reed to her lips, she blows.

The red powder sprays perfectly,
a strong, narrow blast
that sticks to the wetness of the wall,
absorbed by the moon-milk there—
the soft white wetness that seeps from the rock.

Her heart beats.
She has covered only one finger and her thumb.
She bends to the powder,
refills the reed,
puts it to her lips.
And blows.
Two more fingers.
Good.
Again she bends, and when she blows this time,
her hand is done.
She steps away in awe.
She made the mark.
She is part of the cave.

She hurries.
A mark is not enough.
She must make magic;
she must make the deer
as they are hunted,

and she knows the hunting will begin very soon.
But for this magic to work,
she must be in darkness.
The dark light of the cave mouth is not enough.
She takes the torch back from the rock
and walks into the blackness.

As she climbs over boulders,
and slides in wet mud,
and turns to look behind her
every once in a while
to see how small the cave mouth has become,
she grows aware that something
something,
some *thing*
is waiting for her in the heart of the cave.

She can feel it.
She can almost hear it,
but she pushes it away,
because she needs to make magic.

The light from the world outside has gone.
She has come far,
and now she is in the place that connects to the magic.
This, the place the teller of tells has spoken of:
the place that connects this world and others,
where words are not enough to say anything,
where only actions can speak;

where magic made on the walls
can make meaning in the world.

She finds a place to plant her torch,
and takes the charcoal from her bundle.
All she has is two thick sticks,
but that is more than she will need.

She chooses a rock.
She likes it.
It bulges,
and in that bulge she sees the curve of a stag's back.
It was made for the magic,
and she places the tip of the charcoal on the rock.
Her first mark is good.
Her first mark is so good,
she can already see the stag on the wall,
before she's even made it.

She has made its back,
but her line is light.
She makes it again and makes it hard;
she makes it fast and she makes it bold,
and the back is done and it too is good.
Then a sweep of the neck,
a turn, a line,
and there is the head,
erect and proud,
held up just as it will be

when the spear strikes.
Good.

Now she makes the antlers.
Like branches, grown from the head,
strong and fierce, and she does them well.
The beast is almost alive in the rock.

She moves to the foreleg,
and her marks are power;
the lines are strong,
full of magic, and then,
then she notices something she had not seen before.

A mark on the wall
that was already there.
A mark that frightens her.
Her heart pounds and she grabs the torch.
She spins around;
she cries out as if someone is there.
She's alone.
She's alone, but there is still the matter of the mark on
    the wall.

She takes the torch closer, and now she gasps.
A hand.
A negative print of a hand.
A black hand.

Now the torch is closer,
she can see that the hand is not alone.
There is another.
And another.
Her breathing comes fast as she goes farther along the wall,
and the wall is covered with black hands.
Unlike the red hands,
with their marks inside,
these hands are empty.
Just the black powder outline, and . . .

Now she looks again, she knows why the hands scare her.
They have fingers missing.
All have thumbs,
but here is one with a half finger gone.
Here is one with half of two fingers missing.
She looks at them all.
Each misses at least one half finger.
Some have two stumps.
Some have three.
And here's one with stumps for all four fingers.

She doesn't understand.
She doesn't know what it means.
She doesn't know who made them,
but she senses something is wrong.

She runs, back to the light,
dropping the torch as she approaches the world.

She runs to the edge of the cliff shelf,
and there is the lake.
And there, she can see the people,
who have left their boats.

And there
she sees others,
other boats.
Heading for the far lakeshore.
And in them, other people.
Other
people.

She runs.

XVIII

Across the lake,
the people hunt.
They have allowed themselves
to judge the wind on which their scent will carry.
They have allowed themselves
to grow into the grass,
and for the sun to move so their shadows do not show.

He who leads the hunt
lies in the grass,
his spear light in one hand,
his spear thrower loose in the other.

He crawls.
Stops, waits.
Listens.
Then crawls again, and the people move behind him.

It takes an age, to move like this,
but the rewards will be greater.

Then, though the people have made no sound,
cast no shadow, and been careful with their scent,
there is a stampede.

The deer run.
the great uncountable many of them,
all run, at once.

He who leads the hunt leaps to his feet,
and cries out.
He sees the deer running, terrified,
bolting away, and he turns to see
what has caused this chaos,
and as he turns
a spear lands in his chest.

He clutches it as if he needs it,
and gives a small cry,
falling to his knees,
and then to his side,
where he lies in the grass, panting fast.
with wide eyes.

The people who are near him scatter in fear,
and then the others are on them,
without warning.

They have spears, no bows,
but they do not need them.
They throw hard and well,
and the people are taken with barely a sound
as spears land
again and again and again,
thrown hard and well.
Thrown well, despite the fact
that the throwers have parts of their fingers missing.
One of these others leads the rest.
He has four stumps where his full fingers should be,
but his aim is true.
He pulls his spear from a woman on the ground
and stabs her in the face
to finish her.

XIX

From the cave of the black hands,
down the widening shelf she runs.

On a turn in the shelf,
she glances at the water,
at the plains, and her heart runs loose and free.
She stops at the sight.
For with her very good eyes, she can see the people die.

Horror holds her for a moment,
and then she knows what she must do.
She runs.

To camp, she runs,
and her guess is a good one,
for soon, the shelf reaches the forest floor,
with the lake shore close through the trees,
and she knows the way back to camp.

But still she must hurry,
the way is long, though easier by light.
She thinks about the dead boy, the dead old man,
she thinks about the people
who went across the water,
and those who stayed at camp.
It is them that she must warn,

and sooner than she hoped,
camp comes toward her through the trees.

It is empty.
No one there,
and then she remembers that they will have gone to find food,
even the very young,
even the babies, carried at their mother's neck.

She staggers around the smouldering fire.
Twice she runs,
in desperation,
and something is screaming at her from deep inside,
but still, it will not be heard.

Should she look?
Should she wait?
Should she hunt for them, or wait for their return?

She stands silently now in the dawn forest.
Her chest heaves, not from the running,
but from fear.
She stares at the soft sandy earth
beside the fire.
She stares at it, seeing the end of her stick make its mark.
She wonders. She begins to dream.
And then . . .

A crack, and a voice.
A stick breaking on the summer-dried floor,
and a voice, but not a voice she knows.
She hides,
she slips from the camp,
and choosing an easy tree, she climbs.
Out of sight.

X X

They come.
Not the people.
The others.
They come through the trees.
Not from the lake,
but along the shore
and she knows they are more
of the ones who killed her people on the plains.

They sound different from her people.
Before she sees them, they sound different,
when she sees them, they look different.
They walk differently. They wear different furs.

Naked, she clings to her treetop,
and with horror she waits as two

stop beneath her tree.

They smell different,

and she is clever enough to know that she might smell different
   to them.

So she shivers in the high wavering tree,

as they pour into camp,

and prowl.

They touch nothing; they merely look

silently.

Holding their spears

lightly.

She wonders why they don't take the food that's there,

the furs and the tools.

And then she knows:

they want to kill.

Then, the people return.

She hears their sound coming through the forest.

They are singing.

They are singing the songs of the hunt magic.

No, she thinks. *Do not sing!*

But they sing as they come back to camp,

and the others have heard them, too.

They steal away,

hide in the green,

and even though she saw where they went,

they are invisible now.

Even the two others who stood at her tree,

she can no longer see,
but she knows they are there from the smell.

XXI

This is the moment.
This is the moment when she fails.
As the people come back.

She stares down from the tree
and all she can see is the sand by the fire,
and her stick tip touching the sun-dry earth,
so easy to make a mark.

And as the people come back,
the others slide from the green,
and throw their spears with barely a sound,
the last of the people begin to die.

She doesn't help them.
She would only help them die.
There's horror mounting
in her throat
and her belly,
and as she realizes that the two are gone from under her tree,

she slips to the ground,
ready to run.

She takes a last look through the leaves
to the fire pit,
where blood is welling in the sand—
blood from the body of the woman.
The woman is still, just one among all
who die that day.
But as she looks through the leaves
at the killing and the dead,
this woman puts a picture in her head,
of what it was to be young,
before the bleeding,
before the drawing,
before the talking,
what it was to be young
and to be held
in the arms of the woman from whose belly she came.

She watches her bleed in the sand.

They are all dead, or dying soon.
No one is left, not the young or the weak,
so she turns, and runs,
away through the trees
and green leaves,
and blades of grass

where tiny snails spin spirals around themselves,
as if they know a secret.

XXII

The last of the people runs.
Blindly, she runs and is at the water,
and sees boats arriving from the far lake shore.

Her hopes are dashed before they can even rise,
because the boats are not hers.
More of the others
come back from the killing on the plains.

So she turns and runs through the trees,
still running blind,
and then she hears a shout,
and despite her sense
she looks back.

Two of them have seen her:
the two from her tree.
One points; they sprint.
She bolts,
but her legs won't move as she wants them to;
feeling the fear from seeing the faces of the two.

Faces painted with tight black lines,
round eyes, down cheeks:
magic made on the skin,
and she knows it must be killing magic.

That is the magic that makes them powerful,
and strong,
and fast and feared.
In that moment, too,
she saw
the way their fingers stop short.
Knuckle-cut fingers, and yet still they hold their spears
with strong hands.
More killing magic: the mark of the hands.

She hears them closing in,
and though her legs are strong,
she's growing tired.
Yet there is no choice
other than to run and to live,
or stop and die.

Then.
There!
As she runs, she sees the shelf down which she came.
Up there, on the high forest shelf, clinging to the cliff,
is the buzzing body of the lion.
And somewhere in the grass beside it;
her bow. Maybe an arrow, or more than one,

and an idea;
a picture in her mind
of her killing these two,
comes to her with such sudden power than she runs faster than
    ever before.

She turns and starts to make the climb,
but they have seen her turn,
and follow.

She will need to put some time between them,
time in which to find the bow,
time in which to fit an arrow,
to roll onto her back and let it fly.
She pictures it all in her mind,
as she runs, and then she does nothing but run.
There is nothing in her head now.
She is the runner,
and though the two can see her ahead,
she puts space between them,
space and time
that she will use to kill them.

Then.
For some reason.
She stops.

She is by the entrance to the black-hand cave.
She stares into the blackness,

looks back once more,
and then
she steps inside.

XXIII

Just inside,
by the mouth of the maw,
there lie her fire sticks on the cold clay floor.
She takes them in hand,
and the dropped torch,
and pushes inside, pursued.

They falter as she reaches the cusp of light,
beyond which is pure magic blackness.

She is the one who goes ahead,
when others fall behind.
She has been in the deep cave once,
and made magic,
as she made the stag on the wall.
She has dreamed her whole life of what lies in the inmost cave
and she has no fear of what that might be.

But they do.
They stop at the mouth.

They are not magic men.
They have magic on their skin,
but that was made by another's hands.

Theirs is to hunt and kill,
to swim and fish,
to run and trap,
but out in the sun-bright day,
not here.
Not here, in the cold, wet dark
where time doesn't move.
It's here that the magic comes
from out of the world,
from the deepest part of the dark,
and they are afraid.

Hearing no sound behind her,
she stops and turns.
She sees them
outlined against the day-bright light.
She knows why they have stopped,
and that is enough to give her heart some strength,
and yet to fill her belly with fear.

They stand that way for an age,
here in this place where time barely moves,
and, with every step, deeper into the blackness
moves more slowly still.
For deep in the darkness,

in the inmost cave,
lies the prize,
the secret.

The two stand,
then step a step,
then stand.
Back away.
Come forward again,
and she makes to run into the dark, past the black hands
and her red-black stag,
when the world shakes.

The world moves.
The world thunders and the sky outside burns a thousand times
    more brightly.
Something rips it apart,
pounds the mountain,
and the rocks around start shaking so hard she falls to her
    knees.

A sound louder than a thousand suns
tears through the sky and into the earth.
The shaking world begins to crumble.
The two,
fear-frozen in the cave mouth,
fall.
Above them, the rocks crumble,
collapsing.

So easily,
they die.

She watches.
Light flickers through the rock fall.
Dust and debris obscures her view,
but as silence returns and the world stops shaking,
the light, and the world outside with it,
has gone.

She is alone.

XXIV

The last of the people
lies on the floor in the darkness.

Choking clouds of dust roil back to her,
and she lies, heaving her lungs and spluttering her throat.
Around her is nothing.
She can see nothing.
She *is* nothing.
But rebirth.
She feels for the floor,
wet clay and water pools,
and waits for the choking to stop.

When it does, she laps at the water and washes her face.
She shivers.
She stands, if only to know one thing;
which way is up.
The cold skitters across her skin again, and water drips from
    her hair
and her fingertips.
She will die in the cave.
That part is easy.
But before she does, perhaps,
there is something else.
Something that's been lying in wait for her,
and her alone.

She kneels, and finger-sees her way across the floor.
She fails.
She starts again, more slowly,
moving in an ever-widening circle,
turning and growing,
not knowing that above her head
a spider is spinning a giant web,
turning and growing, in a line that will not end.
Then,
she finds them; the torch and her fire sticks,
resting on dry rock.
She does not find the fire bow,
but it can be done by hand,
and, though it takes a little longer,
a red glow appears in front of her between her flying fingers.

She pushes on, spinning the stick between her palms,
and the glow becomes brighter,
and flicks into flame,
and soon the torch is alight once more.

She lifts it close to her skin,
feeling its warm breath on her breast.
Fire flickers in her eyes.
She's alive.
She walks.
There, at the cave mouth,
the way is blocked. It will never be opened.
So she walks
into the heart of the mountain,
hunting for that final understanding.

She walks past the black hands, past her red-black stag,
and she keeps on walking.

She walks where time never moves,
so there is plenty of space for her thoughts to come.
She climbs over rocks, and scrambles up slopes,
lets herself jump deeper and down
into the heart.

The snail goes with her,
and the ferns.
The falling falcon and the spinning bow.

The eddies in the water of the lake
light her way past the spiderweb.

She begins to understand.
She understands many things.

She remembers that she made magic of the stag,
and it did not work.
She knows why,
because though she put her red hand mark on the wall,
she did not place a mark *inside.*
The old man had his two lines,
and yet she made no mark inside her red hand.

She did not connect to the cave.
She did not become one with the cave,
and thus with the magic.
But now the cave has her,
and she will become one with it, forever.

She should have made a mark inside her red hand.

She comes to a place,
so vast her torch cannot touch its walls,
nor find its heights.
The floor is flat, but slopes gently down,
so she follows the path that lies before her,
and there, in the far wall,

lies a crevice,
a tunnel, leading still farther.

From the tunnel ahead whispers pour from the dark,
calling her on,
calling her in.
She approaches the split
the slit in the wall,
and though it's barely wider than she is herself,
she lights her way with the torch,
and goes inside.

There, immediately,
she sees:
hand prints.
Marks.
No animals, no beasts.
Just marks.
Dots and lines,
crossing and forking,
in black and in red.
Waterlike waves,
spotted points.
Mark after mark after mark after mark.

She walks past them all,
toward the end,
as her torch starts to fail.

She sees the sand by the fire pit,
back at the camp.
She sees her stick tip in the sand,
and now she finally knows what it means.
What it *could* mean,
to make a mark in the sand.

If there was a way,
she thinks.
To make a mark in the sand.
And that mark to be known by all.
And that mark to have a meaning.
A meaning known to all.
There could be different marks
for different meanings.
Then there could be a mark to mean *go*
and one to mean *follow*
and one to mean *find*
and one to mean *help*.
And then, she thinks,
there could have been a mark to mean *run!*
And if she had made that mark in the sand,
then her people might have seen it
and run,
and not died in the sand
by the dying fire pit.

Now that she understands,
it seems so easy.

The marks in the sand.
They could be charcoal on rock,
or charcoal on deer's dried skin.
They could have used them to say
go here,
do this,
I am there.

They could even be used, she thinks, to *dream.*

But this is an idea that will die in the dark
before it even leaves the mind of she
who goes ahead,
when others fall behind.

She who goes ahead when others fall behind moves on.
Through the bone,
the black marrow of the earth,
toward the end.
She reaches it, just before her torch fails for good,
and there,
high on a wall,
she sees the uttermost secret of the innermost cave.
This is the divine heart soul fountain face,
where the blinding light takes us
and saves us all,
and upon it
a final mark.

Giant and high,
black on the moon milk.

She stands and stares,
trying to understand it;
the turning circle,
the circling line
that never meets its end,
the ever-widening line,
round and round.

Then.
The light is gone,
the last beat of the flame flutters out and is gone.
She sits down.
Places the torch on the ground.
Stares into the blackness.

Slowly, she thinks,
I will die slowly,
in this time where space does not move,
in this space where time does not move.
She does not fear, she does not cry out,
she thinks only one thing:
if I could do it again,
I know what mark I would make in my hand.
I know that now.

And as she stares,
her eyes show her things that are not really there.
Lights flicker and fizz across her mind, as her eyes
try to see where there is nothing to be seen,
here in the space where time does not move.
Bright colors flicker and fizz:
lines,
dots,
crosses,
hatches.
And spirals.
Spirals like the one that hangs above her head, invisible.

The cave had waited for them to come,
and eventually, they came.
They came and made their marks in the dark.
And long after the people stop coming to make their marks,
long after the world grows empty and quiet,
long after everything has stopped walking,
or sliding, or even crawling;
long after all that
the cave will still be there.
Waiting.

Now, here
is nowhere; the nowhere where she lies in the dark.
And here, though she is in the place where time does not move,
her life moves, regardless.

So then it is time
for her to go ahead,
through the gate,
and into the void that lies beyond.

She goes.

QUARTER
TWO

THE WITCH IN THE WATER

1 ◉ APPROACH OF EVIL

IN THE MIND OF THE MINISTER WAS DEVILRY.

He spied on the landscape passing the window of his carriage, and what he saw was not the green dale, not pasture surrounded by low stone wall, not farmstall, nor woodland, nor wavering grass, but wasteland. A spiritual wasteland.

Father Escrove stifled in the carriage, whose two horses and deaf coachman had borne him with appalling lack of speed from the city and out into the world, to this countryside. He fumed silently, and despite the wicked heat he sat as far from the open window as he could manage, as if he feared contagion from the day outside.

Outside, beyond his window, was sinfulness. It was not even a matter of certainty; it just *was*. Evil lay barely hidden in those hedgerows, behind those barns, under the eaves of the farmhouses passing by. All across this green nature, the Devil had surely found a comfortable resting place. Satan *could* and *did* rise from the hay fields and creep from the forest at any time; seethe his way into some simpleton's soul and take root there. Even now, *the beast* was, without question, approaching through the thick hot air.

He dared move himself a touch closer to the window; the motion of the carriage and the heat inside neatly conspired to send

him a little drowsy, but he fought back. He sniffed the air outside. Heavy. Scented. Grass and dung in the heat.

Forgetting the deafness of the driver, he called out.

"How long?"

His words melted and slipped onto the sun-hard mud track
behind the clopping horse hooves.

There was not one breath of wind; the stale air sat on the earth
and the dale, and the minister's carriage as in an oven.

They were on the top of the world; on the high dale, somewhere at Black Top, he guessed, poking a skinny finger at the
map he'd been given. All around the high, flat pastures spread
away in easy-rolling levels of green, cut through only by weather-
worn walls of stone. There were few trees; the winters up here
saw to that. The winter wind made it hard for anything to hold,
but now, in the summer, the minister felt pressed closer to the
sun, and he sat back in his seat, hating.

Sliding satisfied into his thoughts were memories of his work;
his calling. Images of unrepentant sinners; some faces he could
remember, others he could not, but that mattered little. What
mattered were the numbers of those who he had brought to some
kind of redemption at the end of a good length of twisted
English rope.

Successful. That was what he was, he knew, and that was why
he had been elevated to Rural Dean, with all that that brought.
And what that brought was the opportunity to show the arch-
deacon that his faith was justified in this excursion to the wilds,
and to this place. Welden—no doubt some foul and rotting

sore—had had the misfortune to experience a hiatus; their vicar having upped and died without so much as a moment's warning, leaving the isolated settlement at risk of spiritual decay. And until a new appointment could be made to the hilltop house of God, it fell to Father Escrove to guide the sheep to safety.

They passed the church now.

St. Mary's. He sneered at the churchyard; the dead vicar already underground these past weeks. A man who had failed where he would not.

Away with his thoughts for a time, it took a jolt in the carriage to stir Escrove into piercing the world outside with his gaze once more; they had turned from the pitiful mud track of the green dale onto an even smaller one that set off swiftly down the side of the valley to his destination.

This valley, Welden, was steep-sided; seemingly scored into the landscape by God's chiseling fingertip, winding its way through the dales with Golden Beck at its bottom. Welden Valley was sanctuary to all the life of the place. Outside the brief moment of summer, the wind and the cold kept most life tucked into this groove in the earth; here, on its tiring slopes were the woodlands, the houses, the farmsteads, the mills, and the manor of the squire; Sir George Hamill.

As they turned from the main track to the smaller, Father Escrove saw something.

In the corner of the field to his right lay an area where the grass was kept short, and there, cut into that turf, was some sort of pattern low in the earth; a series of lines not even a foot deep.

He strained his neck to make it out, but could not measure any meaning in it.

Then the carriage jumped over a rut and he hit his head on the window frame.

"God's teeth," he muttered, grimly.

He thought for a moment about what he had come to do.

Then, he smiled.

2 ◉ THE LANG CANDLE

DESPITE THE HEAT, ANNA TUNSTALL KEPT THE windows of the cottage shut while her mother lay on the table. Tom Tunstall watched nothing happen from the kitchen door. Over the last three days he had seen his sister do many things. He had watched with eyes wide as Anna had taken three threads as long as their mother was tall, and twisted them into one. He'd seen how she had wrapped the thread in wax till it was as fat as his little finger, and then how she'd coiled it up on itself, like the adders did under the ferns in Callis Wood, though more loosely than the snakes.

He'd seen her set the lang candle on a small board placed on his mother's belly, pull the center of it up, and light the wick as summer late darkness came. Anna had allowed just one third of it to burn that night, a third the second, and last night, the final third, the flame describing a slow spiral over the course of the three days.

Now Anna sat still on the stool in the corner of the cottage, staring across her mother at the wall. Only once had she stirred, when Tom crept near to their mother on the table, as near as he dared, only for his sister to shoo him off.

"Don't, Tom. And if you have to, walk widdershins by her."

Tom had retreated to the kitchen door, from where he had

kept his vigil these past days. If he had been older he might have understood that his sister was simply tired, but he was young, and neither was he quick.

He looked at his sister as she fell asleep slowly on the stool, her head lolling forward, so that her long red hair hid her face. Her left arm slipped from her lap and fell to her side, but it did not wake her; one fingertip merely touched the dirt of the earth floor of the cottage.

A bad thing came into Tom's head.

He looked at this mother of his, who had not moved for three days, and now his sister was still, too. His mind got to working.

Very gently, he left his place by the kitchen door and approached Anna, and remembered what she had done when they'd come home to find their mother lying on the floor. She'd put her ear to her mother's lips, as if listening.

Tom didn't know what he was supposed to listen for, but he crept up to his sister and lifted two of her long thick ringlets of curling red hair aside, bending his head toward her face.

Then there was a sharp tap on the door, which opened.

Anna's head shot up. Her brother was by her.

"Tom . . . ?" she asked, but Tom had scurried away to the kitchen door.

She stood and saw that there were people coming into the cottage.

The first of the mourners.

Joan Tunstall's funeral was about to begin.

3 ◉ THE TRYSTING TREE

JACK AND ELIZABETH SMITH WERE FIRST.

Anna bid them in, and she even smiled, though she knew Jack was only come because her mother owed him some money. Scared to let death cheat him of twopence.

At least they'd left their children to prattle outside, but nevertheless she could hear Harry bossing the twins around just beyond the garden wall.

Elizabeth's eyes had landed on Joan Tunstall. Anna had wrapped her in a winding sheet from her toes to her head, leaving only her face exposed to the hot room. Despite this tight wrapping, the heat had not been kind.

"She reeks," said Jack to no one.

He wanted badly to let his eyes run over the redheaded Tunstall girl, so he could later imagine his hands doing the same. She was plenty old enough now to be looked at, after all, but the body of her mother made him uneasy.

"The house is terrible hot, Anna," said Elizabeth.

Jack barked once.

"Hot! Spend all day in the smithy before you call this hot."

Elizabeth turned to Jack.

"Yes, husband. You're right."

"Acourse I'm right."

Anna watched Elizabeth Smith cower before her husband, whose face, it was true, was permanently red as if scorched by his blacksmith's fire. Anna wondered how long he would manage to wait before asking for his twopence.

More people entered the cottage.

John Fuller, who'd been master to her father when he'd still lived, and John's wife Helen, thin and gray, who smiled at Anna.

"Hot in here, Anna," said John, wrinkling his nose.

"Yes, but the windows must be shut," said Anna.

Helen agreed.

"No breezes above a body. Where's little Tom?"

Anna started as if remembering her brother for the first time in days. She knew Helen was kindly to children, even though Anna's mother Joan, the village gracewife, had delivered four dead babies of Helen Fuller. No more had come, alive or dead, but still Helen Fuller smiled at the sight of a young child.

"There!" said Anna. "Tom, come."

Tom stayed where he was by the kitchen door, and Anna let him alone. More people entered the door, and the small room became full, so that people edged closer to Joan.

With surprise, Anna saw that even Adam Dolen was there, though there was no sign of his wife, Maggie or their daughter, Grace.

Three empty days of silence and now this noise. Neither the emptiness nor the noise seemed real to Anna, but she wasn't aware of thinking that; it was only important to stop people passing anything over her mother's body. Sweat ran from Anna's neck and down her back, itching against the threadbare cloth of her long black dress.

She tried to speak, but found her voice too frail to be heard.
She tugged at John Fuller's sleeve.

He turned and his eyes softened.

"Anna?"

"Mother ought to go now."

John nodded. His wife was trying to talk to the idiot boy. He
wanted to touch Anna's skin, but he could feel her mother watching him from two feet off, even though her eyes stayed dead shut.

Instead, he turned to the room.

He clapped his hands and everyone stopped talking. Though
he didn't own the mill, half of the room worked there, and therefore they worked for him. They did as he bid.

"We'll take Joan to the tree now."

The villagers worked.

Helen Fuller and Elizabeth Smith opened the window that
looked over Welden valley, while the Byatt brothers fetched in
a single wide oak floorboard. They stood by as Anna finished
winding the sheet over her mother's face, and then Tom was suddenly at her elbow.

"I want to say goodbye to Mother," he said to Anna, and Anna
died, wishing the room was empty of people and that she could
wind her mother's face away alone.

But everyone was waiting.

She unwound the cloth a way, till Joan Tunstall's closed
eyes showed.

"Go on," Anna said.

Tom whispered something, and then as Anna began winding again, he reached up and tried to help his sister, his clumsy
hands slowing her, but calming her some, too.

That done, Anna stepped back, pulling Tom by the shoulders, squeezing them tightly.

She watched as the Byatts and Jack Smith and John Fuller lifted their mother onto the floorboard, and passed her out of the now-open window to the other villagers waiting outside.

Then came the cry of "to the tree!" and away they went.

Somewhere above thirty of the villagers had come out, come out from their homes dotted through the woods in Welden Valley.

Anna clung to Tom. They came behind the others. Tom's mind was empty. Anna wondered at the size of the wake; perhaps they'd come because they'd liked Joan Tunstall. Perhaps they'd come because they were afraid of her, even in death—the gracewife, the cunning woman. Anna had seen almost everyone there come through their door in the year before her mother's death; they all used Joan for this and for that. For swollen knees, or to bring a fever down, to take an ointment that would make a husband a better lover, or for some herbs to stop a wound going bad.

The Tunstalls' cottage was at the top edge of Callis Wood, near the top of the valley, above them were the tentergrounds, where Anna spent so much time working for John Fuller. Below them were the trees, lining the steep valley sides like green velvet in a rich lady's coffin.

The funeral party moved down the path that led beside Tunstall Cottage, zickzacking through the trees, left and right, left and right, to the valley floor where Golden Beck flowed.

The tall trees were towers around them; the floor was flat with flagstones where the narrow river ran left, artificially underground for a fifty-yard stretch before emerging at the wheel of Fuller's Mill.

They turned to the right, and a short walk led them to the trysting tree; not one tree in fact, but two that had grown close together, and somehow the trunks had fused near the bases, leaving a perfect neat archway between them. Above this natural arch, the two trunks grew apart again and thrust up to join the leaf top canopy of the forest.

No one alive had a memory of a time before the trysting tree, and thus it had existed forever. Therefore it had been made either by God, or one of the older sort. Therefore it was magical.

The villagers wasted no time.

Two of the men went to the far side of the tree, while the four who'd carried Joan through the woodland bent and passed the body, floorboard and all, through the hole, through the heart of the trysting tree.

Without touching the ground, Joan emerged from other side, a little safer than before she went through.

Tom clung to Anna's side as they watched.

Adam Dolen was there, then. Fat.

"Shame it is, to bury your mother while there's no vicar in the house."

Helen Fuller heard him from where she stood.

"What difference does it make? We know our business as well as the vicar did."

Adam said nothing else because he was too slow to think of anything to say before the procession moved off again.

Back down from the tree, they made their way over the flags that hid the river, then followed the path that led around beside the mill pool, past Fuller's Mill, along the valley bottom with Horsehold Wood on the left and the river on the right. Beyond the river, Arton Wood clung to the hillside, all the way up to Dolen's farm, where Grace's mother no doubt sat, stewing.

On the procession went, all the way down to Gaining Water, and as they turned to take the path back up through Horsehold Wood to St. Mary's Church, someone started to sing the song.

So it was, singing, that they carried Joan Tunstall's body into the churchyard, and placed her in the hole that Anna had paid Old Harry threepence to dig.

They left Joan Tunstall in the ground then, and while Old Harry started to pile earth in on top of her, the villagers went across the track to the field at the edge of the tentergrounds, to dance.

Anna hung back awhile, watching the earth go in.

She glanced at the little mound, much smaller, nearby; that was where Grace Dolen's baby had gone, a month ago. She wondered if it was just bones in the soil now, and she saw them in her mind—tiny white bones in the dark earth.

By the time she pulled herself away, saw that her brother had gone ahead, and went to join the others, the dancing was well started.

The villagers formed a circle, an open circle, holding hands all, but with a gap.

They faced inward, toward each other, and moved to the right, to the right hand, and stepped sideways, spinning the circle round and round, always to the right. Anna joined them, as she should, putting her left hand into Helen Fuller's right. Now Anna led, dancing and dancing, to the right, to the right, trying to meet the end of the open circle, but never, never reaching it.

They danced to the right "in the same way they believed blood spirals to the right," through the generations, passed from parent to child, but always to the right.

They sang, and they danced the spiral dance, and three people watched them.

The first was Robert Hamill. Second son of Sir George, recently returned from France.

Watching Robert watch the dance was Grace Dolen, who had come across the valley from Dolen's Farm to scowl out of the woodland edge.

And watching all of them, from his stifling seat, was the minister, Father Escrove, whose carriage had just then arrived in Welden Valley.

4 ◉ A MIND SMEARED ACROSS THE HEAD OF THE MILL HAMMER

GRACE DOLEN'S THIRSTY EYES WERE STILL ON Robert Hamill as the Smith twins approached her. Hettie and Hester Smith weren't dancing with their brother and the others. They didn't want to dance. They were still and cool girls, who watched and whispered. Though barely eight, something dry in them had identified Grace Dolen as a source that they might be interested in. They latched on to her without knowing why, but now stood a few feet away, watching her watch Robert watch the wake dancers at Joan Tunstall's funeral.

Their brother Harry was dancing; he was a loud, energetic boy, tugging too hard at the hand to his left as he pulled to the right.

The sun was slowing the pace of the dance; foreheads ran with sweat and bare feet crushed the dying grass as they circled on.

Grace knew, as everyone there knew, that the dance had a purpose. Whoever was the first to fall could be asked a question, any question, and not only did they have to answer, they had to tell the truth.

Someone had fallen, and it was enough to distract Grace from gazing at Robert for a moment. From the distance at which Grace watched, it seemed a dream as Anna Tunstall stumbled in the heat haze and put her hands to the harsh grass. Young Simon Bill was the first to hop over in front of her.

Grace sucked her lip, wondering what question it was that Simon put to Anna. She knew what she'd have asked her, given the chance.

"You're Grace with the dead baby," announced Hester Smith.

"Aren't you," added Hettie, in an equally empty voice.

Grace shifted her gaze back to Robert Hamill. She was wondering how much she could see of him at the manor house. He was just returned, the week before, from France, where his father had sent him to learn something about trade and travel.

The twins didn't twitch so much as an eyelid as they considered Grace Dolen. She leaned against a tree at the edge of Horsehold Wood, slowly chewing a thin stalk of pale brown grass.

"Why did your baby die?" asked Hester Smith.

"Did you kill it?" asked Hettie.

Grace didn't appear to have heard either question.

She shifted her weight from one hip to the other and her fingers unconsciously stroked her belly where the baby had been. So something good had come of the death, then, she thought. How lucky for her that the boy had died just as Lady Hamill was looking for a wet nurse for her own son.

Lady Hamill, the second Lady Hamill, young wife to Sir George, with a child that needed milk, and there was Grace on the doorstep of the manor the following morning with her baby gone in the ground and milk hanging in her breasts, ready. What luck.

Of course Grace had taken a clip round the ear for being so

bold as to stand on the front doorstep of the manor, but once she'd found her way to the back, she'd been installed in the nursery to feed Lady Hamill's son. That meant, from time to time, that she was even allowed in the house proper, even as far as her Lady's bedroom, to show the baby to its mother once in a while.

Grace knew where Robert Hamill's bedroom lay. She had seen the door, and though it had been closed, she thought powerfully about how to get beyond it. Robert was young and not half the men that the vigorous Byatt brothers were, whichever of them it had been who had given her a baby. But Robert was rich and, unlike his older brother Samuel, he was unwed, and Grace held unlikely desires of securing him.

The twins made one more try.

"Ma Birch says you killed your baby so you could let her ladyship's baby suck at you instead."

That was Hester Smith.

Grace slowly turned her head to look down at the Smith twins, who stood upright in their rough, long white dresses, their eyes as unblinking as owls.

"Did you do that?" asked Hettie.

Grace spoke so quietly that the twins barely heard.

"It was Joan Tunstall that killed my boy," she said, and then she pushed herself away from the tree and started back to the manor house, for she had only been home across the valley on an errand, and could not afford to be gone long. The Hamill baby would want feeding soon.

5 ◉ STONE FOOT

THE DANCE WAS DONE.

The heat of the sun had soaked into everyone, and while some sat on the grass of the field with their legs out and propped up with their hands behind, others slunk away back into the green valley, and its coolness.

The sound of Golden Beck had drawn them, and Harry Smith had forgotten to torment his twin sisters for a time while he and other boys bathed in Gaining Water.

Robert Hamill waited.

Everyone had left but Anna Tunstall, and her quiet brother Tom.

Tom had wandered away from the dance and was walking round the lines, the lines carved into the turf up by the road.

Anna watched him winding his way round and round, and then called.

Her voice drifted as far as Robert, and there was no wind, so Tom must have heard, too, for he was closer. But he didn't move.

"Tom!" she called again. "Thomas!"

The boy kept walking the lines of the maze.

Anna's shoulders dropped, and her hands, which had been on her hips, dropped to her side, then she slowly walked to where Tom was, took his hand, and started home.

The track that led from the road ran straight to the gates of
the manor, and then on, right past Tunstall Cottage, but Robert
saw that Anna pulled her brother the other way, back past the
churchyard to the path up from the valley.

She was retracing her steps. The journey they'd made an hour
or so before, with a body on a floorboard.

Robert followed, keeping his distance.

Down to the beck, where a short way away the sound of stupid boys floated over from Gaining Water.

Anna still held Tom's hand as she led him back along the path
by Golden Beck, past Fuller's Mill, where tomorrow being Monday she would have to find herself again.

She didn't stop and then, just as Robert expected her to turn
up the path that led through Callis Wood to the cottage that was
now hers, Anna made straight ahead, past the trysting tree, and
then farther, pulling Tom along with her.

They walked for half an hour along the valley floor, and only
the trees and Robert Hamill saw them go. Robert wondered
if she knew he was following, so he dropped way back, trying
to use tree trunks to hide himself, leaning his head around
only when he thought it was safe.

A little way on and finally, she stopped.

There was Stone Foot; a tiny bridge across the beck, made of
two long and narrow blocks of stone laid end to end. They met
halfway on a pillar that had been set into the bed of the stream.
There was no handrail. At either end of the footbridge, two squat
stone bollards formed an open gateway across the path. The
bridge had the latent power of a Methuselah, an ancient and
patient thing.

Just above Stone Foot, the stream had made a pool for itself over the course of the last ten thousand years; much smaller than Gaining Water, but much quieter, too.

Robert pulled himself in tight behind a large scrub oak, and looked.

Anna came off the path, and Tom followed her onto the grassy bank above the pool. Despite the thick woods all around the valley, this secluded pool was a rare spot in full sunshine; sunlight stole over the rippling water sending beams even as far as its shingle bed.

Anna kicked off her clogs, and Tom did the same.

They were speaking, or at least, Anna was speaking to her brother. She was pointing at the stream, and then Tom pulled his clothes off and jumped into the water without a moment's hesitation.

Anna laughed, loud enough for Robert to hear; a sound as golden as the stream.

Anna pulled the hem of her dress up and for a dizzying and eager moment Robert thought she was going to take her clothes off, too, but she merely dangled her feet over the bank and into the water, then lay back with her hands over her eyes because her face was in full sun.

Seeing his chance, Robert Hamill approached.

6 ◉ PRESENCE

TOM LOVED SWIMMING, AND ANNA LOVED TO HEAR
him splashing and tumbling in the water; truly, simply happy. It
eased her difficult thoughts. The cool water ran around her
feet, sunlight poured onto her pale freckled face, and Tom's
laughter took her away somewhere where she didn't have to
worry about what the future held for them.

But there *was* a decision to be made.

Should she go on working for John Fuller, carrying cloth from
the mill hammers up to the tentergrounds every day? Or should
she try and keep her mother's gifts alive, scraping a coin here
and there from the villagers who paid a call?

Fulling work was foul business. Unloading the woollen cloth
from the ponies that walked up the valley from Deepdale. Heft-
ing the cloth into the mill. The stench of the urine in the baths.
The grinding of the mill gears as John slipped the hammers into
action. The pounding of the hammers on the cloth, hour after
hour until, in some way Anna knew not, John would announce
the batch to be done. Stronger and more water-hating than it had
been when it arrived.

Then the washing and rinsing in the millstream, and carrying the sodden wool up the track from the mill, past the manor
lands and onto the tentergrounds.

That was the one part of the process that Anna didn't mind so much; up, out of the narrow valley, to the open dale where she would hang the fulled cloth up on posts, where it would dry, stretched out on tenterhooks. Up there, she felt a little braver and less captured.

Otherwise, she hated the job, though John Fuller was as kind to her as he'd been to her father. It was steady money, that was all, and the alternative . . . ? To rattle around the cottage, putting some of the things her mother had taught her to practice, only making money when someone came to knock.

She knew some herbs and she had taken to the art of their preparation naturally. The ditches, riverbanks and woods of Welden Valley were overflowing with the plants that could make and mend. Knapweed: good for those who are bruised from a fall, or to heal green wounds. Feverfew, good for wounds, too. Meadow Saffron, which used indiscreetly, could be poisonous. The fresh leaves of young ferns; which purge the belly and expel waterish humors. Or cause abortions. All these powers lurking in the leaves of the valley.

With time she could become a skilful gracewife, she believed. She had assisted her mother very often, most recently to deliver Grace Dolen of the scrawny runt that had died within the month.

Anna still felt surprised by that; how such a scrappy thing had come from between the plentiful thighs of Grace. She had expected a plump calf to emerge that morning, not the sickly babe that never increased. Joan Tunstall had done everything she knew for the baby, but it would not come on, and in the end, all she could say was that she had given Grace Dolen an easy,

short and painless birth for a boy who was not destined to prosper by God's hand.

Despite such setbacks, which were after all just the way of nature, Anna's heart called to her to become her mother. They had
the same hair—the winding red. They had the same pale skin,
with a band of freckles across the nose that looked so out of place
on a woman the age that Joan had been. But most of all they had
the same *desire*—to find out what was to be found out. To uncover things covered, to explain the mysterious and to put these
findings to service in order to help people against the dangers
of the world, which were, to put it at its plainest, legion.

And that was the way Anna's mind was wandering, through
avenues alternately sunlit and leafy-dark, trying to weigh up
whether to take the risk, when the sun was suddenly gone from
above her.

Her eyes opened, and she expected to see a cloud; but there
was someone standing, looking down at her, blocking the light,
silhouetted against the hot blue sky.

"How long have you been there?" Anna said, angry at having been crept up upon.

She rolled onto her stomach and scrambled to her feet, then
saw who it was.

"Oh," she said. "I'm sorry, sir."

Robert Hamill, second son of Sir George, stood in front
of her.

It took her a moment to realize that he didn't seem cross
with her.

Anna hesitated, unsure of what to do. Sir George's second son
seemed to be staring at her, but to what end she had no idea. She

didn't see herself as he did; her hair flaring in the sunlight, her long toes, bare and wet on the bank. The curves under her so-thin dress.

She turned, saw Tom still splashing in the pool. He ducked under for a second and then erupted in a fountain of stream water.

"Tom!" she called. "Time we went."

But Tom didn't hear.

Anna gave Robert a small curtsy and moved along the bank, closer to her brother.

"Tom!"

"Anna Tunstall," Robert said. "Aren't you?"

Anna stiffened slightly. What did he want with knowing that?

"That's your brother," Robert said.

"Tom," murmured Anna, without thought. Then she turned and shouted.

"Thomas! Get out now!"

Now Tom heard. He stood up in the shallows of the pool, and saw there was someone with his sister. Water dripped from his fingertips.

"Get out, Thomas, we have to go home."

Tom started to climb out onto the bank, but before Anna could take him his clothes, Robert Hamill was speaking to her again.

"I'm sorry for you," he offered.

"I ask your pardon, sir?" Anna said.

"You buried your mother today, and I'm sorry for that."

Anna felt herself looking at Robert now, properly.

He wasn't so old and he wasn't as tall as his brother Samuel.

Nor as arrogant, that was clear to see. He seemed a much gentler sort of creature, in fact, now that she risked meeting his eyes.

"Thank you, sir," she said.

Robert ignored that.

"Here," he said. "I've something for your brother."

Before Anna had time to reply Robert dug into the pocket of his doublet and approached Tom, who sat on the bank staring at the water.

"Thomas?" Robert said. He bent down near him as if speaking to a lamb. "I've something for you. It's a gift."

"What is it?" Tom asked.

"Look," said Robert, and finding a large flat stone nearby, set it in the grass of the bank.

Then he held out the thing he was giving to Tom, a small wooden disc on a spindle. He flicked it between his fingers just above the stone and there it spun, standing up on its point.

Tom clapped his hands and laughed, watching it spin till it began to wobble then skitter away and fall off the edge of the stone.

"Do it again!"

"Do it again, *sir*," Anna said seriously, then realized how silly that sounded. "I mean, if it pleases you to."

She dared a smile at Robert, but Robert was already taking the little spinning top up in his fingers, sending it into its dance on the stone.

Anna came closer and now she saw that painted on the top of the disc was a line that curled in on itself just like the line of the turf maze up on the edge of the tentergrounds.

She saw that the line moved, moved inward, forever, always

getting smaller but somehow always there, never disappearing. Or so it seemed.

Robert saw that she was fascinated and when the top fell over this time he picked it up and showed her the painted line.

"It doesn't move," Anna said.

"Only when it spins," said Robert. "It's an illusion of sorts. I found it in the market in d'Auville. That's in France," he added, wondering if Anna might be impressed by his adventurous life.

She showed no sign of knowing what France was, or caring.

"Do it again," said Tom.

"*Sir*," said Anna.

Robert laughed and spun the top again, and again, and again, until he taught Tom to do it for himself.

Anna watched, unable to move. She couldn't take her brother away from Sir George's son, and he showed no sign of leaving, so she waited, watching as the young man played with her brother.

Finally, as Tom sat staring at the spinning, shrinking spiral, Robert straightened and looked at Anna.

"I have something for you, too."

"Me, sir?"

He didn't say anything else, but fished in his pocket and pulled out something on a chain. He held it up.

It was a heart, delicate and dangling, and it spun in front of Anna's eyes. She guessed it was silver.

For some reason that she did not know, her heart began to pound.

"It's for you," said Robert, but he held it closer to his chest. Then he reached for Anna's hand, and she tried to pull away, but he took it and put the silver heart into it as the chain fell through her fingers and swung for a moment. She'd never seen anything so precious.

"It was my mother's," he said. "My late mother."

Anna started shaking her head.

"No. No, sir. You cannot give me this."

"But I do."

Terrified, Anna didn't even hear how Robert's voice shook as he told her to keep it.

"I cannot. Why would you give this to me?"

"I would have hoped you had known that," Robert said.

Anna shook her head again, but Robert wasn't done.

"I have seen you, Anna Tunstall," he said. "I saw you before I went away, two years last winter. I saw you then. And I have traveled since. Across England. To the sea! To France. I did what Father bid me do and I learned the French tongue and I am back in Welden now, here, and in all that time never did I see such a woman as you."

He stopped, and Anna knew what he was saying.

"But you can't . . . You . . . Oh!"

She pushed past Robert Hamill, who spun after her, surprised, to see that Tom Tunstall was fitting on the grass.

His eyes had rolled back in his head, his body jerked as if his arms were working front to back. He shuddered, horribly, and Anna was crying out as she tried to fish for his tongue with her fingers.

"Tom! Tom! I'm here, Tom."

She leaned in close and spoke to him over and over.

Tom kept shuddering, silent.

Robert took a step closer. A small step.

"What happened? Anna? What is the matter?"

Anna called to her brother, again and again, and now she managed to get his tongue free from the back of his throat. She moved the stone on which the top had spun away from him and let his arms and legs jerk free, and all the while kept talking to him, as calmly as she could, though she felt anything but.

Robert saw the boy lose himself and a puddle formed in the grass under him.

"What is the matter?"

Anna called over her shoulder.

"He does this. It will pass soon. It will pass," she said, talking more to her brother again than to Robert, who took a step farther away again.

The three stayed that way.

Robert standing on the hot grass, Anna crouched over Tom, who shuddered still, but eventually, his movements eased and he flopped flat on his back, staring infinitely up into the sky.

"That's good, Tom," said Anna. "That's good. You are well again."

Robert saw how the boy seemed to sleep now, exhausted, and Anna sat beside him leaving her hand on his chest, which rose and fell gently and smoothly.

She looked up.

"He is well again," she said. "Well enough."

But she couldn't look away from her brother, nor did she want to see what was waiting on Robert Hamill's face.

Robert stared for a long time.

He noticed something in the grass, and stepped forward. He

picked up the silver heart from where Anna had dropped it and came and knelt beside her, though the smell of her brother was unpleasant to him.

"I want you to have this," he said, and put the chain over her head, then pulled her thick red hair from under it so the heart fell onto her black breast.

He stood, and with one final glance at the boy, he smiled at Anna and stole away.

Anna hung her head, and her hair curtained her face, shutting her in.

She knew she must go after Robert Hamill and return the gift. A piece of silver! He should not have given it, and she should not accept it, but she was tired, and needed to stay by Tom. Their mother had died but three days before; they had only just put her in the ground. She knew she should get up. But she was tired. She did nothing. So that was how Anna Tunstall came into the possession of the silver locket that had once belonged to the first Lady Hamill.

7 ◎ THE DEVIL IN WELDEN

BY THE END OF SUPPERTIME, FATHER ESCROVE knew the Devil was at work in Welden. In fact, he had learned all sorts of things about the community, such as the fact that John Fuller did not own his mill but merely leased it from Sir George; a twenty-year lease that was soon ending, such as the fact that the first Lady Hamill had died giving birth to Samuel and Robert's sister Agnes, now eleven years old, and such as the fact that Jack Smith down at Gaining Water smithy beat his wife whether she needed it or not.

He knew all these things, but these were not matters that interested him greatly. Not yet, at least.

Sir George had had some short warning of the arrival of the Rural Dean, and had prepared a fit feast to welcome him that evening. Three geese and a squealing-loud piglet had passed away that morning in readiness for the Father's appetite, and yet Sir George seemed to have made a mistake.

He assumed that all men loved food as much as he did, because he had never, despite his wide travels, met a man who did not eat well when given the chance. And yet it appeared that Father Escrove was not like other men.

Sir George and the minister sat at opposite heads of the long table in the great hall, and each prepared a set of mental notes about the other. The minster's set of notes was by far the longer, while Sir George's ran out a little way past the thought that Father Escrove was skinny, hard, and dangerous. Quite what form this danger took had not yet entered Sir George's mind, whereas on the other hand, the man of God knew exactly what the danger in Welden was.

The danger was the evil of a parish that was operating without God, and yet Escrove did not blame Sir George. The old knight was feeble; he stumbled around his manor on that failing leg of his; some injury sustained in the wars. He had allowed his village to descend into the dung heap, but the minister knew that the real blame lay not at Sir George's door, but at the door of the church; St. Mary's. Whoever that vapid vicar had been (and Escrove could not now remember his name), he was undoubtedly the miscreation responsible for permitting Satan to stroll up this winding darkening valley, unchallenged.

If only the bloody weakling priest were not in the ground, Escrove would have taken great care and pleasure to put him there; he had been the one who should have stood with a shining sword ready to lop off the head of the Monster; yet had instead seen fit to do nothing while that beast grew in every festering corner of this sordid little place.

Escrove pushed a piece of pork across his pewter plate, and estimated Lady Hamill, halfway along the long side of the table. What was she? Twenty-five years the junior of her husband? Thirty? *Forty?* It was a wonder the old dog had been able to put a baby into her, but that he had evidently done, as Escrove had had to be shown the damn thing before supper, brandished at him by some fat serving girl with an inappropriate name.

The sons, Samuel and Robert sat either side of their step-mother, mute as mud. Their sister, Agnes, did not eat with the grown-ups, but had been fed and put to bed much earlier on.

"And how long will you abide here, Father?"

It was the lame-legged old dog, speaking to him from the length of the table.

Escrove didn't hesitate with his reply.

"As long as the Lord wills it."

"Yes," said Sir George, his fork hovering in midair. "Very good.

"And what is it you intend to do here, Father?"

"The Lord's will."

"Yes."

The fork, hovering.

"And—?"

"Yes?"

"What is the Lord's will?"

Now Escrove didn't reply, and his silence was more dreadful than any words. Samuel and Robert studied their empty plates; Lady Hamill, barely a year older than Samuel, found herself unable to look away from the minister's eyes. A piece of pork fell from Sir George's fork, onto the floor.

"There has been no priest in St. Mary's," whispered Father Escrove, "for nigh three months. Whether the sinfulness I have already witnessed, merely from my carriage ride here, had been allowed to flourish before that time, or merely since he departed, I do not know, and I do not care. But before I leave this parish not only will there be a vicar in the pulpit once more, but every man, dog, and worm in this place will know the fear of the Lord."

He rose from the table.

Sir George rose, too, wincing as the weight went onto his leg.

"Very good, Father."

Escrove clicked his fingers at an old servant who stood by the door.

"Show me to my rooms."

With that, he was gone, and the air behind him trembled.

8 ◉ GRACE

THE OLD SERVANT, WHOSE GIVEN NAME WAS EDWARD and who had no second name, had seen many things in his years, so he flustered little at the manner of the minister.

But he had stood and listened to everything that had passed up and down the table over supper, and as he made his way to sit in a cool corner of the kitchens, he enjoyed himself a great deal by telling everyone there what had escaped from the minister's lips. He told how the Father had presided over the trial of, by his own modest accounts, at least thirty women, and how pleased he was to say that he had put every one of them at the end of a rope.

Further, he claimed to have unmasked the Devil working in several men, too, though that work was by far less satisfying, he explained, than the purification of the weaker sex. With his own eyes, Edward went on to recount, Father Escrove had witnessed a woman turn into a bundle of writhing snakes, and seen the Devil hovering over the shoulder of a woman accused, even while in the courtroom that was trying her. Finally, Edward finished with a whisper, Father Escrove had uncovered a hideous coven in which babes were fed from women giving not milk, but blood.

Such things being so, Father Escrove knew just what to do in the face of evil: exterminate it.

The kitchen listened with some glee to these tales, Cook even pausing awhile to hear the stories, and in the corner sat Grace, with her ladyship's son at her breast, sucking away.

A dozen times Cook had told Grace not to bring the child into the servant's part of the house.

"If they catch you, girl, you'll be out on your arse," she'd said, a dozen times or more. But Grace got bored feeding the boy up in the nursery, all by herself. She liked to come to the company of the kitchen to hear the gossip.

It didn't cease to amaze her how this noble little gentleman kept growing off nothing more than her milk, day by day, when the feeble boy that had come out of *her* hadn't gained so much as a fleck of fat in his short time on Earth.

Anyway, the fattening baby was now sucking in his sleep, so she pulled him off, put herself away, and hastened from the kitchen, along the passage, up the back stairs and to the nursery. There, she put the baby down in its crib, and turned her mind to more interesting matters.

One floor down and at the end of the corridor lay Robert Hamill's bedroom. There was no time to waste. Supper was done and he'd be in bed soon, if not already. This was an opportunity for which she had waited. She tiptoed down a floor and then along to the door, where she tilted her head and listened through the wood. She could hear movements inside; a jug and a basin of water, the soft sound of a window being opened. She knew she had attraction for men; both Michael and Steven Byatt had proved that point. Several times. She pulled the waist of her dress down, a tug, to expose an inch or two more flesh. Then, without knocking, she opened the door, and strode in to find Robert Hamill in his britches, washing at his basin.

He stood up straight, his eyes wide, and then, as his stepmother's wet nurse came in, shut the door behind her, with the top half of her dress way down from her shoulders, his eyes grew wider still.

He stared at her.

She said, "Hello, Master Robert," and smiled what she supposed was an invitation.

Then he screamed, "How dare you!" at her, closely followed by "Get out at once!" when she was too stunned to move the first time.

Blood rushed to Grace's face as she understood that Sir George's second son was not the least bit interested in her. She hurriedly pulled her dress back into place and ran from the room to her own tiny bunk in the attic, where she lay sobbing until the stars faded from view.

9 ◉ THE GIVING GROUND

MONDAY WAS HARD ON ANNA TUNSTALL.

She took Tom with her to Fuller's Mill while she worked, because they no longer had a mother to look after him. Anna wasn't sure that John Fuller would allow Tom to loiter about the mill all day, and on the way down just after dawn she lectured him on that issue.

"You must be good, Tom, and not get into trouble, Tom. Or John Fuller will send you packing, and then what will you do all day while I work? Tom? D'you hear me, Tom?"

In fact, that at least had been fine.

Tom sat in the shade of the trees that were the edge of Callis Wood, and played all morning with the spinning top that Robert Hamill had given him. Whenever Anna came outside she checked on him, and worried. She watched him staring at the ever-decreasing spiral that the top made as it spun, and worried that that was what made him have the fit the day before. She had never worked out why they came, nor had her mother, but they seemed to be set about by all sorts of odd things. And some nothings, too. But Tom seemed well today, although he stared at the spiral endlessly. Whenever the time came to take a load of cloth up to the tentergrounds, she got Tom to walk up with her, and worried that he seemed weak after his attack, weaker than he usually was.

But when work was done, Tom was fine and had become no bother and furthermore, as they were leaving, Helen Fuller had come out of the mill house and pushed a large wedge of cheese wrapped in nettle leaves into Anna's hands.

"Don't tell John," she whispered, smiling, and sent them home.

But on top of a day's work, when Anna got home she found Ma Birch sitting in the sun on the step of Tunstall Cottage, wanting the poultice that Joan used to make for her knees.

So Anna set to making that, with some old flour, some dried mugwort, and a little yeast to give it warmth. When she was gone, there was a knock at the door and there were the Smith twins sent by their mother to ask what was good for bruises, and just as she got rid of the twins there was another knock.

"Please God, what?" snapped Anna, and flung the door open.

There was Robert Hamill with a face like a lovesick sheep.

Anna did her best to smile.

"Yes, sir?"

"Don't call me sir, Anna," said Robert Hamill, second son of Sir George to Anna Tunstall, the laborman's daughter.

Not knowing what to say to that, she said nothing.

He looked through the door, beyond Anna's beauty, and saw Tom playing with the top on the hard earth floor.

"Come for a walk with me," he said.

Anna hesitated.

First jewelery, now walks. But he was the squire's son.

"I'll give you this back," said Anna, and from the neck of her dress pulled out the silver heart.

She held it out, but with consternation she could see that Robert was already shaking his head. He took it from her, but then slipped it straight back over her head again, and as it sat about her neck she felt a shortness of breath come into her.

Her arms hung limp by her side; she could not lift a hand. This was Sir George's son who commanded her.

"Leave it be," he said. "And come for a walk with me."

Anna still did not move, but he was waiting. Watching.

"Very well," she said, quickly and small.

"Very well indeed," said Robert, smiling.

They walked in silence from Tunstall Cottage along the track that led along the top of Callis Wood. Anna walked with her head down, so her hair protected her gaze again. She said nothing by way of reply to his attempts at conversation, and presently he stopped trying.

When they crossed the track down to Fuller's Mill, the trees were no longer called Callis Wood but Horsehold Wood, and from here it was a short walk to the path that led to St. Mary's.

"Oh," said Robert, seeing the churchyard ahead of them. "Perhaps you would not have come this way."

Anna shrugged.

"I wanted to come here today. I want to come here every day if I can. To see Mother."

Robert gave a nervous little nod.

"Your father is dead, too, Anna?"

"Some few years ago."

Robert nodded.

He tried to sneak a glance sideways at Anna when he thought she wouldn't see. That hair, the way it curled to her shoulder and hung upon her black dress. Her pale skin. He remembered seeing her slender calves the day before as she dangled her feet in the water. With the sunlight behind her, he was able to see the outline of her legs through the cloth of her dress, even black as it was. The blood stirred within him.

"I will speak plain then," he said.

Anna had reached the gate of the giving ground, beyond which the bodies of the dead were slowly releasing their souls to heaven, or other places.

"You have no father to speak for you and your mother is gone, too. I do not think you are foolish, Anna. You must be wanting for support. I can offer you such support."

Dear lord! thought Anna. *What does he mean?*

"My lord," said Anna, "I do not know what you mean."

Overnight, as she'd lain awake in bed, walking through the events of the day of her mother's funeral, nothing seemed as strange as the boy Robert giving her a silver locket. In the end, she had decided that it was his way of trying to buy some time with her body on the forest floor, and yet now here he was speaking of even wilder things.

"I can make you a good life, Anna. You will want for nothing. My father is a rich man. I myself have already—"

"Your father . . . ?"

Robert was not listening.

"I can make you a good husband, Anna. You will want for nothing. I can see to that."

"Husband?"

"Yes. I am making you a proposal. You will come and live at the manor to be my wife."

"The manor? You'll take me to the manor?"

She was so dumbfounded she could not think.

"You'll take me as your wife? To the manor?"

"That is my proposal."

"But—you can't! What do you think? Your father is a knight! Mine was a laboring man. You cannot surely believe your father would agree to such a thing."

"I will speak to Father. I will get him to understand that I wish it to be."

"You want me to be your wife?"

"I do."

"And you'll take me to the manor?"

"I will. Until such time as I move to my own property."

"And you'll bring Tom with me, will you?"

Anna felt the blood of her own body stir in the evening heat now.

She saw Robert's face, his mouth moving, his eyes dead, as he spoke some words, which were these; "I shall see that your brother is well cared for. We can perhaps send him to the poor house in Deepdale. I will pay a doctor to look at him. Perhaps something can be done."

"But he's not to live with me?" Anna asked, trying to keep her voice smooth.

"You can hardly expect that. No, Tom will be ably cared for elsewhere when you come to the manor."

That was that.

Anna forgot that she was William Tunstall the laborman's daughter, and that she was speaking to the second son of Sir George Hamill.

"How dare you? How dare you!" she cried.

She swung herself through the church gate and shut herself in.

"You would take me away from Tom? To be your wife? I would never marry you. Not ever! Even if it were such a thing that could happen! You fool!"

Robert's face burned at her.

He snatched the gate open and went in after her.

"You get away from me, Robert Hamill," she said, but Robert came on.

"Have a care what you say," he said, and grabbed her wrist. For one so slight he was strong, and he twisted her wrist so she fell to her knees.

"Stop that," she shouted. "Stop that."

But he did not.

He pulled back her lovely long red hair in his hand, tipping her head and then he planted his mouth on hers.

She tried to pull away but he grasped her hair all the harder, and then she bit his lip so deep that she tasted the blood that welled into her mouth before he pushed her away.

He staggered back holding his mouth, blood dripping between his fingers onto the dry grass of the giving ground, and while he stood there, surprised, angry and rejected, Anna made good her escape. She did not stop running till she slammed the cottage door behind her and threw the bolt, and the echo of both came back from the far side of Welden Valley.

Tom looked up from the floor. Suddenly the stupidity of what she'd done rushed into her. If Robert Hamill decided to be vindictive, he could probably get his father to throw them off his land, and then, even this pitiful hovel and the few things they owned would be lost to them.

She stared at Tom for a long time before she realized he was speaking to her.

"Will we eat, Anna?" he said.

Anna shook herself. Her hair hung damp on her forehead; there was heat in her chest. She looked at her young brother.

"Will we eat?" he said again, and Anna could only think of the stupid thing she'd done.

10 ◉ SIN

SO THAT'LL BE HIM, THOUGHT ANNA.

She'd come out of the mill with a bundle to tie, to take up to the tentergrounds, and sensed something. Someone.

There he was, and God, he was as thin as they'd said. Like Anna he was draped in a long black dress, but there the resemblance ended. The cassock hung off him like a shroud on a scarecrow. Where Anna's skin was pale, his was sallow and gray, and what little hair he had left clung to his skull. But he was tall, and his eyes seemed to have found her the moment she left the mill.

He was standing in the trees, at the edge of Callis Wood. He stood perfectly still and Anna didn't know whether to acknowledge his presence or just go about her work. They'd been talking about him yesterday. Down at Gaining Water smithy. She'd gone there with the two pennies her mother had owed Jack Smith, since she'd managed to get Ma Birch to pay for the poultices she'd been having. Anna didn't want Jack Smith to have anything over her, not even tuppence. At the smithy, she'd found Jack and Elizabeth talking to John Turner and Adam Dolen about the minister who'd arrived at the manor house.

Anna kept her distance from Adam Dolen, but he was the one in the know. Since his Grace was living at the manor house now, he boasted, she knew everything that was going on there. She knew all about the Rural Dean, and why he'd come.

So Anna had given Jack the two coins and hurried away.

And now here he was. Standing in the sun pools that flittered down between the thick green leaves of Callis Wood. Watching her.

Her heart pounded.

But Father Escrove turned, walked away along the bank of Golden Beck, and was gone.

11 ◉ RIGHT- AND LEFT-HANDED MEN

DUSK IN WELDEN VALLEY. OWLS HOOTED IN THE half-light. The faintest of breezes twitched the tops of the trees. Golden Beck danced on as it had since water first curled its way through the cleft of rock that wound its way down to the place where Deepdale now sat.

Anna Tunstall sat in Tunstall Cottage. Tom was playing outside in the late evening warmth while she boiled herbs. Her mother had believed there was a cure for Tom's fits, and had tried many varieties and mixtures of plants, but without success. Despite the heat of another fierce day of sun, Anna bent over a pot on the fire, stirring, watching the tea revolve at the end of her spoon, believing the answer lay in there, somewhere. The endless turning hypnotized her for a while; she gave up wondering if she'd ever cure Tom, and began to think about herself. She still knew she ought to find a way to give that heart back to Robert, but it felt lighter about her neck now. It was by far the most special thing that had ever entered her life and at the very least, she knew she couldn't leave it lying around for Tom to find and start asking questions about. So for now it could sit as safely under her dress as anywhere, and she'd give it back as soon as ever she could find a way to make him take it.

Helen Fuller was putting food on the kitchen table at the mill house. She called to her husband, John, but he didn't hear her. He sat by the now-silent hammers in the mill room, wondering how he could afford to renew the lease on the mill if Sir George put up the rent, as he'd said he would.

Left-handed Jack Smith was beating his wife because of something she hadn't done, and outside the smithy, little Harry Smith was thumping Hettie Smith with his fat left fist while Hester stood by, unblinking.

Sir George Hamill was returning from a constitutional walk with Hector, the wolfhound. Sir George's walks were slow, but Hector was very old, and they suited each other as walking companions. Sir George reached his right hand out to stroke Hector's shaggy head.

In the manor house, lying on his bed, Robert Hamill stared at the ceiling, as he had done hour after hour. When the old servant Edward was sent to fetch him to supper, Robert said he was sick, and would not eat.

Grace Dolen heard that news from Edward.

She stole up to Robert's room again, and this time, in his misery, he did not send her away. Instead, he poured out his tortured heart to her, and she listened eagerly, joyfully drinking in everything he had to say, though she was careful not to smile. The boy was miserable, but she saw he had become angry, too, and she knew that was something she could use.

It was a hot night. All Robert's windows were open, as were the windows of his little sister, Agnes, who sat awake on her bed, listening in the dark as her brother cried and sobbed and spoke to the wet-nurse called Grace. She didn't catch every word. But she heard enough to make her excited, because here was her brother Robert telling Grace that he had been bewitched, and some other things besides.

And here was Grace replying, saying, "Yes, sir. She is a witch."

Much later in the finally cool night, with only the sound of owls and the rushing of Golden Beck for company, a figure slipped through the trees of Horsehold Wood, heading down into the valley, a stick of charcoal in their left hand.

12 ◉ THE CURVE OF LIFE

THE AXLE OF THE WATERWHEEL OF FULLER'S MILL was thick, almost two hands across. Its end was a flat smooth disc of age-pale wood, which constantly turned. And somewhere in the night, a line had been cunningly marked on that disc; a single line that wound to the center and, always spinning, seemed to forever shrink to nothing, and yet never disappear.

Tom had scampered ahead that morning, down the track through Callis Wood, to the mill.

He was enjoying his days sitting in the sun, watching Anna come and go, listening to Helen Fuller talk to him sometimes, and splashing in the millrace when the sun got too hot.

So when Anna arrived at the mill, she found Tom surrounded by a small group of people: John and Helen Fuller, John Turner, Anne Sutton, and from Deepdale, just arrived with a load of cloth on a sweating pony, young Simon Bill.

Anna saw that they were half watching Tom, and half watching the thing that he was staring at, fixedly, without blinking; the spiral on the axle end.

"Who set that there?" said Anna.

No one gave her an answer. There was something about the line that provoked silence. They all stared at it, and then they all stared at Tom Tunstall.

"Come. Come here, Tom!" Anna called, and tried to pull Tom by the arm.

He resisted. Without words, but he shook her off.

"It's time to work," Anna said to John Fuller. "Is it not?"

He turned to her, dream-held.

"Hmm," he said, quietly. "Yes. Time . . ."

"Who set that there?" Anna asked again. "Helen, who? Did you do that?"

Helen shook her head.

"Anna?"

She didn't seem to be seeing Anna Tunstall, though she stood right in front of her. Then her eyes brightened a little.

"Anna? Anna."

"Helen, it's time to be at work."

Helen stirred.

"Yes. You are right, Anna."

But she didn't move.

Anna shook Tom's shoulder. Nothing.

She stood in front of him, and slowly he leaned around her, to keep his eyes on the axle, and then Anna spun him hard, forcing him to look away.

"Gentle with your brother," murmured Helen, and Anna angrily marched up to the axle end, and pulling a rag from her pocket began to rub at the charcoal line. She rubbed fiercely, but couldn't remove the burnt wood marks, yet she did enough to smear it, spoil its form. Hide it.

She turned back to the group.

"It's time to be at work!" she yelled, and she watched in amazement as the five of them seemed to wake from a sleep, stand and stare at each other for a few moments and before hurrying off to be at their business, as if they were embarrassed.

Anna turned to Tom, who was now sitting on the flags outside the mill, staring across the water of Golden Beck.

She tried to speak to him, but he was lost somewhere.

She held him and kissed the top of his head and tried to speak to him again and there was John Fuller at the door of the mill house, shouting, "Anna! We don't pay you to nursemaid your brother!"

So she left Tom sitting by the water as the sound of the fulling hammers starting their day's pounding battered them both.

13 ◎ SIR GEORGE IS DEFEATED

"THERE IS A PESTILENCE HERE," SAID FATHER
Escrove, "but it is not a bodily one. It is a pestilence of the soul."

He stood square in front of Sir George in the arching high
hall of the manor, while Sir George, sitting in his dining chair,
rested his leg. He'd been on it too long recently, and the heat
didn't seem to help things. It ached terribly and whenever it did
he relived the pike going into it as if it was happening now, and
was not something that happened thirty years ago.

And to add to his trouble, there was this black creature in
front of him, buzzing at him like a blowfly.

"These are good people," began Sir George, but he was weary,
and the minister's patience had run out.

"Good? There are no such people. That is something I have
learned through my work. There are no good people. There are
only people who haven't been caught at their wrongdoing yet.
And this parish is full of them. There is wickedness on every
side. Heathen dances on the high ground, right in the face of
the church! I know of at least two burials that were conducted
outside of Christian ceremony! There are bastards on every side;
sins of lust and lechery!"

Here he looked with full meaning at Sir George, to give him

to understand that a wife young enough to be his granddaughter was, in his eyes, a wickedness.

Sir George sighed.

"It is not so terrible as you say."

"Not so terrible?" snapped the minister. "Nay, you are right. It is worse! How dare you lecture me on God's business? You have allowed such devilment to foster itself here, under your nose! Do you deny these things? Do you defend them?"

"No, of course not. But it is only dancing. Some license with the law . . ."

"You call these things acceptable?"

Sir George was being backed into a corner and he knew it.

"No," he said. "No. Of course not. But these are simple people. They do things their own way, sometimes and—"

"And not the way of God?"

Sir George said nothing, because there was nothing he could say to that. But the minister was not finished.

"I have come here," he spat, "to restore a priest to the church, to restore the name of God in this village and, by God, I will do that. You can either assist me in my work, or obstruct me, but I will do these things either way. And if you do not assist me I can promise you that life will be all the harder for you. This may be your land here, but the law of God trumps the law of England! Or had you forgotten that? Here, tucked away in this valley with your good people?"

Sir George Hamill hung his head and sighed. How his leg ached, and how he wished this devil would be gone.

"You are a Justice of the Peace, are you not?"

Sir George knew that Father Escrove knew that he was, so he didn't trouble to reply.

"You are a Justice of the Peace. You have the full power of the law in your hands, and a refusal to do so could be greeted with the deepest concern by the king, could it not?"

Sir George troubled himself to give the faintest nod of his head.

"So?" asked the minister. "I can count on your assistance?"

When Sir George lifted his head again, his eyes were glistening.

"Yes, Father," he said.

14 ◉ WITNESS

THERE WERE SCREAMS.

Outside the mill.

Anna ran from the dark hammers and saw Tom in a fit, scraping himself on the flags, his head banging on the stone. The Smith twins were there, watching, and their brother Harry, as were Adam Dolen, Ma Birch, Anne Sutton, and others, all watching Tom on the ground.

Anna ran, pushing roughly past them to get to Tom, where she began to calm him, speak to him, settle him, hold him while the fitting passed. It took longer this time to bring him back and while Anna spoke she felt all the eyes around her, staring at her, staring at her brother, and she turned and shouted.

"Go away! I hate you. Go!"

Her shouting only upset Tom more. He struggled in her arms, so she clung to him whispering as calmly as she could.

"Tom. I'm here, Tom. I love you, Tom. I'm here."

Over and over, until eventually the shudders became only shakes, and the retching and wracking let his muscles alone.

Now, Anna turned, and saw that the crowd had left her, just as she'd wished, though she saw Adam Dolen still watching her from the trees across the far bank of Golden Beck.

There was a voice at her shoulder.

She turned, looked up to see John Fuller.

His face was empty.

"Take him home, Anna," he said.

"But there's still half a day's work to be done," she said.

John shook his head.

"Not today. Take him home."

It took Anna half an hour to get Tom back to the cottage. He ambled along, stumbling frequently. He said not a word, didn't even seem to recognize that Anna was speaking to him. Slowly, step by step, she got him up the track and back home, where she lay him on his narrow bed.

"I've something for you to drink," she said. "Tom, did you hear? I've something for you to drink, that will make you well."

Tom's eyes were pointing at the ceiling, and stayed that way.

Anna looked at him a moment longer, then went to the pot and began to get a fire going to let the tea warm before he drank it.

When it was ready, she propped him up on the bunk and held the cup to his lips, letting him sip it slowly, letting the tea slip into him steadily, and she prayed that it would make him be properly alive again.

He lay back down again when the tea was done, and then he slept, deeply.

They came for Anna that afternoon.

The sun had moved round to beat on the front of the cottage, pouring burning light into the dark space, setting bright

squares on the earth floor inside, when there was a thump at
the door.

Just one, and then the door flew open.

With the glaring sun behind them, Anna couldn't see who it
was outside her house.

She could only see a raggle-taggle crowd, and from their silence, she sensed danger.

"What do you want?" she said, but she received no reply.

They came in to get her.

She tried to shut the door, but someone put a boot against it
and they were inside the cottage.

By force they took her outside and she yelled, "What do you
want with me?"

Again, there was no reply.

Now she saw who had come. There was Adam Dolen and
his wife Maggie. There was Jack Smith. There were the Byatt
brothers. There was William Holt and John Turner. And there
was Grace, standing off to the side, glaring at Anna.

"What have I done?" screamed Anna as they began to drag
her down the track.

Still they didn't answer. They didn't need to.

Grace stalked into the cottage as they went and wanted to
burn everything.

She stared at Tom on his bunk, who seemed to have slept
through it all, slept in some place very far from the waking world;
his chest rising and falling slowly. She looked at the herbs hanging from the roof beam, and at the jars of remedies that Joan
Tunstall had made. It was one of those things she'd smeared
across Grace's sick baby, those things that had killed it.

She saw the pot of tea hanging above the fire and she kicked out at it, sending it flying, spilling the contents all across a wall and onto the floor.

She spat on the boy Tom as he lay on his bed, and then she hurried after the others, for she did not want to miss a moment.

15 ◉ THE WATER GIVES ITS ANSWER

THEY DRAGGED HER SO HARD AND SO FAST THAT her feet barely touched the ground, and though she begged for answers, to know what they wanted and where they were going, and why, they all held their tongues.

Their hands however, were not still, and Anna screamed as Jack Smith for one let his hands visit places they had dreamed of at night as he lay in bed beside his wife. She fought all the more as he touched her and that only got her a slap across the back of her head, which made her want to be sick.

She wrenched her head round and one last time she screamed at them.

She looked Jack Smith in the eye as she screamed, but there was nothing there to see but hate, and then they were by the pool just above Fuller's Mill.

Anna cried out. There was not even anger left in her now; only wild wild fear.

"What are you doing?"

"The water will give its answer!" Adam Dolen yelled. His face wobbled as he flung his words at the woods beyond the pool.

John and Helen came out of the mill house and started toward the crowd, but Adam Dolen swung his fist at them.

"Get back!" he snarled, and they did. "We're going to swim her."

Anna screamed, again, again, and then they had her on the ground. Hands grabbed her ankles and her wrists and she was lifted off the flags into the air, where they begun to swing her backward and forward.

She wailed, incoherent sounds pouring out of her, as they let her fly. She was in the air for an age it seemed, and all was silence but for the rushing of Golden Beck filling the pool. Next moment she hit the water, the shock of the cold gripped her, but the only thought in her head was of Tom, who could swim like a fish, where she had never learned, had never had time to learn.

Her woollen dress sucked itself into the water, and she went under straightaway. She fought against it and managed to erupt from the pool, screaming even as she tried to gasp at the air.

She batted her hands against the surface, sending great splashes into the mosquito air, but it was not enough to keep her up.

"If the water takes her . . ." slobbered Adam Dolen.

He didn't finish his words. They all knew what was happening.

Grace stood on the bank now, screaming at Anna in the water. She had managed to work herself into a frenzy, had even managed to convince herself that she cared that her baby had died, and she wailed as angry tears poured down her cheeks.

"You killed my boy! You killed my boy!"

She picked up a stone and hurled it at Anna, who had come up for a second time. The stone missed by a handsome margin, but it didn't matter. Anna was going down, and secretly Grace started to grin as Anna was about to die. Her drowning would prove her innocence, but Grace didn't mind about right or wrong, she only wanted Anna hurt and dead.

Anna went under for the final time.

She tried to hold her breath as she frantically flailed under the water. She'd seen Tom make the slightest movements, and glide along, whereas all her efforts did nothing.

She stared up at the sunlit surface of the pool, where the world shimmered through the water. She could see Grace leaping about, and then, as she sank deeper, Anna's gaze drifted dimly down, where, on the rock wall of the far bank of Golden Beck, under the water line, she saw a huge spiral line carved into the stone. A spiral.

Under the water, a spiral, illuminated by a single sunbeam that penetrated the depths.

The witch in the water was not yet dead.

She tried once more to fight against the weight of her clothes, as the last bubbles of air popped from her mouth, and she tasted the beck entering her mouth.

Then there were hands under her.

Too desperate now to even understand, she fought against them, but moments later felt herself being pulled up, and to the side. She was at the bank, with an arm under her, around her, a thin arm.

She coughed and choked and spluttered water. She heard a voice in her ear say her name.

"Anna."

She turned.

"T-Tom!"

She clawed for the bank some more, and Tom pushed her, so that she managed to climb onto the bank, where she lay heaving and spewing the cold water from her.

Tom clambered out of the water after her, and sat by his sister.

The crowd stared.

Not moving, not speaking, they stared, not knowing what to do.

Grace shoved her father, and Adam Dolen took a step forward, but John Fuller put his hand out and held him by the elbow.

"No more, Adam," he said, and he said it well enough for Adam to stop.

Anna lay on the ground still, Tom sitting there; his hand on her head, gazing at his sister.

"I'm here," he said. "You'll be well soon, Anna. I love you, Anna."

And then Anna began to cry, though she didn't want to in front of these people who had tried her in the water, but she did, she wept. The crowd, Adam, Jack, and all of them, turned their faces to the earth and slunk away, leaving only Grace to stand and hate Anna.

"You won't," spat Grace. "You won't."

But what it was that Anna wouldn't do, Grace didn't say. John Fuller came and shoved her in the back, sending her packing, and no one saw the black charcoal marks on her left palm.

Anna rolled onto her back and found Tom's hands with hers.

He laughed quickly and happily.

When they could stand Anna up on her feet again, John Fuller helped Tom to take her home, though they went in silence the whole of the way.

That night, Anna didn't sleep. All through the long hours, she expected the cottage door to burst open, and the crowd to come back.

All through the long hours, she lived again and again in the water; feeling the cold holding her, tasting the water in her mouth, the surge of panic as she knew she couldn't swim, and would drown. But for her little brother, who had somehow woken, and found strength, and run down the valley to throw himself straight into the water, she would have.

Above everything else, she wondered about what she'd seen under the water; there on the wall of the rock beneath the surface, hidden from view, the spiral.

She was afraid, and she wondered what it meant.

She'd grown up with the spiral maze on the tentergrounds.

She'd danced widdershins in circles with the rest of the village, just as much as any of them. But then that mark had appeared again, on the toy that Robert Hamill had given Tom. And then again on the axle of the waterwheel.

And now here it was, on the rock, under the water of Golden Beck, and it scared her. There was some magic about that mark, something old and powerful, she was sure, and though, like her mother, she had always wanted to know what is not known, and uncover the covered, and find out everything she could about the world, something deep inside told her to be scared, and she was.

16 ◉ THE NAIL

THESE WERE THE BRIGHT HOT DAYS IN WHICH ANNA'S fate was sealed. The sun scorched the grass of the tentergrounds. Trees wilted; branches of the tall ash by the churchyard cracked and simply fell off in the dried air, even the level of Golden Beck seemed to fall slightly, though not enough to expose the carving it had long been hiding.

The strong colors of early summer were gone. In their place were pale browns and greens that faded further every day, and if there was only one strong color left, that color was black, the black of the minister's cassock.

This was the time when Father Escrove began his work in earnest, and he was as shrewd as he was eager.

He had heard about the ducking of the gracewife's daughter. It made him smile, to think of these simple people. Their enthusiasm was undeniable, and yet their methods were crude, primitive. There were much more subtle ways of bringing justice, much more powerful. And having heard about the ducking, and how the inevitable conclusion was made inconclusive thanks to the intervention of the girl's brother, Father Escrove grew very interested in these goings-on indeed.

So his first visit was to the nursery of the manor house.

There he found Grace, with the third Hamill son sucking at her breast. The minister suppressed the desire to wrinkle his nose, and instead placed himself by a small window that possessed a broad view of Welden Valley.

He'd waited some days since his arrival before getting to his work, and he knew now that that had, as so often before, been a successful strategy. It was important to listen, to hear what people had to say for themselves. For it could so often be used against them.

"Girl," began Father Escrove, without looking at her. "You have a babe of your own?"

Grace looked up from the Hamill boy. She could just see the minister's profile as he looked out of the casement. Didn't he know she'd lost a child?

"No, Father," she said. "It passed over."

Escrove nodded.

"So you came to wet nurse here?"

Grace nodded. Then she remembered the minister wasn't looking at her.

"Yes, Father."

"I am sorry for your loss. It must have been a . . . torment to you."

Grace nodded.

"Why did your baby die, child?"

Grace's eyes widened.

Oh God, she thought. *What happens if I say?*

"It was born sick," she said.

"And it did not recover?"

"It ailed every day."

"Till it died?"

"Till it died, Father."

"And what caused the ailment of your baby?"

Grace hesitated. Was it just so easy as to say it? Could it be? Still she hesitated.

Father Escrove turned in his chair, and now he looked straight at her. She lifted her head and found she was looking straight into his eyes, which held her, fixed her, and she stayed that way as she became aware that the minister was saying something to her.

"Do you think there was some malign influence on the infant? Child?"

Grace found herself nodding.

"Every day I took it to Joan Tunstall."

"Joan . . . ?"

"The gracewife. She died just last week."

"And every day you took the child to Joan Tunstall, and every day it got sicker?"

Grace nodded again. Still she stared into the minister's eyes and she felt small. All she wanted to do was to please him.

"Father?" she said.

"Yes, child?"

"The gracewife? She was a cunning woman, too. And she was helped. By her daughter."

"Her daughter?"

"Anna Tunstall."

"Anna Tunstall. And is she a cunning woman, too?"

Grace nodded.

"Yes, Father. The cottage is full of it."

"So, child. This Anna Tunstall. She helped bewitch your infant?"

Grace smiled inside, but outside, her face was a mask as she looked the minister in the eye and said, "Yes, Father. I'm sure of it. My mother swears so."

Father Escrove doubted very much whether a wench like this Anna Tunstall would have a coffin for her funeral, but if she did, the first nail had just been hammered into it.

17 ◉ GAINING WATER

FATHER ESCROVE MADE HIS WAY DOWN THE TRACK that wound through Horsehold Wood. Wood pigeons called to each other through the leaves of the scrub oaks, tall flowers thrust rude parts up from the darkness of the forest floor to find light and insect lovers. Golden Beck rang louder and louder as he approached, and with that sound, the sound of hammering grew louder, too.

He turned the final corner in the track to see Gaining Water smithy directly by the waterside, a large pool spreading beyond it, which quickly narrowed into the neck of a waterfall that dropped down toward Deepdale.

Through the open door of the smithy he saw the fire of the furnace, and in the hands of the smith, the fall of a hammer on glowing metal. Escrove enjoyed this infernal picture. He was at God's work, after all, and any malefactors he found would soon be enjoying the same scenes in Hell.

The way forward, of course, was to pick people off, one by one. The way to do that was to start at the weakest end of the chain. And Father Escrove had heard some things about Jack Smith.

He watched for a long time, through the door, waiting for Jack to finish his hammering. At last, the metal he was beating grew too cold to work. He thrust it into a glowing bed of coals, then stalked out of the door to cool off while it softened again.

He saw the minister right away, standing. Waiting for him.

"Father?" asked Jack Smith.

"Would you talk to your priest, Jack?"

"Of course, Father. What would you talk about?"

"I would talk about a girl named Anna Tunstall."

The minister noted that the blacksmith stiffened slightly at the name.

"What of her?"

"You swam her in the pool at Fuller's Mill?"

"There were many of us did that," Jack Smith said hurriedly. "It was not only me did that."

Jack saw that the minister was nodding. He sounded understanding.

"Of course, of course. And you must have good reason for doing what you did."

Jack Smith felt his mouth dry.

"We did," he said.

The Father was smiling at him, broadly.

"And what were your reasons?"

Jack Smith felt his tongue like a rough ball in his mouth.

"She's a witch," he said, very quietly.

"How do you know that? Did the water reject her?"

The blacksmith looked back inside his forge, and the minister coughed, just once, to get his attention back. He swung round and found that the minster's eyes were fixed on his.

"No, Father. That is . . . She was saved before we knew whether the water had made its choice. But she is a cunning woman, all right."

"You know that?"

"Everyone knows it!" cried Jack. "A cunning woman, just as her mother was. Everyone goes there!"

"Everyone?" asked the minister, and Jack knew he'd made a mistake.

"Many do."

"Do *you*?"

Jack Smith thought about the pots of herbs sitting on the shelf in the smithy kitchen.

"No," he said. "Never."

"And you would testify to this? About the girl?"

Then Jack Smith thought about Anna—her long hair, those slender legs he'd once seen as she danced the spiral dance and the wind lifted her dress. He thought about those wide lips and he thought about the number of times he'd imagined them on him. He remembered how she'd felt under his hands as they'd dragged her to the water. He'd managed to feel her softness. Oh God, how he wanted her. Oh, how he hated her. Bitch.

"Yes, Father," he said. "I would."

The second nail. And the third was even easier to come by.

18 ◉ WHAT FEAR CAN DO

FATHER ESCROVE ASKED TO BE INTRODUCED TO Jack Smith's wife.

They found her in the kitchen and Jack was stupid enough not to be able to stop himself looking at the jars of herbs on the shelf. But the minister didn't seem to notice.

He was smiling easily at Elizabeth Smith.

There were three brats in the room. A lumbering boy and two pallid girls who looked just like each other.

"Perhaps our conversation is not for innocent ears . . . ?" said Father Escrove, and Elizabeth shooed the children outside. They ran out, and then all three crept back and sat under the open kitchen window, a rare truce agreed in an unspoken moment.

The tall man of God was speaking to their mother.

"And what do you know of her?"

"Anna?" asked Elizabeth.

"Anna. Just so."

"Not so much. They live up there by the tentergrounds . . ."

"And your view of her?"

"Why, I . . . I don't know."

"She is an evil woman, is she not?"

"Anna? Evil? No, that's . . ."

"That's curious," said the man in black, cutting into her words with his own.

"C-curious, Father?"

"Curious, when your own husband here says that she is."

There was a long silence then, during which the children ached to peep over the windowsill, but dared not. There was something in that room that stopped them, and though they couldn't have named it, they felt it.

Fear.

Into the silence, Father Escrove said, "have you had an accident, Elizabeth?"

"Accident?"

"How come you by that bruise on your neck, Elizabeth?"

"Oh, that. An accident, yes. I stumbled and fell and hit on the table."

"It must have been a strange fall that placed your neck on the table," said Father Escrove, and then there was more silence, which the minister ended.

"So, your husband says the girl is practicing wicked matters. What do you say to that?"

Then there was the longest silence of all, after which Elizabeth spoke, quietly.

And she said, "He is right. She is a wicked girl."

Then Father left, striding out of the smithy, but not before he said one last thing.

"Be careful how you stumble, Elizabeth."

The children watched his black dress switching away through the trees by Gaining Water, and then he was gone.

They understood nothing.

19 ◉ FULLER'S MILL

FATHER ESCROVE WALKED ALONG GOLDEN BECK, taking the tiny path by the river bank, stepping over the hefty tree roots that crossed it from time to time, shaded from the heat of the day by the oaks and the steep valley sides.

He was satisfied with his morning's work, but in order to bring things to a head, there was one more testament he wished to obtain.

It took him a quarter of an hour to come to Fuller's Mill.

The sound of the hammers pounding the wool in the baths of piss came from inside, and something of the smell, too.

There was no one in sight.

Maybe she was here. This was the place she worked. But there was no sign of her, nor anyone else. The place seemed deserted, free of people, as if the mill itself was alive and running things ably.

Father Escrove approached and peered in a window. There was a man and a woman tending the fulling. But not her.

He walked around the side of the mill to the house and rapped his peeling knuckles on the door.

Nothing.

He rapped again, and now the door opened and the wife, Helen Fuller, was there.

"Father Escrove," he announced. "I am Rural Dean. You may have heard of my presence."

Helen nodded dumbly.

"Is your husband here? I wish to speak to him."

The woman seemed confused.

"Your husband, madam? He is the tenant of the mill?"

"Yes—yes," she stammered. She turned back into the house. "John!"

It didn't take much.

It didn't take long.

Within half an hour, John Fuller was where the minister wanted him to be, although the minister was surprised, and a little irritated that it had taken that long.

The man who employed Anna Tunstall, and who had employed her father, seemed reluctant to bear witness against her. And he was cleverer than the others. He managed, for twenty minutes, to avoid the traps that Father Escrove set him, always just avoiding condemning the girl, without condoning her either, and damning himself in the process.

But there is an Achilles heel to everyone, Escrove believed, and John Fuller's was one of the first he had discovered on his arrival in Welden.

So it had been a very easy matter to convince John Fuller of the seriousness with which Sir George wished to pursue the roots of evil in the parish. That the Father not only had his full backing, but that Sir George had explicitly stated that everyone in his parish should lend their full support to these investigations, or be deemed to be preventing the minister from doing his good work.

And, seeing the fear in John Fuller's eyes, it had been a very easy matter indeed to make one last step. It was something Father Escrove dropped lightly into their conversation, as if it were a passing matter, something irrelevant but somehow just worth mentioning, and he saved it for the end.

"Of course," he said to John Fuller. "You are the tenant of the mill? Sir George is your landlord? I assume it would not do, it would not do at all, to anger your landlord? Especially at a time when the rent is to be discussed . . ."

John Fuller wept openly then.

He wept, thinking of the gentle man who used to work for him, William Tunstall, who had not been evil, but who had taken some weak decisions in life and ended up a laborer in a mill.

And he thought about William's daughter, Anna.

"So," said Father Escrove. "I can assume you will not obstruct my work?"

John Fuller shook his head, just the slightest movement.

Father Escrove wasn't done.

"And the girl is not to work here, not while her innocence is in question."

John looked up.

"Not work here?" he said. "Innocence? And if her innocence is proven, then she can come back and work?"

Father Escrove smiled.

"Certainly," he said. "Certainly." Then he added. "Though I very much doubt that will be the case."

20 ◉ WITCHCRAFT IN ENGLAND

ANNA WAS ON THE TENTERGROUNDS AND ENGLAND lay beneath her feet and her fingertips as she hung the damp cloth on the tenterhooks to dry in the sun. Cloth that she had already hung flapped and beat in the breeze that wisped across the dying grass of the fields, and she knew it was a perfect day for drying.

The poles on which the tenterhooks were fixed were planted in the ground at a slant, leaning away from the wet weight they had to bear. The hooks were fixed to the top of these poles by short lengths of twine, and for the first time Anna saw the twist in this twine, how the threads spiralled around each other, like the tendril of the vine winds around whatever it can find to cling to.

Tom was at home, resting, she hoped.

His fits had come more often than before and it seemed he was keen for sleep through the long hot days. She wondered if she would ever be able to help him. Her mother never had found the solution, and Joan had been a far more skilled woman than she.

She wondered if she could earn enough money at Fuller's Mill to pay for a doctor to come from Deepdale to look at Tom one day, and that thought gave her hope, a hope for the future.

* * *

If she could, Anna kept her back to the sun as she worked. Her skin burned easily and this summer seemed to want to do her harm, just as it was scorching the world around her with the onslaught of heat, day after day after day.

She was nearly done with the new bundle, and began to hook up the last damp cloth, looking forward to the cool walk back down through Callis Wood, with the dry cloths to take back with her, much lighter than the ones she'd fetched up from the valley floor.

They came from all sides.

Jack Smith and his violent boy came along the wall of the churchyard, where Anna's mother lay rotting.

John Fuller came up from the Mill on the track that kept Callis Wood from Horsehold Wood, and from the trees of the latter came Adam and Maggie Dolen. Others followed, word having been spread by the mouths of those without thought: the Smith twins, Ma Birch, Anne Sutton.

But it was John Fuller who Anna saw first as she turned, heaving the dry bundle onto her back.

"John?"

"Anna. You're to come with us."

He didn't look at her, but at a spot near her feet.

Anna stared at him. She tried not to look at the others, for they filled her with fear.

"John?"

"To the manor. You're to come to the manor. Leave the cloth here, Anna."

So, this time, Anna walked quietly with her captors.

She led the way. They followed behind her, as if she were the priest leading her flock, and though she walked quietly, inside she was screaming.

21 ◉ DAMNATION ·

THE HALL OF THE MANOR HAD BECOME A COURTHOUSE.

The dining table had been moved to one end of the room under the high window, and behind it sat Father Escrove, flanked on one side by Sir George, on the other by Samuel Hamill, Sir George's heir.

Lady Hamill, Robert, and Agnes sat in chairs to the side of the table, their servants behind them.

The room was packed, and the villagers stared about them, for almost none of them had ever been privileged enough to be invited over the front step of the manor house, never mind the hall.

In a small clearing of the people, in front of the table, Anna Tunstall stood with her hands clasped together to try to stop the trembling.

The man in black didn't look at the girl in black.

He had his eyes turned down to some papers on the table before him, and was writing slowly and carefully with a quill.

The whole room waited while he completed his task, methodically.

Finally, satisfied, he looked to Sir George on his right-hand side.

"These things must be done true. Yes, Sir George?"

The old knight closed his eyes. When he opened them again, he saw that Father Escrove was at last looking at the girl before them.

"Her hair," Father Escrove quoted, "'in wanton ringlets waved, as the vine curls her tendrils.'"

His words fell onto the floor between him and the girl, who wanted to do nothing but run, though she knew that was impossible. Twenty strong men stood between her and the door.

The minister made his opening address.

"This land is full of witches; they abound in all places. I have hanged five or six and thirty of them. There is no man here who can speak more of this than myself. Few of these witches would confess it. Some of them did, against whom the proofs were nothing so manifest as those that denied it.

"The Devil is a spirit of darkness; he deals closely and cunningly. You shall hardly find any direct proofs against such a case, but by many presumptions and circumstances you may gather the truth in. They have on their bodies diverse strange marks at which the Beast sucks; for they have forsaken God, renounced their baptism, if ever they had it, and vowed their service to the Devil. And they have inflicted their powers upon the innocent.

"Therefore, we call forth witnesses, they who have reason to know that the girl before the table today is guilty of these many perverse crimes."

Here Father Escrove pointed at Grace Dolen.

"Come forward," he said solemnly. "Speak."

Grace did as she was told.

She found a good deal of that sadness she had summoned

before, and so she made a pitiful sight as she made great show of being unable to look at Anna, for terror.

"She killed my baby," she whispered, and the congregation gasped.

Anna shook.

"No," she said. "No."

The minister screamed across the table.

"Silence!"

And Anna fell silent.

Encouraged, Grace had more in her that she wanted to say.

"She killed my baby. Her and her mother did it. They made it sicker every day."

"We were trying to help!" cried Anna, and Father Escrove roared at her again, scaring her into silence once more.

"They smeared potions on him. They said it would cure him, but they killed him!"

Grace's eyes were alight now and she no longer seemed scared of Anna.

Father Escrove pointed at the accused.

"You smeared potions on the infant of this girl. Do you deny it?"

"No," said Anna. "No, but it was to help him."

Father Escrove bent to his quill and paper.

"She does not deny it."

He lifted his head.

"Your mother was a cunning woman, yes?"

Anna nodded.

"And you are a cunning woman, yes?"

"We only ever tried to help people—"

"Answer the question! You are a cunning woman! And you practice evil crafts for that!"

"No!" cried Anna. "No. We only ever helped people. That's all. Nothing more."

"Be silent!"

Father Escrove pointed his finger at her again.

"Be silent. Bring forth the next witness!"

He swung his hand at Maggie Dolen and her husband.

"Your daughter's babe was killed, just as she describes?"

Maggie Dolen seemed to have lost her tongue, a rarity that the village was amazed to see. But Adam Dolen had not.

"She did kill the boy," he said. "Her and her mother."

"My mother is dead!" cried Anna. "Let her be!"

"She does all sorts of evil up there—everyone knows it."

"What sort of evil?"

"There are pots," said Adam Dolen. "There are things in pots, and herbs, and liquids. And all to do harm."

"No!" cried Anna. "They do no harm. And you know it. You came to my mother yourself. You came to get a paste for your sore foot! *You came!*"

Anna turned to the room, desperately.

"You came! You all came! You all came for something. Tell him! Tell him you know it's for good."

But none spoke. Not one of them, though some had the decency to look at the floor when they felt Anna's eyes settle on them.

In the silence that followed, Adam Dolen felt a clever idea appear in his head.

"All sorts of things in that cottage," he said. "And there are books."

"Books?" asked Father Escrove, leaning forward.

"Books. Books that have evil in them."

"Why, I can't even read!" cried Anna. "What would I want with books?"

"Silence! The accused will be silent!" screamed Father Escrove, and his anger was so terrifying that Anna was struck dumb.

"Let us speak," said Father Escrove, "of the brother of the accused."

Anna's head flicked up. *Tom? What of Tom?*

"I have it here recorded," Father Escrove was saying, "from the witness of several persons here present, that Thomas Tunstall, brother to the accused, is prone to strange shakings and disturbances of both body and mind. That is so."

And that, no one denied. Not even Anna, but Father Escrove wasn't finished.

"And that these disturbances and symptoms, far from being natural, are indeed of unnatural origin, and do show nothing more or less than the truth that the boy is possessed by spirits!"

Father Escrove rose to his feet and pointed at Anna.

"You have caused this! You have dallied with the Devil and your brother has suffered! Possessed! Infected! And you cannot deny it!"

"I do!" shouted Anna, her voice hoarse from screaming. "I do! I deny it. Tom has a sickness. Nothing more! He has a sickness. That I will cure!"

"With your wicked potions, no doubt! You play God with your own flesh and blood! You invite Satan into him, and then would run for fear when you are unable to send him out again! You foul creature!"

The minister thumped the tabletop with his fist, over and over again, as he assailed Anna with words she could not refute.

He dropped back into his seat, his chest heaving for breath in the sweltering room. Sweat ran freely from his brow.

The room seemed to hover for a moment, held in thrall, and then Father Escrove said, in little more than a whisper, "bring forth the next witness."

He lifted that dreadful finger again, and this time the crowd was struck with awe as they saw on whom it fell.

Agnes Hamill, only daughter of Sir George.

"Step forward, child," said Father Escrove, and the terrified child stepped forward.

"Please, Father," said Sir George, but the minister cut him such a look as to send him slumping back into his chair.

Agnes stared at the minister, who smiled in return.

"Agnes, my child. Will you please tell the court what you heard your brother say to Lady Hamill's wet nurse in the night? Tell us, child, tell us loudly and clearly."

Samuel Hamill was staring at his little sister.

Robert Hamill shifted uneasily in his chair.

Agnes spoke.

"He said she was a witch."

"I did not!" said Robert, and then all eyes were on him, including those of Father Escrove.

"You did not?" he said, his eyebrows raised. "Did you not say 'she has bewitched me'?"

Robert stared wildly at Grace, then quickly lowered his eyes.

"What did you mean by that? 'She has bewitched me' You have lately been sick, have you not? You did not dine with us, for this sickness. Do you deny that?"

"I do not," said Robert, quietly, "but I did not call Anna a witch."

"Anna? You know her name?"

"We all know her name," said Robert quickly.

"I see," said Escrove. "So what did you mean when you said she had bewitched you?"

Robert's mouth opened, but he said nothing. He fought to find an answer.

"Please," cried Anna. "Tell him! Tell him what you did."

Father Escrove leaped.

"What? What is this? What is she speaking of? Have you spoken with this wench?"

Robert was shaking his head. His mouth was a grim thin line. The minister's eyes held him and Robert could not look away, of which he was glad, for it meant he could not look at Anna, who he had desired.

"No!" he said then. "Of course not! Why would I ever have spoken to a girl like her?"

"Quite so!" said Father Escrove. "She lies, just as they all do. To use lies against the innocent. The court will witness this!"

Anna broke into sobs, and her head hung as her tears fell.

Escrove stood.

"Enough!" he declared. "We must try other means. Such evil women have marks upon them—the place where the Devil sucks. It is merely enough to find these marks to have proof of malice. Strip her."

The room tensed, and a terrible silence descended.

No one moved.

Escrove pointed at Elizabeth Smith, Anne Sutton.

"Strip her. Find the marks."

So it was that Anne Sutton stepped forward eagerly, and Elizabeth Smith less so, and with the help of the men, they began to silently wrestle Anna from her dress, in a soft dumb silent theatrical of a fight, in which hands groped and feet scuffled on the wide floorboards of the hall.

They had the dress ripped at the back and pulled down, and Anna stood covered only by her shift, and suddenly Samuel Hamill stood, pointing, and said one word.

"Stop!"

The dumb dance stopped and Anna stood hunched over, breathing hard, Swinging from her neck was a silver locket in the shape of a heart.

Father Escrove turned to Samuel.

"What is it?"

"My mother's locket. That is my mother's locket."

Sir George sat up, leaning forward, peering.

"Bring that here," he said, and Adam Dolen wasted no time wrenching it from Anna's neck with a fat fist and brought it to Sir George.

He looked at the locket in his hand, and then lifted his head to the room.

"It is," he said. "It is."

Anna cried out to Robert, one last time.

"You have to tell them. Tell them you gave that me! Tell them!"

"Ridiculous!" roared Father Escrove, who rounded on Robert with eyes ablaze.

"You would have done no such thing, would you? To give your mother's jewel to this vile slattern! Ridiculous."

And it was all that Robert Hamill could do, as his father, his stepmother, his brother, his sister, the minister, and all the villagers of Welden stared at him, to mouth the words that killed Anna.

"No . . . Ridiculous."

Anna collapsed on the floor. Falling to her knees with her dress rent about her waist, her hair hanging in ringlets around her, and she knew without question that she was lost.

"Anna Tunstall," the minister said. "You have been brought before this court and found guilty. Of practicing treason against your masters. Of overlooking Robert Hamill. Of inducing the possession by devils of your brother. Of the murder of the Dolen baby by means of witchcraft. The sentence is death. You shall now be taken from this place and be hung by your neck until you are dead. And may God have mercy upon your wretched soul."

22 ◉ ROPE

THE WAY THAT FATHER ESCROVE LIKED TO HANG
people was simple.

The usual method, of course, was to give the condemned a
long drop, enough to snap the neck, which would result in a few
moments of jerking, and then stillness from the body while the
crowd vented their fervor and delight.

The minister did not favor this approach. It was too easy, and
too quick and did not make the best use of the death to strike
fear into those who had witnessed the execution.

Anna's hair was shorn from her head. It fell to the floor in
turning coils of red, and lay still, all movement from it gone
for good.

She was stripped of the remains of her dress.

Escrove watched all this. He looked at his witch, and hate
crawled within him, and twitched.

In her white shift, they carried Anna from the manor across
the field to the tall single oak that stood beyond the main road—a
sentinel high above the dales.

The world was burning that day, as hot as any day yet. The

earlier breeze had fallen away, and the air was thick and smelled of scorched grass. Grasshoppers called to each other and the sound of grunting came from the men who swung a length of rope over a high branch of the oak—Jack Smith, the Byatts, Adam Dolen.

Anna Tunstall was forced to climb a ladder that led to the branch, and there, from another ladder, Jack Smith slipped the noose over her neck. Already, she found breath hard to come by.

"Not too long!" called Father Escrove from the ground, and Jack Smith grunted in satisfaction, shortening the length of rope that hung free from the branch.

He climbed quickly down, and Anna stood on a high rung, her hands tied behind her back, trying not to fall, though it would have only sped matters along if she had.

She looked up.

The tree arched over her, and the sky over the tree.

She saw closer things.

She saw the rope round her neck, and its short journey to the branch.

She noted how it twisted, round and round, that same shape.

The spiral dance.

The spinning top in her brother's hands.

The waterwheel.

The carving under the water.

The rope at her neck.

It was all the same thing; the same sign, and now she knew what it meant.

* * *

A little way away, in Tunstall cottage, Helen Fuller sat with Tom Tunstall, and wondered if he truly understood what she'd told him, what was happening to his sister.

She held him, though he seemed not to be crying, and she held him as tight as she could, as, over the windless air, she heard the voice of the minister call out, and a second later a muted cheer rose up above Welden Valley.

Helen Fuller held young Tom Tunstall tight.

"You're going to come with me, now, Thomas. With me, and John. You'll be with us now. You'd like that, wouldn't you?"

But there would be time later to explain that.

For now, she held the silent boy tighter still, and wondered when she'd ever stop crying.

QUARTER
THREE

THE EASIEST ROOM IN HELL

Saturday, March 26

MY ROOM OVERLOOKS THE SEA, TO THE NORTH AND the east.

Verity's, to the south and the east. Between our two rooms is a third smaller bedroom with an easterly view, which I will use as my study, and where I am writing now. I will put my desk in here when it arrives from New York. Otherwise all we have is a pair of suitcases each that made the journey with us. The Long Island Rail Road sped us as far as Greenport so that after these weeks of planning and letters to and fro, it is strange to arrive here so suddenly. Of course, from Greenport we still had some few miles out here, but Doctor Phillips had sent a man to meet us with a horse and buggy. Verity loved that, and I couldn't help smiling seeing her so happy. In New York we might just have climbed into a taxi, and though we are only a few hours away, it was a good reminder that things here are somewhat different.

Greenport, the end of the line, proved to be a bustling little town with a fine station, and I even saw a turntable on which the locomotives can be turned around before their trip back to the city. There is a ferry terminal, too, with boats to New York and the Connecticut coast. But even the short ride, eight miles or so, from there to Orient Point, showed our destination to be even further removed from modern society.

At one point, the land of the North Fork tapers, so there is sea but a stone's throw away on either side, and our driver showed us how the land is so low-lying that it is no wonder that floods across it are not uncommon.

Then the land widens once more and climbs a little, forming the headland. A road to our right leads to Orient itself, but our driver took us straight on, to the place that is to be our new home.

The building itself is as remarkable as I had been told. While all around are various outbuildings: the sheds connected to the farm and gardens, workshops, the crematorium with its tall chimney, and so on, the landscape is otherwise somewhat bleak and windswept, aside from the Kirkbride building; so ornate, majestic and, I truly believe, inspiring. Six full floors with their tiered wings tower over the grounds.

Here we sit in our rooms, with a bathroom of our own and even a small kitchen, at the eastern end of the seventh floor. This floor is shorter than the others, and covers only the central block of the building so that we have a view over the roofs of the sixth floor.

It is a fine view. Each of our three rooms has a door leading out to a balcony of all things! With a finely wrought white wooden railing safe enough for me to allow Verity to sit outside if she wishes. The balcony runs right round the building, so that I could stroll along to Doctor Phillips' rooms in the center if I wished, and there I might converse with him as two gentlemen on the deck of a liner, not as newly arrived employee talking to venerable employer.

All in all, it is a place that would suit the Vanderbilts, or the Astors, or the Du Ponts, were it on the South Fork of the island.

From my vantage point up here, and close to the gods I fancy, it takes some little effort to remind myself why I have come, what my work will be, and that in the building beneath and behind me are some three thousand insane, all sent here because society has no more hope for them.

I must end. Verity is calling for her father. I record in this journal only the brief hope that I may do well enough to send one or two of the insane back to the society that rejected them.

Sunday, March 27

I SLEPT WELL. I WOKE TO FIND VERITY AWAKE before me and dressed, standing looking out at the sea from the balcony.

I told her it was too cold to stand there in the stiff breeze, but she laughed at that, and only the idea of breakfast would bring her inside.

Breakfast appeared in a hatch in the hallway. This "dumb waiter" connects to the kitchens seven floors below. Verity laughed at that, too. She wanted to climb in, saying it was like a tiny elevator, and that she wanted to surprise the cooks.

I smiled but there was in me half a belief that she actually meant to do it. This place is vast; there are all sorts of mischiefs she might run into. I wonder if I have ever lived in such luxury and style. I know that Verity has not, with food appearing like magic, as if a genie made it happen, and with soft beds and views that a billionaire would not be able to fault.

"This morning you must entertain yourself," I said as we ate. I told her that I had to meet with Doctor Phillips, because tomorrow I start work, properly. And tomorrow Verity will go to the schoolhouse in Orient and we can settle down into a normal life.

After breakfast, I left Verity to play in her room. I paused in the doorway.

"Perhaps you could read awhile," I said.

"Perhaps, Father," she said.

I started to leave and then I paused again.

"Don't climb in the dumb waiter," I said.

She smiled at me and I left her to playing with her dolls while I went along the corridor to find Doctor Phillips, in his rooms at the west end of our floor.

In the center of the building is a most remarkable thing.

From the ground floor, all the way up to the seventh, is a giant curved stairwell. Therefore from the entrance hall, up to us, here, is a vast open cylinder, with a staircase that winds up and up, each elegant turn bringing you to the floor above.

It forms an enormous spiral staircase, though with interruptions at each landing. On the seventh floor however, on the landing at the midpoint of the corridor between Doctor Phillips' rooms and our own, the architect's idea of the spiral is allowed its true form, for here a beautiful free-standing wooden spiral ascends from the floor, thrusting up into a glass domed cupola, from which light floods down.

I haven't been up these steps as yet, but even from the landing I can see another place from which one could view the surrounding landscape: a circular walkway inside the cupola, with no other purpose than to admire the view.

I found Doctor Phillips hard at work at his desk, despite the day and the hour. His rooms are of course the mirror image of ours; except that he uses the room equivalent to Verity's as his office, a larger space in which to work.

He greeted me warmly, I felt, and asked after our travel and other matters in a sincere way.

"I trust," he said, "that all the arrangements were suited to your needs?"

I told him they were.

"Good," he said. "I like for things to be done well. And it is right that you are well cared for here. At the end of each day you will find that you have earned it. You enjoyed your breakfast, I hope."

I told him it had been excellent.

"If a little cold after its journey up seven floors," he said. "I generally eat in any one of the dining rooms. However at the weekends I take the chance for some privacy over breakfast. You may choose where you eat, although there is the matter of your daughter."

I nodded. It is a remarkable part of the system here, that I was to invite my family to live with me, and of course, with no mother at home to care for Verity, that was a major consideration in my acceptance of the position. I want her close at hand.

"I have no family," said Doctor Phillips, and a moment's reflection showed the truth of that to me. There were no photographs of wife or children either on his desk or on the walls. His rooms had the air of a college man—nothing feminine was in evidence, nothing was there that did not need to be there, save for an engraving on the wall of an antique map of Long Island and another of the North Fork of the island.

Doctor Phillips saw me looking at the maps.

"Oyster Ponds," he said, and I must have looked confused. "The former name of Orient Point. And before that, Poquatuck, to the Indians. And before that . . ."

He smiled. "Who knows?"

Doctor Phillips is a tall man, as tall as me I think, though he stoops a little from age. He is perhaps sixty. He has a tired look about him, and his eyes are circled underneath in dark blue.

"As I was saying," he went on, "I have no family, and so these things are unimportant to me. But such are the demands of the work here, that for those that do, it seems only well and proper that the family comes and abides here, too. Besides that, it is part of our grand plan that the insane are reminded of the normalities of the world outside. It will be helpful for them to see a father and daughter living happily, help them to remember such simple, honest structures, help them to strive in their return to mental well-being."

That made much sense to me. I have seen in my work before, in New York, how a patient might come to us relatively well, and yet how a few months in the hospital seemed almost to have dragged them down to the level of those for whom there truly is no hope. It seemed to me as if the very system designed to heal these poor souls was responsible for their demise.

Part of the "cure" here at Orient Point, a very large part, are these ideas that were Kirkbride's: the large, ennobling architecture, the ample light available in every ward, the modelling of normal society upon which the insane might copy and so build their road to recovery.

"Of course," Doctor Phillips went on, "I hope I don't need to tell you that at no time should your daughter be allowed to talk to the patients, nor should she even witness the existence of some of them."

He appraised me for a moment or two, until I stammered out, "No—no, of course not."

"Look!" said Doctor Phillips.

He was standing by the window and I joined him.

There, we witnessed something quite touching.

A wagon arrived in front of the asylum. I recognized our driver from yesterday, and now his black mare had been joined by a piebald, for they were pulling a larger, low cart, upon which sat a group of children, and a solitary woman dressed in dark indigo. They seemed tiny, looking down as we were from seven floors up, but I could see two things about the children. Firstly, they were poorly dressed, very shabbily indeed, and secondly, each one held a large bunch of flowers.

When the carriages stopped, they climbed out and filed down the drive of the asylum in a solemn manner, away from the building, the woman in indigo following at some distance as if her presence was barely required.

"Orphans!" said Doctor Phillips, smiling. "From the orphanage at Greenport. They come to us once a month. All part of the care we provide here at Orient Point."

The children turned through a gate in a neat hedge and now I saw their destination: a rather bleak-looking cemetery, just one part of the vast grounds here.

I must have looked mystified, because Doctor Phillips hunted round on his desk for a while, leafing through tidy piles of papers, until he found a newspaper cutting.

"Look," he said. "We got ourselves a write-up."

He handed me the paper as I watched the children begin to place their offerings on the graves, one flower for each.

My eyes still half on the children, I glanced at the cutting from the *Daily Suffolk Statesman*:

> The little inmates of the orphans' home at Greenport, under the supervision of their matron, gathered a lot of wildflowers, and decorated the graves of the insane dead, who have been buried at the asylum cemetery. The deed was a worthy one, and to the little ones is given a great deal of credit for doing this act of mercy to the unfriended dead.

I gazed down at the orphans, dressed in their paupers' clothes, brown and gray, and I thought about Verity, dressed in the finest clothes I could find in New York, and that comparison made me feel uncomfortable, I admit.

I told myself how good a nation we are to have such institutions as state insane asylums and orphanages and inebriates homes, and how lucky these people who live in them are to have such a safety net. That's what I told myself, and yet I felt little better.

Doctor Phillips was smiling down at the children going about their duty, and then, with horror, I saw another join them. As if my thinking about her had conjured her up, there was Verity, at the edge of the cemetery, under a stooping tree, watching the orphans.

Doctor Phillips' warning about Verity rang in my ears, and I felt my cheeks start to burn with just the thought of shame if he saw her. I glanced at him, wondering what he would say if he caught sight of Verity roaming the grounds on her very first morning.

"Now," said Doctor Phillips. "We should continue our interview. Perhaps a tour would be the thing."

I readily agreed. He had not seen Verity and I was only too glad to get him away from that window.

As we turned away, I took one last look at my daughter and saw that she was not alone. She had been joined by a man. From my distant viewpoint I could see nothing about him, save that he was dressed in a gray suit, and was pointing at the orphans, gesturing as if explaining something to Verity.

Doctor Phillips was waiting for me, and I hurried after him.

Sunday, March 27—later

I WAS PRAYING THAT VERITY MIGHT HAVE SEEN sense and returned to her room, or at least to have disappeared before Doctor Phillips or someone else caught her at large, as Doctor Phillips pulled a key from his jacket pocket.

Despite the grandeur of our accommodations, there are of course small reminders that this is not a hotel but an asylum; the most notable of these on our floor being the iron bars that seal us off from the six floors below, set into the landing just in front of that wonderful spiral staircase. Only three people have a key to the gate here: Doctor Phillips, the head warder, and now, myself.

As Doctor Phillips turned the key in the lock, invited me through, and locked the gate behind me, I wondered how it was that Verity had managed to escape our rooms. Looking back through the bars as we headed for the floors below, I saw the dumb waiter set into the wall of the corridor and I felt anger and disbelief, equally.

She couldn't have. But how else then had she got out, unless she'd convinced the head warder to let her out?

"The floors and wings of the asylum are carefully organized," Doctor Phillips was saying, and I reminded myself that I have a new employer to impress.

I joined him at the door to the west wing of the sixth floor.

"The wings divide the sexes. In here, and the five floors beneath, are the women. The men are housed in the floors in the east. From here you can really see the benefit of the Kirkbride system. See how much light each corridor receives?"

That was obvious. Compared with the dark squalor of the hospital in New York, Orient Point is flooded with light. The idea is ingenious. Rather than just have two long wings stretching away from the central block of the asylum, each wing runs for no more than a hundred feet before turning ninety degrees and then immediately ninety degrees again back to its original direction. What this results in is therefore a series of staggered corridors, and each one has full-length windows at either end, through which the powerful light of Long Island Sound pours in. Seen from above, the asylum must seem like a formation of strange oblong geese in a V, and in the center, the glass cupola with the staircase winding down like a screw into the building.

"We arrange the patients by floors, according to the degree of their disturbances."

Doctor Phillips peered through the glass doors of the women's wing of the sixth floor.

"These are our most docile customers," he said. "Those with profound melancholia, for example. As you can see they are of outwardly normal appearance, and may have even survived in society for some time before their commitment here. Note how the wide corridors permit social interaction. All corridors are at least twelve feet wide. The main arteries are no less than sixteen."

I joined him and looked through the glass.

I saw a group of three women standing at the far end of the first corridor, by the window. They were talking to each other and if not exactly chatting away as if at a temperance meeting, they would have indeed appeared nothing but normal on an urban street corner.

"The men are on this side," Doctor Phillips said. "Would you like to meet one or two?"

I told him I would, and after he unlocked the door, we strolled along the corridor of the men's wing, until we arrived at a particular room.

He knocked and without waiting for a reply, we entered.

The room inside was cramped, but ample enough for a single bed, a chair and a washstand. A small man sat on the bed, and rose immediately as we entered.

"Jonathan," said Doctor Phillips, and the man nodded. I could see at once that he was disturbed. He had extreme nervous reactions and yet was eager to please and answer all the questions that Doctor Phillips and I posed, albeit with one word answers, in general.

I thanked Jonathan for his time, and we left to continue our tour.

"You'll see how Jonathan, like all other patients on the sixth floor, wears his own clothes. Of course they all have to be tagged with their owner's names, but otherwise this enables these patients to feel a certain degree of normalcy."

That was true, I thought: *normalcy*. Though that normalcy is somewhat of an illusion. Even on the sixth floor, I noted that Jonathan's door has no handle on the inside, and therefore can only be opened from without. Also, there are bars on his window.

"The same is true of patients on the fifth, fourth, and third floors. So the majority of patients here wear their own clothes, or if they have damaged or lost their own, we provide them with simple alternatives. See this lady here."

We were at the third floor landing, and he pointed through

the glass to a woman standing by the door, in a plain white dress with a pinafore. She had no hair on her head, none at all, and stood motionless, but for her hands which she wrung together endlessly.

"From here down, the final two floors, we house our most intractable patients."

"Everything is well thought out," I said.

"Of course it is," said Doctor Phillips somewhat tersely, and I felt I ought to make amends.

"Things are nothing like this in New York," I said. "It's very gratifying to see such grand aspirations."

"Year after year, our society is producing an increasing number of lunatics," he said. I winced slightly at the old-fashioned word. He seemed not to have noticed. "We grow embarrassed by them and seek to deal with them in ever new ways. So now we have moved out of the city, for the most part, to places such as these. With air, with land, with nature all around, with honest work for the patients to engage in. In our embarrassment, we give the *lunatics* new names. So, some years ago, the Orient Point Lunatic Asylum spent four hundred dollars on a new set of letters to be welded over the gate. Now we are an Insane Asylum. In the next decade no doubt we will have to spend six hundred dollars changing our name again.

"But it is all for the best, perhaps. Our ways are changing. Here we use new ideas and new methods and cast aside the grim medieval notions of the madhouse."

He paused.

"The first floor."

We had completed our circular descent down the floors and

were now at ground level. From here, sounds of human voices floated down the wide, sunlit corridors. I could hear sobbing, and also the occasional cry and shout. I am used to these things, from my days in New York, but it is strange to hear these sounds in an environment that does not seem to match. Even the Kirkbride ideal has its extreme cases, I suppose. As if to emphasize that point, just as we made to leave, a naked man ran across the end of the hall, saw us, and ran out of sight again. I saw him for no more than a second or two, I suppose, but that was more than enough to see the dirt on him, and the wildness in his eyes.

"Shall we?" suggested Doctor Phillips, and we moved on, the noise of something or someone banging repeatedly dying away as we came to the outside.

The front of the buildings face south, and from here a wide lawn slopes away to the beginning of the gardens. I could see patients pruning hedges, weeding flower-beds, with warders supervising, dotted here and there, so distinct in their white uniforms.

I stole a look toward the gate behind which lay the cemetery, but I could see no sign of Verity underneath the tree.

"Our patients, those who are able to at least, take part in a variety of meaningful activities at Orient Point. They help with the grounds and ornamental beds. Our head gardener is a wonderful man who has infinite patience. Behind the main building is our farm. We keep livestock—sheep mostly, some goats and cows. We grow all our own vegetables, and have a fruit orchard, despite the perishing winds from the sound. The bulk of all this is done by the inmates here, with the lightest supervision possible by staff."

We continued our walk, passing some single-story buildings to the flanks of the main one.

"We have carpentry workshops and metal shops. There are washing rooms and drying rooms. Rooms for ironing and rooms for baking. There is an infirmary, a mortuary. In short, we have everything here that a small town would have."

"Even a cemetery," I said.

"Just as you saw."

"And a crematorium, too."

"Just so. There is the question of choice, when it comes to these matters. There is also the question of money. Not every patient has relatives who are able to afford the cost of a burial. Cremation is a considerably cheaper option."

Then, as we rounded the corner of the main building once more, Verity appeared.

She was standing talking to that man, the one in gray.

He looked up immediately as we approached, and smiled.

"You must be the new assistant superintendent," he said, and held his hand out. He nodded to Doctor Phillips.

"Yes, I'm Doctor James," I said, and shook his hand. "Doctor Phillips, may I present my daughter, Verity? Verity, this is Doctor Phillips. Say hello."

Verity did us proud. She gave a little curtsy and said, "How do you do?" in the sweetest way that I swore Doctor Phillips could not possibly be angry either at her, or me.

"A pleasure to meet you, young lady," said Doctor Phillips. He turned to the man in gray. "Charles."

The man turned back to me.

"I'm so sorry, forgive me. I'm Charles Dexter."

I nodded, offering him a smile, taking him to be one of the junior doctors who I had not yet met.

"A pleasure," I said, and then we were joined by the head warder, a man called Solway whom I had met only briefly when we arrived.

He bowled round a corner and stopped when he saw us. He said nothing.

Doctor Phillips turned to me.

"I think that's enough for one morning, Doctor James. We will see you on the wards early tomorrow and we can begin our work in earnest. I look forward to that. For now perhaps you should take Verity to see the sights of the island. The coastline is quite pretty I think, and it's a pleasant day for March."

I had the feeling I was being dismissed. There was perhaps something private that Doctor Phillips wished to discuss with Dexter or Solway, or both.

I took Verity's hand and bidding everyone a good morning, we set off. I decided to head back up to our rooms first because I had a conversation to have with her about her escape.

As we stepped into the entrance hall, however, I remembered that I had meant to ask Doctor Phillips if I could receive an advance on my salary. I would not have done so if matters were less pressing, but I had left New York with some financial trouble over me.

"Go straight upstairs and wait for me by the gate," I told Verity, and for once I was glad she did just what I said, because as I stepped out again and round the first corner of the building, I found a terrible scene.

There stood Doctor Phillips, his hands on his hips. He stood a little way away from Solway, who was bent over Dexter, who half lay on the ground as the head warder rained a series of blows about his head and his shoulders. Blood was running across his face from a cut above his eye.

Dexter tried to ward off Solway's fists, but Solway is a tough character, and kept up this assault. I heard Doctor Phillips speaking to him.

"What did I say, Dexter? What did I tell you?"

Dexter did not reply, but as he struggled under the blows, he saw me staring at the three of them, and managed to stumble out some words, still with that same smile with which he had greeted me earlier.

"Doctor James!" he cried, and his eyes were bright. "Welcome to Orient Point!"

Monday, March 28— early morning

TODAY I WILL BEGIN MY WORK AS THE ASSISTANT superintendent of Orient Point, but I will do so with a clouded mind.

I slept badly.

On my first night I had been tired from the journey, but Sunday's events had stimulated my thoughts, so that I could not find an easy path to sleep.

Of course I asked Doctor Phillips about Dexter.

My arrival seemed to bring an end to his assault by Solway, who then escorted the injured man off to the infirmary to have the cut above his eye dressed.

"Who is that man?" I asked. "Is he not then one of the doctors?"

"Such can be the drawback of those patients who wear their own clothes," he said. He showed no hint of concern at having been discovered meting out this punishment to Dexter. "It can be hard to tell them apart from the rest of us . . . to the untrained eye."

This last remark I felt could only be directed at me.

"He's a patient?"

"Of course. One of the most awkward we have. In some ways."

"But he seems to be normal. Rational."

Doctor Phillips raised an eyebrow at me.

"Seems?" he said. "You ought to know better than seeming, Doctor James. Charles Dexter is a constant source of friction in this hospital. And he is dangerous."

"Dangerous?"

"I use my words accurately," he said, "in all things."

That was the end of the interview, and he left me. Of course I forgot to ask about my salary, and must find the courage to do so at the first opportunity.

* * *

Verity and I walked as much of the coastline as I could bear, and I asked her how she had escaped from our rooms. I told her that she had to obey me, and she said she was sorry and didn't think she was doing anything wrong.

"This is to say nothing of the danger," I said, trying to worry her, just a little.

Her eyes lit up.

"The danger?"

"Of traveling in the dumb waiter. You could have been hurt, Verity. Or worse."

"But I didn't go in the dumb waiter," she said and then I had to remind her that we don't lie.

"I'm not lying!" she said.

I was patient. Everyone deserves that.

"Then how did you get down from our floor?" I asked, pointing out to her that there was only one explanation. "There's no other way."

"Unless someone let me out," she said.

"Who?" I asked. "Only Doctor Phillips, Solway, and I have a key. I was with Doctor Phillips and I know Solway didn't let you out."

Verity said nothing.

"Did he," I stated.

Verity looked really worried. I could see she wasn't playing games.

"Did he?" I asked.

"You've told me not to break promises," she said.

"I have," I said. "What of it? Have you made a promise to someone?"

She nodded and looked even more worried.

"To whom?"

"That's the promise. I can't tell you."

"Verity, you have to tell me the truth. I'm your father. We must have no secrets."

"But you said never to break a promise."

I held my breath for a moment.

"Yes," I said. "You're right. But if you are telling me that Solway let you out and made you promise not to say anything about it then that is a bad thing. Are you saying that?"

"Father, please. I can't break a promise."

I could see it was hurting her, both to think of breaking her word and to keep things from me. So I let it go.

"If that's what happened," I said, "you need to make a new promise. Which is not to do anything that you cannot tell your father about. Do you understand?"

She nodded and I let her go and paddle in the freezing ocean until I dragged her back to our new home, wondering all the while if Solway really had let her out, and if so, why?

In the night, I heard the sea. I must have been so tired on Saturday that it did not disturb me, but last night I could not hear anything else but the constant soft roar of the beach that lies just beyond the grounds of the asylum.

I wonder if it will drive me mad.

Maybe it will save me. Perhaps that's why I've come here. Not because of the promotion, or the salary. Not because it means I can be close to Verity. But because it means I will be close to the sea. Not just close to it. Surrounded by it. Perhaps I have intended to force a cure on myself.

In the smallest hours, as sleep still eluded me, I got out of bed and went to the window. A weak waning moon shone through a bank of clouds that drifted steadily across the sound, and I was about to step out onto the balcony, when I remembered the spiral stair up to the cupola.

A desire to torture myself crept into me, and though I fought it, I did not try to fight very hard.

I found myself at the foot of the elegant spiral that led up to the circular balcony and in bare feet I padded up the smooth wooden steps.

There, from that narrow circular gallery, was a pale night view of the whole of Orient Point and the sea surrounding us on all sides, save for that one narrow and low stretch where the road comes in from Greenport.

I stared at the blackness where the sea lay, unseen in the dark, and I thought long and hard about Caroline, my beautiful wife.

Monday, March 28

I SPENT THE MORNING DOING ROUNDS IN THE company of Doctor Delgado, one of the junior doctors. He told me that Doctor Phillips wished me to start with the men's wards, and we began on the sixth floor, working our way downward. Doctor Delgado is a young man and I asked myself why I didn't feel as I should be feeling. As assistant superintendent, I am Delgado's superior, and yet, as he spoke to me, I sensed that he didn't see it that way. Perhaps I'm being arrogant. We are all engaged on the same mission here. But, something made me uncomfortable, and it is the sense that I cannot seem to gain respect from others.

Of course, it's natural. I know little of the hospital. Doctor Delgado has worked here for four years, he told me, and therefore knows everything. He had a story about every patient, even the newest ones, and he was not shy about telling me these tales. I grew to dislike him before we had even finished the first ward.

All the way, however, was something more pressing in my mind. I found myself thinking about Dexter, who had seemed perfectly rational when I met him, albeit a very brief meeting. I have worked with the insane for ten years now and never met anyone as composed as he seems. I assumed therefore that he would be housed on the sixth floor, for the least disturbed of all the patients, but as we passed room after room and Delgado gave me his withering opinions of man after man, in their rooms and to their faces, Dexter was not among them.

We made our way onto the fifth floor by way of a no more than functional set of stairs at the far end of the wing, and once again I expected, with each door that opened, to greet Dexter. I found myself wanting to talk to him, and guessed that he would be somewhere on this floor, since he had not been on the one above.

But he was not. We progressed slowly, ever downward, floor by floor, and our slowest progress was on the third and second, where the forms of madness displayed by our patients grew more extreme. Now the inmates were clothed in simple white pajamas, as on a hospital ward, though the clothes were gray from frequent washing. Delgado laughed at one or two, was angry with others, and even shoved one unfortunate man back into his room, which was much more akin to a cell than the rooms on higher floors, slamming the door on him.

"Idiot," Delgado said. "But that's why he's in here, right?"

He grinned at me.

Still we had not found Dexter, and it was close to lunchtime when we reached the first floor.

The sights behind the doors on the lowest rung of Orient Point were ones I was familiar with from New York. Yes, their rooms might be a little bigger and brighter and they might not be shut in with other patients, but the terrible sad scenes were just the same. These rooms had, for the most part, been stripped of all furniture. There were no washstands or bedframes, just mattresses on the bare floor, for the patients' own safety, so they did not do themselves harm.

Then, toward the end of the wing, farthest from the center of the building, we finally found Dexter.

Delgado opened the door, and there he was, sitting on his bed, propped up on a pillow with his hands behind his head.

As we entered, he showed no sign of noticing us, which gave me a moment to regard him closely. Here was another tall man, with gangly limbs, emphasized by the fact that his suit was rather small for him. His eyes were large and somewhat round. They spoke of nights lying awake with the moon. The cut above his eye had dried but bruises had welled up around his neck and forehead.

Finally, he stirred.

"Doctors," he said, turning to us.

"What did you do this time, Dex?" asked Delgado, with the air of one trying to provoke. Dexter responded amiably.

"Something I had apparently been told not to do," he said.

"You freak," said Delgado. "Don't be smart with me."

"Doctor," I interjected. "Please. Let's let Mr. Dexter speak for himself."

"*You* let him," said Delgado. "I think we're done for today."

He turned and left the room with a sour look on his face.

I turned back to Dexter. The door was open, and I stood on the threshold.

"Won't you come in, Doctor?" Dexter asked.

Once again, I had the feeling that I was the one taking orders when I should have been the one giving them.

"I'm fine here," I said. "In fact, why don't we take a walk? It's a sunny day."

Dexter raised his eyebrows.

"Would Doctor Phillips think that a good idea?"

Damn this, I thought.

"Doctor Phillips has given me no such instructions and since

I am second here, I think if I invite a patient for a walk there is nothing to prevent us. Don't you?"

Dexter smiled and got to his feet.

"Besides," I said. "Your room, though comfortable, must get tiresome occasionally."

Dexter's room is unlike the others on the first floor. He has not only a proper bed, but a chair, and a tidy desk. There is a washstand with a good china jug on it and, most remarkable of all, along the wall above his bed is a narrow shelf crammed with books, so many that they are piled on their sides along the top of those ranged conventionally. Fascinated, I tried to glance at some titles, but Dexter was speaking to me.

"On the contrary," he said. "Sometimes it's the only way I can get any peace around here."

I wondered at the use of the word *peace*, since just next door one of his peers was emitting a constant low moaning. Other, wilder sounds came from along the hall—the cries of the insane and the harsh shouts of warders. I am used to such noises, of course, from my work in the city and so I put the sounds from my mind.

Dexter was appraising me.

"But I've reached a good place to stop work for the day," he said, and then, as if we were two old friends deciding to take a stroll, "Yes, why not?"

He even picked up a fedora to put on his head.

"It's not as warm as it ought to be," he said. "The winds that come in from the sound can cut you in half."

"Work?" I asked, as we made our way along the corridor. "What are you working at?"

"A novel," he said, simply. "It's to be my first."

"That's admirable," I said. "To use your time here to such good effect. What did you do before you came here?"

We had reached the door to the grounds, which Dexter held open for me.

"After you," I said.

Dexter shrugged, and I followed him out.

"What work did I have?" he asked. "Is that what you mean?"

"Yes."

"This and that. Needs must, so they say. But what I was *before* I came here is what I am *now*."

"And what's that?"

"A poet."

"Oh," I said. "A poet."

"Yes," said Dexter. "I've been a poet for as long as I can re-member. I have written a number of short stories, too. A great number, in fact. I am finished with that form, however, and cur-rently I am engaged in writing a novel."

It was now that I began to see hints of a disturbed mind in Dexter. I doubted very much whether he had written short stories as his tone had something of the delusional about it. Nonetheless, in all my years, I have never come across such an intriguing delusion, and one that could perhaps be beneficial to the patient, if used correctly. So I pressed him to tell me more.

"And you were planning some part of the novel, were you?" I asked. "When Doctor Delgado and I came in. Dreaming up some scene or other to incorporate in the book when you write it?"

"When I write it?" Dexter asked, and for the first time, he

sounded confused. "Not when I write it. I *am* writing it. I was writing it when you came in just now."

"But you have neither pen and paper, nor a typewriter."

"Doctor, I am not stupid. I am writing it *in my head*."

"That's fascinating," I said, eager for him to say more.

"I am writing it in my head. I had just finished a chapter when you came in."

"You mean to say you are dictating the thing to yourself, in your head? But how will anyone read it?"

"I don't need anyone to read it," he said. "Furthermore, I have perfected the art of novel writing. I have studied it endlessly and now that I come to do it myself, I see that I am writing the most perfect prose ever written. It is sublime—it redefines beauty, in fact. And since I have the whole thing in my head, I therefore have no need to write it down. I intend to write this way from now on, in fact. Perhaps another novel, although I might return to poetry, one day, I suppose."

He stopped walking for a second and gave me a smile. It was modest, and so charming that I could not but be infected with something of his contentment.

"It's going very well," he added.

He walked on, leaving me staring after him, trying to work out if he was a madman or a genius.

I hurried after him.

We walked together, and chatted for some time.

"Tell me, you have a fine collection of books there, in your . . . room."

I hesitated as I avoided using the more accurate word.

"Fine? You call that a collection of books? A library? It's a shelf, no more. But I managed to keep one or two nice pieces."

"You don't have enough to read? I could get you more books, perhaps."

"You are a strange kind of doctor," he said. "Most professionals I have spoken with appear to think I read rather too much. Doctor Phillips only tolerates my books because I read from them to the other patients."

"That's very kind of you," I offered.

He brushed my compliment aside.

"It's surely only a decent thing to do. Once a patient arrives here, it is all too easy to slip from mere frailty to genuine insanity. Many of them stop receiving any kind of mental stimulus. Many cannot read, or find it too hard to concentrate. I read what I can to them. Fairy tales, the great poets. Twain and Dickens!"

I clapped Dexter on the back, heartily.

"That's wonderful," I said. "Do you see results from your reading? Are there improvements in the patients' demeanor?"

Dexter looked at me strangely, as if amused by what I'd said.

"Come now," he joked. "You're the doctor, aren't you?"

"Yes," I said, feeling foolish. "Of course. Of course. But I wonder what *you* have perceived in those who you read to. Do they appear to become healthier?"

Dexter stopped walking. The gentle smiling peace on his face fell away, and he spoke softly.

"Doctor. We are lunatics here. All of us. What hope is there for any of us? Do you know how many people ever leave here on their own two feet, restored to equilibrium? Or should I say, how *few*? We are those who are without hope. But when I read, I see, in just one or two faces, the return of something more noble."

"Yes?" I asked. I felt the need to clear my throat. Dexter waited for me to do so, and to speak again. "And what is that?"

"It is their soul, crying for peace. It appears in their eyes, like a ghost surfacing, crying for help. And then, when I stop reading, the mad waters rush in, and wash it away once more."

Tuesday, March 29

IF THINGS ARE GOING WELL WITH DEXTER'S WRITING, life is not being so kind to Verity. Yesterday was her first day at the schoolhouse in Orient and it was not a happy one.

When I finished my afternoon's work, I came upstairs to our rooms to find Verity in her room, crying. Solway had let her in when she'd returned from school, and there she'd been ever since, miserable.

"They're mean," she said.

"The other children?"

She nodded, the poor creature, and I sat down next to her on the bed. What does one say to a sad child? That these things will pass? That life is unfair but that it must be faced anyway? That it is foolish to take heed of what unkind people might say or do?

What do any of these things mean to a crying child of eight years?

"I expect tomorrow will be easier," I said, and to that Verity said nothing.

Wednesday, March 30

I WAS WRONG.

Verity had no easier time of it on her second day at school, nor her third. Her classmates are stupid, she says, and very mean. They taunt her, and when I asked about what, I was angry to hear her reply.

"They say I'm crazy. I'm a crazy girl living in the madhouse."

Tuesday had seen me working the floors of the women's wing, and it was only today that I found myself talking to Dexter again.

I found him in his room, writing his book.

"Why are you living on this floor?" I asked.

"One moment, please," he said. "I need to stop at the end of a paragraph . . ."

He looked into the wall as if seeing something, and then, a few seconds later, he rose to greet me.

"This floor?" he asked. "No reason."

"Come now," I said. "All around you are, for want of a less prejudiced term, the desperate insane. And you are sitting here with your books and your furniture, an island in the storm. Why?"

Dexter waved a hand at me.

"I have a fear of heights," he said. "I asked to be put down here and Doctor Phillips was good enough to oblige me."

The subject seemed closed and I decided not to push things for the time being.

"Why was Solway punishing you?" I asked, instead.

"Just as I told Delgado yesterday, I was doing something I was told not to do."

"Which was?"

Dexter shrugged. "Speaking to your daughter."

I found myself speechless then.

"That's all, I swear," said Dexter.

"Doctor Phillips told you not to speak to my daughter, even before we arrived here?"

"He did."

"And for that, he beat you?"

"He had me beaten," corrected Dexter, holding up a finger.

"That's . . ." I said, and then remembered I was speaking to a patient.

This evening, I went along to Doctor Phillips' rooms, because there were two things about which I wished to speak.

The first was the question of an advance against my salary, which Doctor Phillips very kindly told me was impossible, but that since the month end was soon approaching, I would receive a week's pay within a few days. I did some quick calculations in my head and decided I could afford to let that subject drop, and that brought me to my second one.

I asked Doctor Phillips straight out why he had told Dexter not to speak to Verity, and his manner immediately worsened.

"I told you on Monday, I believe, that Dexter is a dangerous character. I would not have him near your daughter and I would think you should not either."

"I have weighed the risks of bringing Verity here," I said. "And since I have spent my life trying to convince the general public that they are at no more risk from the insane than any other member of society, I would be a poor politician who did not put his words into practice."

"And there I would agree with you, Doctor James," he said. "But, for the exceptional case of Charles Dexter."

"That may be so, Doctor Phillips, but beatings? That's not how I imagined things were done here."

That was going too far, and I knew it at once. The superintendent grew quietly angry with me.

"What you imagined in your comfort from New York is hardly the point, wouldn't you agree, Doctor? And I am superintendent here; it is my judgement of how things are run that matters and, as I told you on Sunday, I recall, I like things to be run well."

"Just what is it that Dexter did? Is he criminally insane?"

"If you want to know whether he murdered someone or some

other act equally dire, the answer is no. But I judge him to be a menace to himself and others here, and I intend to make sure he does not upset the apple cart. It is a continual battle to see that he does not. And what is your diagnosis, Doctor James? Have you not noticed various telltale symptoms? Or do you think he's the sanest one among us?"

Doctor Phillips was not only goading me, but testing my medical capabilities. I knew I needed to succeed here and, in truth, I had seen one or two things about Dexter.

"I would say that he is suffering from General Paralysis. There are some signs of tremors in his hands, which he fights to control. His speech is slurred at times, occasionally noticeably. I would like to test it to be sure, but I thought I detected in his eyes some signs of Adie pupils. If that were the case the diagnosis would be certain, but what I have seen, coupled with these delusions about being a poet, is enough to make me suspect General Paralysis of the Insane."

"Very good," said Doctor Phillips. "Just so. Dexter is suffering from neurosyphilis as a consequence of the tertiary stage of the disease. But you are wrong on one count."

I could see he wanted me to ask, and feeling that I needed to appease him, I obliged.

"I am?"

"Oh, yes," Doctor Phillips said. "I had thought you a better-read man. Charles Dexter was a poet before he came here, a notable one. I have his collection, *On Drowning,* somewhere. It was heralded, by some, as the greatest new writing since Whitman, before Dexter's illness. I can lend the book to you, if you would like to educate yourself."

I didn't care that Phillips was taunting me again. No. This wasn't taunting. This was a cold blade slicing into me.

"Yes," I said. "I think I would like to read that. Very much."

Phillips gave a derisory snort, but he stood and began hunting along the shelves in his study for Dexter's book.

"Tell me, Doctor, why is Dexter housed on the lowest floor of the asylum? He told me he's afraid of heights . . . that you agreed to this arrangement?"

"He told you that?" asked Phillips, turning back to me with a book in his hand. He tossed it at me casually, and I scrabbled to catch it. There was something derisory again in this action, I felt belittled, and for some reason I felt it belittled the book of poetry, and its creator, too. With surprise, I realized that I have already come to care about Dexter. It is never a good idea to feel too much for your patients. If you followed every madman down his dark flight to death you would soon be destroyed. But, and it is quite simple, I like Dexter.

Doctor Phillips' action angered me, and in that anger I decided to press him for answers.

"Dexter tells me you warned him not to speak to my daughter. I would like to know why."

"I have already told you that. I consider him to be dangerous."

"Doctor Phillips," I said, taking my courage in my hands, "You may be in charge here but, as your assistant superintendent, I would like it to be noted that I do not approve of beating patients under any circumstances, never mind for something as trivial as this."

He stared at me then, and my courage withered under that stare.

"Noted," he said, drily. Then he seemed to relax a little. "Very well, Doctor James. You have made your case, and I concede that we may have dealt with Dexter somewhat harshly."

"I just think such actions could set him back in his recovery. It will damage his self-esteem, which must already be very low."

"Perhaps so," said Doctor Phillips. He came round the desk to me and took my elbow in his hand, gently guiding me to the door. "Perhaps so. I tell you what. In order to rebuild this self-esteem, I shall apologize to Dexter personally."

I turned to him.

"That's a noble gesture, Doctor Phillips. One I'm sure will not go without reward in the form of Dexter's character."

He nodded.

"Bring him to me tomorrow and we'll have a chat about all this. The three of us. Agreed?"

I agreed, and left.

I feel I have achieved a small thing for Dexter already. This apology can only serve to enhance his sense of status, and while Doctor Phillips clearly operates in some ways I find difficult, it is a rare man who can admit his mistakes and make amends for them.

I will go to bed soon, I just want to read a little of Dexter's poetry. It may help me to understand the man better.

Thursday, March 31

I CURSE MYSELF THAT I AM STILL SO NAIVE.

I have been played with, on all sides it seems.

My elation over my success with Dexter's punishment lasted only one night, and even before I slept, I found I was unsettled by the man's poetry.

On Drowning is a strange piece of work; not all the stories concern water or the sea, though many do. The poem that gives the book its title is the third in the collection. A long and formless piece, I found, which hints at unknown things. Over the course of several pages, Dexter's words wove some sort of terror into me, but exactly what that terror is of, I cannot say. All I can report is that his words, in some way, disturb. Everything is shadows and the suggestion of monstrosity, of horror in the water, of something dark and powerful beneath the waves, something—there is no other word for it—malevolent.

This morning, I went along the wards as lightly as I could, making one or two instructions to the warders over various patients, yet all the while I was eager to get to Dexter's room.

I found him writing, as usual, though this time he was standing and looking up out of the mediocre window, at the sky.

He turned as I opened the door.

"Can you hear the sea?" he asked.

I listened, but all I could hear was the sound of doors

clanging nearby. It seemed an odd coincidence to me that he should speak of the sea when the night before I had been reading his poetry, which appeared too obsessed with things aquatic.

"Can you?"

"Sometimes," I said. "It's louder the higher up the building you go."

"Well," he said. "What shall we talk about today?"

I smiled, because there really is something disarmingly charming about his open manner.

I decided to return his manner with playfulness of my own.

"I have a surprise for you," I said. "Will you walk with me?"

"A surprise? You are the strangest doctor I have ever met," he said. "And I have met one or two."

We came out into the hall and instead of turning for the doors to the outside at the eastern end of the building, we made for the central hall. Thinking back, I should have noted a slight change in Dexter even then, but I was busy with other thoughts, for he had just asked me a very interesting question.

"Tell me, Doctor," he said. "What is your opinion of psychiatry?"

"I would rather you tell me yours," I said. "Do you know something of it?"

"I have read a little," he said.

"And your conclusion?"

He waved a hand above our heads, and round about. I could almost feel the weight of brick and steel above us.

"All this," he said. "All this *matter*. To try to correct the ineffable disturbances of the *mind*. It seems . . . odd, at least, wouldn't you say?"

"You think psychiatry a more effective treatment? You think it would serve you better?"

He tilted his head toward me.

"Where are we going, Doctor?"

"A short walk," I said. "Your view of psychiatry, if you please."

"Well," he said. "Do you know, that it is almost twenty years since Messrs. Freud and Jung visited our shores for the first time? You might think we had advanced further in our treatment of *mental* aberrations. That we might be trying to understand these matters on their own terms. Instead, it appears that Doctor Phillips and his colleagues would like to mend the mind in a physical way—as if it were a motor car that has broken down—and wrestle it with hammer and wrench."

I found his words as unsettling as his poetry. They would have hurt if they had been pronounced by some leading man of medicine, they hurt all the more for coming from the mouth of a patient.

"Please, Doctor," Dexter said. "Where are we going? I don't much care for surprises."

He tried a smile, but I could see it was a shaky one. We had arrived at the main entrance hall, the curved cathedral that serves as the spinal cord to the building. I should have noted how Dexter was standing, facing the front door, to the outside, and his shoulders were hunched. He was frowning, almost wincing, as if trying to anticipate some attack from behind.

I also should have noted that Solway and two other warders were in the hall.

"We're going to see Doctor Phillips," I said. "He has something he wants to say to you."

"Outside?" asked Dexter, his voice trembling, and that was the last sane sound he uttered, because when I said, "No, in his office," and turned to the spiral staircase, he began to back away from me, mumbling incoherently.

The change in him was so sudden, so very swift, that I didn't see it coming. Solway and his men ran over and grabbed Dexter roughly, and I understood that they had been waiting for us, for him.

Dexter struggled in their hands.

"Don't be a bad boy, Dex," said Solway. "The doctor told you where he wants you to go, didn't he? So come along and play nice."

They started to force Dexter toward the stairs, and now I saw that Dexter was terrified to go.

"No!" I said to Solway. "It's okay. He doesn't have to go if he doesn't want to."

I was thinking that I had no idea that Dexter was so scared of Doctor Phillips. He'd shown no sign of that the day we'd all met. And then, as they forced Dexter to the stairs, and lifted him so he had to place a foot on the first step, I understood.

It was the *stairs* he was afraid of.

He fought, and fought so hard, that despite the three men accosting him, he managed to break free. But only for a second, then they had him again, and Solway pulled a short baton from inside his shirt and gave Dexter such a blow across the back of his neck that he fell to the floor.

Still Dexter roared and screamed, over and over, though what he screamed was unclear. The commotion attracted the attention of patients of both first floor wards, and on either side of us they thronged at the doors and beat on the glass so hard I thought they would smash through. A great wailing and screaming echoed around and up the hall, and I looked up too then, as a shadow crossed the sun, to see Doctor Phillips on the balcony of the seventh floor, his hands on the rails, surveying the scene.

Still Dexter thrashed, and violently, but Solway had him on his front now, his arms twisted behind his back.

Solway barked at the two other warders to "see to" the other patients, and that they did, charging into the wards of both the men and women, pulling people by their hair, dragging them away from the window in such a rough manner that many just scurried off to safety.

I begged the head warder to stop.

"Please, Mr. Solway, please!"

Solway took no notice of me, at least not directly, for then he spat into Dexter's ear, saying, "Let's show the doctor what you're really afraid of."

He rolled Dexter onto his side, still twisting his arms so badly that he had utter control over him, and he pointed Dexter's face up, up into the curved space of the hall, where the staircase ran round, floor after floor, forever, or so it seemed.

"Look!" hollered Solway. "Look!"

Dexter's eyes were wide open in terror as he looked to the very top of the building where that fine spiral staircase ascends into the cupola, and then he screamed a long and empty scream, a howl right from the bottom of his mind, that spoke of unnameable horror at the world before him.

Thursday, March 31—later

I HAVE JUST RETURNED FROM A MIDNIGHT EXCURSION.
Once again, I could not sleep.

The day was a long and painful one after Dexter's episode.

The whole thing, I realized, had been a setup to humiliate both Dexter and myself, to show me that I knew nothing and that Dexter is as mad as Phillips believes him to be.

It seemed that wherever I went in the whole vast building, I could hear the cries of one lunatic above those of three thousand others. Dexter's wailing lasted all morning and most of the afternoon, during which I not only had to work but also had to endure my most patronizing lecture yet from Doctor Phillips as he painstakingly and with great deliberation took me to pieces in front of Doctor Delgado, two other juniors, and Solway.

Dexter, according to Doctor Phillips, has an immense pathological fear of the spiral form. When shown even a simple drawing of a spiral, he grows uncomfortable. Forced to hold one, he becomes wild, and in the face of something as powerful as the staircase of the hospital, he loses all control, and becomes violent if unrestrained.

I made the mistake of asking Doctor Phillips if he knew the cause of this behavior.

"Is there some trauma that Dexter experienced? Did something happen connected to a spiral staircase, perhaps?"

"There does not have to be a pleasing little explanation

for everything in life, Doctor James," he said. "The man is a lunatic. Do not look for method in his madness, for there is none."

I tried not to hang my head, nor to look as defeated as I felt, but I felt pretty rough and it must have been obvious.

And Doctor Phillips had one last barbed remark for me, before he was done.

"To seek the rational where there is only irrational might itself be an act of madness. No, Doctor?"

This evening, I sat and listened to Verity read for a while. She is improving all the while and despite her slow start in life, she makes me proud every time she finishes a chapter. She refused to speak of school today and I didn't have the heart to push her. Instead, I told her to wash herself up and get to bed, and when she was ready, she trotted over and gave me a peck on my cheek.

"Good night," she said.

"Father," I said, and she nodded.

"Good night, Father," she said, and I told her to sleep well.

But sleep didn't come for me, and in the middle of the night, I rolled over and saw Dexter's book by my bed, in the half-light.

I put my hand out for it, but my hand hovered halfway, and then refused. Instead, I found myself climbing the spiral stair to the circular balcony, and began to pace.

In Connecticut and elsewhere, on houses near the sea, are

those rooftop verandas known as widow's walks, from where the wives of sailors would gaze out to sea, hoping for sight of their husband's ship safely returning. And from where the wives of the drowned would gaze at the waters that took their husbands away.

Such did I feel, only with the roles reversed. *I play the widow*, walking around the cupola of the insane asylum, a fearful sentinel staring out at the sea with no more anger now, but just a hollow endless pain.

I had begged Caroline not to go. Not because I feared for her on the voyage. Because I could not stand to be without her for two months. But her English grandfather was dying, and wished to see her again, and would pay for her crossings.

She made it to England before her grandfather died. He got to see her. But I never got to see her again. Somewhere in a storm a way off shore her ship sank, all hands lost.

Even now, after all this time, I still cannot shake the knowledge that she is down there somewhere. My drowned wife. Her body is still there, at the bottom of the sea, and even though I know what horrors will have happened to her body since then, it changes nothing. She is down there.

Thursday, March 31— later, continued

STANDING ON THE WIDOW'S WALK, I STARED AT THE sea for a long time, or at least where I imagined it to be. Then, I slid my hands into the pockets of my jacket, which I had thrown over my pajamas, and my fingers closed around the key to the seventh-floor gate.

Dexter came back to my mind. Before I thought rationally, I was halfway down the main spiral and, no more than a minute later, I was opening Dexter's door.

He was quiet, but not, as I'd imagined, sleeping.

"Who is it?" he asked, and his voice was hoarse, no more than a broken whisper, broken I supposed by his day of screaming. He sounded tired.

"Doctor James," I said, and he fumbled in the dark, switching on a little light on his desk.

"You should not be found in here with me, Doctor," he said. "Aren't you afraid?"

"Of what?" I asked.

"That's a good question," he said. "A very good question. You had better pull the door to, but do not allow it to close, or you will be shut in with a lunatic until the morning, when no doubt all they will find of you is your white bones, with some frantic tooth marks here and there."

"Are you trying to scare me?" I asked.

He sighed softly.

"You're already scared," he said.

"Me?"

"Don't protest," he whispered. "You are scared. Of many things."

"Why do you say that?"

"It's obvious. To one who is terrified himself, it's quite easy to spot a fellow sufferer."

Dexter was already controlling the conversation, and I found to my alarm that I did not care about that as much as I should have. So I forced myself to care, and tried to wrestle the conversation back into my control.

"What happened this morning?" I asked Dexter.

"You saw that for yourself."

"I did. But I'm trying to understand it. They tell me you're frightened by spirals. That the staircase disturbs you. Is that true?"

There was a long, long pause before he answered, but I knew the trick was not to prompt him, but merely to allow the silence to mount until he could not refuse an answer. Finally, it came.

"It is."

"Why?" I asked. "Did you have some accident? Was there something that made you fear the spiral? It is only a shape. It must have some powerful connotations for you. Perhaps a loved one—"

"—a loved one tumbled down the spiral staircase of Montauk lighthouse and crushed her skull on the bottom step? No! Doctor James, no. No. It is not that simple. *I* am not that simple. There is no pathetic cause and effect for me. Unlike you."

I ignored that last remark. Or I should say, I tried to, because I was, by then, already wondering what he knew of me.

"What then is it, about the spiral, that terrifies you so, so much that you are reduced to a screaming heap at the mere suggestion you walk up one?"

Dexter did not answer me directly.

"What is your desire for life, Doctor?"

"I'm not sure what you mean."

"What do you want from life? What are you trying to do with your life?"

What do I want? I thought. I cannot have what I want. That chance has gone. I decided to limit the question to that of my work.

"I want to help people, and I want to improve myself so that I can help people better."

"Noble," Dexter said, and there was no suggestion of sarcasm in his whisper, but, rather, a hint of admiration that brought tears to my eyes.

"What do you want?" I asked.

"I have spent my life trying to fill my mind. I have spent it trying to fill the thing, and yet the more I learn, the more I realize still remains to be understood. I wrote my poetry to explore the world, and in doing so I find I have been nothing more than an ant, standing at the shores of the Atlantic, wondering what lies on the other side. But at least I know there *is* another side.

"So I have tried to open my mind further, and to fill it further, and yet the process appears to be an infinite one, on and on, forever."

He fell silent. I thought about what he said, but could find no connection to spirals. Then I felt stupid for trying to make, as he put it, a simple cause and effect where he had told me there was none.

"Have you ever been locked in the dark, Doctor?" he asked me. "No."

"You should try it sometime. It is remarkable. After a period of time in total darkness, you begin to see things. I am not talking about hallucinations. Your eye starts to show you certain lights and shapes. These are called 'entoptic phenomena.' I read about them in von Helmholtz's recent book. You read German? I would lend you the book, were it not for the fact . . ."

He trailed off and glanced at the shelf above his head. Only now, in the gloom, did I see that all his books were gone. Every single one.

"Doctor Phillips took them away."

"Why?" I asked.

"Because of what happened today."

"That's terrible," I said.

Dexter hung his head, and I didn't know what more to say. The empty shelves gaped at me, like a wound, somehow. No, like a crime, but more than a theft, like a murder. Phillips was trying to kill Dexter. That was the mad and angry thought that came to me as I saw the bare wooden shelf hanging above Dexter's bowed head.

"It's not so bad," Dexter said softly. He looked up. "I am not reading at the moment. At the moment, I am writing my book. Hopefully Doctor Phillips will relent by the time I wish to start reading again, and return my books to me."

I could not speak. All I could manage was a brief nod of my head.

If Dexter noticed my doubt, he made a firm job of hiding it.

"Anyway," he said, "according to von Helmholtz's book, it seems that, denied of any visual stimulus, the eye starts to fire off all by itself, seeing ghosts if you like, and the lights that are seen fall into a few groups. There are lines, and there are groups of dots. There are zigzags. And there are spirals."

"Spirals," I echoed, watching Dexter's hollow face as he spoke in the weak light of the bulb on his desk.

"Did you know that these few shapes are the first shapes that humans ever made? In caves all across the world, at times so distant from us it can barely be imagined, the first men scrawled these shapes onto the rock, in charcoal and ochre, and by some miracle, we can still see them today.

"These marks were made across the world, by different primitive peoples, from Africa to Asia to the Americas and to Europe. Different peoples, separated by thousands of miles. These shapes are inherent in us. Universal. Do you see, Doctor?

"From these marks, comes all art, but also, writing must have come from these marks too. Eventually. Everything has come from these dark caves, from these innermost depths of the mind. Of the mind of the Earth, if you see what I mean."

I didn't. At least, I was starting not to follow Dexter's thoughts, and I was overwhelmed by the feeling of conversing with someone immeasurably more intelligent than I am, of someone who was struggling to keep his words at a level I could understand.

"But why do these marks, these particular marks, the spirals, why do they frighten you?"

"It can be a frightening thing to free your mind as I have done, Doctor. But when you have . . ."

"What? What have you done?"

"It is not a question of what I have *done*. It is a question of what I have *seen*."

"And what is that?"

And now Dexter took no trouble in ignoring my questions and taking things where he wanted them to go.

"Your wife is in the sea," he said.

I said nothing. I stared at him in horror, as down the hall the sounds of the asylum at night washed into me.

"Isn't she?"

Then, I understood.

Suppressing anger, I declared, "Verity told you that, I assume?"

"Verity!" he said. "She is something to be proud of, isn't she? So intelligent! So pretty."

"Answer my question, if you please," I said.

"No," he said. "She did not tell me."

"Then, how do you know? You read about it perhaps. In the papers. You have a remarkably good memory, perhaps you put two and two together."

"Perhaps," said Dexter, in the most infuriating way. "Perhaps I did. Perhaps the sea told me."

"The sea told you?" I asked, strangely happier that we were talking about matters of Dexter's delusions again, and not Caroline.

"Do you know why they built this asylum here?" said Dexter, throwing me again.

"Tell me."

"We are surrounded by water here. But for that spit of land to the west, we are an island. The sea surges all around us, the tides sucking and gnawing at our pebbles. And what powers the tides? The moon. The moon, and what powers us madmen? Us lunatics? The word itself tells you all you need to know."

"There has never been proven any link between the phase of the moon and the behavior of the deranged mind. It is no more than common folklore, an old wives' tale."

"You think so?" said Dexter. "Nevertheless, here we are in this insane asylum, with the sea all around, and everyone and everything controlled by the pull of the moon. And down in that sea, Doctor, are dead things. Your wife is among them, but she is not the most powerful, or the oldest. These things are angry, they are vicious, and they want revenge upon us, the living. We should kill them, but they are dead, and that's the trouble. Killing the dead is very hard to do."

Now I was certainly very intrigued. I pressed Dexter for more.

"What are these things?" I asked.

"You would cry yourself to sleep every night if you knew," he said. "I daren't tell you. Did you not read about what that oyster dredger pulled out of the sound some years ago? No? It caused something of a stir around here. But maybe such fanciful talk never made it to the great and enlightened city."

"You're playing games with me now," I said. "You don't know what you're talking about and instead you want to scare me."

But what scared me more was how Dexter then replied.

"No," he said, and I could tell again he was being sincere. "I truly don't.

"If you want to know more, you could read my poems. It's all in there. There's a poem I wrote. It's called *Poquatuck*. You need read no more than that. In fact, you may like to know that the poem was the inspiration for the novel I'm writing. Once I had the poem done I knew there was more to say. Much more."

I made a note of the title in my head.

"She is down there," Dexter said.

"Stop saying that," I said.

"She is down there. And she wants you. Or rather, she wants to destroy you now. Because you have wronged her."

"I have?" I asked, growing angry, and despite the fact I knew I was being foolish, I could not stop myself. "What have I done?"

"You have offended her. You replaced her. You replaced her in your affections with the girl."

"The girl?" I asked, my lip trembling. "What girl?"

"Verity, of course! You know perfectly well what girl . . ."

"How dare you?" I said, and I shouted, too loud. I heard the sound of keys turning in the lock at the end of the hall. I needed to leave his cell immediately or I would either be found, or have to spend the rest of the night there, and I no longer wished that to be the case.

"How dare you insult my daughter?" I said, as I slipped out of the door, and as I went, and closed it behind me, I heard Dexter say softly five more words that cut me through and through.

"But she isn't, is she?"

Saturday, April 2

I HAVE NOT HAD TIME TO WRITE FOR THE SPACE OF a couple of days, nor have I seen Dexter since our midnight interview. There was much to be done yesterday in the women's wards, and today I found Verity in such better spirits now that her school week is done, that I decided to make good on a promise to her to take her to the movies.

We rode back up the coast a way, where there is a modest but very fine movie theater that stands on the seafront. I was buying two tickets at the box office when I saw Verity reading something on the wall. I joined her and saw a neat iron plaque on which were the following words:

IN MEMORIAM

THIS PLAQUE REMEMBERS THE 20 LIVES LOST DURING THE HURRICANE OF 1922 DURING WHICH THE OLD THEATER WAS SWEPT TWO MILES OUT TO SEA. THE BODIES OF THE AUDIENCE OF 19 AND THE PROJECTIONIST WERE NEVER FOUND, NOR ANY TRACE OF THE OLD BUILDING. THE CURRENT THEATER WAS BUILT IN 1924.

"The whole place went out to sea?" asked Verity, open-mouthed. Then she looked at the tickets in my hand.

"It's hard to believe," I said, "but I bet this new place is as strong as an ox."

We went inside.

"I wonder what they were watching," Verity said.

"What?"

"I wonder what picture they were showing when they went out to sea."

"Verity—" I began. I stopped myself. There were things I would rather not think about and it was easier not to say anything than to approach them.

"What, Father?"

"Nothing."

We saw the movie, which was a very funny picture with Harold Lloyd called *The Kid Brother*. When it was over, I counted my pennies, and bought Verity an ice cream, even though it was a cold enough day to make me long for a hot cup of coffee. Then we rode home, and I decided I had to ask Verity.

It had been playing on my mind since I closed Dexter's door, and I needed to know.

"Verity," I said.

She didn't look away from the view outside the train window.

"What?"

"You remember that man you spoke to? On our first day here?"

"You mean Charles?"

"Yes," I said. "Charles. Do you remember what you spoke about?"

"I guess so," she said. "Mostly."

I thought what to say next.

"Did you talk about us?"

"Us? You mean, you and me?"

"Yes. You and me. And maybe Caroline."

Verity looked at me then.

"I didn't talk about her," she said.

"Did he? Charles? Mr. Dexter, that is. Did he talk about Caroline?"

"No."

"You're sure?"

"I'm sure."

I waited again. I could tell Verity was upset, though she didn't know what she'd done wrong. I suppose this is one of those things that is just deeply engrained in her.

"Did he talk about us, though? You and me?"

"No, Father."

"Verity, you know you mustn't lie."

She started to cry. But I couldn't stop myself.

"I'm not lying," she said.

"You must be lying," I said.

"I'm not! I'm not."

"Then how does he know?" I shouted.

I saw some fellow passengers look at us, and I dropped my voice.

"How does he know?"

"How does he know *what*?" Verity asked.

"Don't be smart with me," I said angrily. "You know what I'm talking about."

"I don't. I don't."

Verity was crying loudly now, but still I couldn't stop.

"How does he know I adopted you, of course! What else?

No one here knows that. You were supposed never to tell anyone."

"I didn't," she wailed. "I didn't say. I'm not lying. You told me never to lie and I'm not lying!"

Then she just began to bawl so much that I realized what I had done. I tried to calm her down and told her I was sorry for shouting and yet nothing I said seemed to help. Gradually, she calmed herself, but we rode the rest of the way to Greenport in a bitter silence.

Saturday, April 2—later

I COULD FEEL VERITY SULKING WITH ME FOR THE rest of the day, and I don't blame her. The only other thing she said all day was to ask me what *In Memoriam* means.

"It means 'in memory of,'" I said. "It's Latin. We use it when we want to remember someone."

"Someone who's died?"

"Yes," I said. "That's right."

At bedtime, she came and stood in front of me in her night-dress, and wished me a joyless "good night." I thought about what I should say, what I could do to cheer her up, but I could think of nothing. For a moment, I even thought I might put my arms around her and hug her, but she turned on her heel once she'd said her piece, and went off to her room.

I watched her go, then called out.

"Verity."

But I must have called too softly for she didn't turn and come back.

I wonder often what life was like in the orphanage, but I hope it had to be better than when she lived on the streets before that. The streets of Manhattan are no place for a small girl to be, but I often get the feeling that the two years in the orphanage are what did the damage to her. Why she is so scared. Why she finds it hard to trust me. And every time I lose my temper with her, I know I am sending her back to the orphanage in some way, just a little.

After Caroline died, and I decided not to look for a new wife, but for a daughter, I lost touch with the remnants of my own family. I know they felt I was behaving oddly, but I know I will never love a woman the way I loved Caroline, though I might love a child as well and as truly. That was my belief, and still is, though I wonder when I will really, finally, connect my heart to Verity's, and she hers to mine.

It was easy to choose her.

Like choosing candy at the store, or the prettiest stone on the beach; there she was on the day I made my visit to the orphanage. And if no one told me she was the spitting image of Caroline, like a miniature version of my own dead wife, well that was only because no one there knew both the woman, and the girl.

When Verity went to bed, I did the same, but saw Dexter's book waiting for me beside the table. It seemed to be telling me that it had all the time in the world, that it could wait for me to read it, whenever I was ready. I felt like throwing the thing out of the seventh-floor window, but I didn't. Instead, I picked it up, and flicked to the table of contents, where the names of the poems were listed.

There it was: *Poquatuck*.

I read.

Poquatuck

Sea-found, wind-worn and wild;
the land will lose.
Here are places so old as to defy memory;
The point, the creek, the inlet.
The old tide mills, dilapidated,
were but a blink in the eye of time.
And there are older things here,
things which the oyster boats dredge from the deep.

There on the headland;
the asylum,
and the asylum boneyard,
where the land-borne dead are corrupted,
harmless bodies are sucked of life;
in the cemetery.

Graves grow from the soil;
the black fingernails of the monstrosity beneath.
It lies far down, under the ground, under the sea,

pushing an arm up,
up to the air
a hand with a thousand fingers; and every fingernail
      a grave.

Deep in the sea, at the other end of the arm
sits its heart-brain,
this being from beyond the stars, from the beginning
      of time:
its mashy form quivers inside the shell
which protects
and resonates its thought-waves across the world
in ancient reverberation.

Spiral-set shell mind,
It blows a soundless horn to us all, a warning:
I am coming.

Dreaming

CAROLINE CALLS TO ME FROM BENEATH THE WAVES.

I am standing on the roof of the asylum, and I jump, and somehow fly down to the shore from where her voice is louder and more insistent.

I am not afraid. I know she is dead, but somehow, in my dream, that doesn't matter. All that matters is that she is talking to me, and that I can hear her voice again, the voice I have not heard since she sailed for England four years ago, and never came back.

This is the shoreline of the Long Island Sound, whose trapped waters have engulfed hundreds of boats over the centuries. Deep down lie their bodies; these drowned souls, and rather like the madhouse, it doesn't matter where they came from or who they were, now they are all alike, now they are equal as they wait out the years, welcoming new souls from time to time.

The wind beats my face; it is spring and the wind is cold, colder still at night. The waves pound the shore in front of me and I become hypnotized by their continual cycle, up and down the beach.

Then, without warning, Caroline is there. She rises from the waves as far as her waist, dressed in the same green dress she was wearing the day I saw her off at the Chelsea Piers, though now the dress is darkened from the water. Her hair, always straight, is sleek and black and salt water runs from her fingers.

"Come to me," she says, and I do.

I walk out into the cold waves. I feel nothing. I keep walking, a long way, and I know I should be underwater by now, but I am only waist high, like she is.

And then we touch, I put my hands into hers and pull them around me and hold her tight. Her wet hair strokes my cheek and I can smell salt and age and other, darker things, which I choose to ignore.

Then we go down. Fast, we sink into the water and I begin to panic that I will drown, but she laughs and puts a hand on my mouth.

"You don't need to breathe, down here," she says, "You can't," and I think, no, of course not, how silly of me.

Down we go, and though we are far below the night waves I can see through the murk around me.

Things are swimming. People. They swarm like clouds of midges that come and go, eager to see who I am, keen to keep their distance, and Caroline pulls me deeper. I know that all around me are the souls of the drowned, and yet only then do I begin to realize that there is something else down here. Something worse.

Now I see that Caroline is winding into the water. As if descending a vast invisible spiral stair, we're winding down, and down, and now the darkness does begin to take hold, and the water presses in on me, threatening to crush me in its grip, and Caroline turns to me and says,

"Why do you want her? Why do you want her? Why? When you could have me . . ."

She holds my hand and is about to pull me to the bottom where something terrible is waiting, and has been waiting through unlit centuries, and I scream.

I scream a stream of mad bubbles, and seeing them rise, I tear my hand from Caroline's and begin to kick for the surface, kicking, pulling with my arms, wriggling up through the water until my arms and legs are screaming, too, burning with pain, and just as I fear I won't ever get back, I land, in my bed, gasping for air.

I roll onto my back and, though I know it was a dream, my face is wet.

Saturday, April 9

THE PAST WEEK HAS HURRIED BY, AS FAST AS MY first week at Orient Point. I am tired, perhaps to the point of exhaustion, for there is never an end to the work and the days are long. Now that I have been here a week I am expected to know everything, be everywhere, answer every query and report to Doctor Phillips each evening with a written summary of the day in my hand.

Verity's week has been no easier than mine, I suspect, and though she is talking to me happily enough again after the business last Saturday, she refuses to talk about school.

"If you need any help from me, Verity," I told her last night, "you need only say."

I hope she doesn't take me up on that offer, for there is no other choice for her than the schoolhouse in Greenport. Perhaps her tormentors will lose interest in her soon and pick on someone else. I don't tell her that. I don't want her to have false hopes.

I have not seen Dexter, to speak to, all week. Once or twice we passed each other in the halls, but he was always being detained by a warder or another doctor. Then, last night, as I made my report to Doctor Phillips, his name came up.

"The case of Charles Dexter," Doctor Phillips said. "It remains an interesting one, does it not?"

I nodded, already on my guard. Phillips has used Dexter once already to humiliate me, and Dexter suffered as a consequence, too. I did not want to offer a repeat of either of those things.

"He does," I said, prepared only to say the bare minimum by way of conversation.

"Come, now, Doctor James," Phillips said. "You surely have more of an opinion than that?"

He fixed me with a needling look.

"His is an interesting case," I admitted. "As are the cases of three thousand other patients here at Orient Point. Is there some matter you are referring to in particular?"

Doctor Phillips seemed to change his tune slightly then. He could see I was not going to be made the fool again, and his taunting manner disappeared.

"I know you think that some of our ways here are old-fashioned, but that is far from the case. As it happens, we are at the forefront of certain techniques, at least as far as the United States is concerned. I am very influenced by one or two European practitioners and, in fact, I have selected Dexter to be the first subject upon whom we will try a new cure, known as malarial treatment. The work in London, on those suffering from general paralysis, is very encouraging."

"Malarial treatment?" I asked.

"You haven't heard of it? I thought you were abreast of all the latest techniques. Macbride and Templeton have published on the subject, as long as two years ago."

"I must have been too busy to—"

"It doesn't matter. It is a very simple procedure and the outcomes of the experiments have been remarkable, at times."

"What is involved in the procedure?"

"As I say, it is a very simple procedure. All that is required is access to a patient suffering from benign tertiary malaria. A blood sample is taken from that patient, and then injected into the general paralytic."

"You infect the insane patient with malaria?"

"Indeed. The subsequent fevers are often high enough to destroy the syphilis bacillus in the patient, leading to recovery."

"Often? And what of the malaria? Does that not prove fatal?"

Doctor Phillips fixed his eyes on me.

"Not in so many cases."

I could do nothing but stare for a moment.

"And why do you select Dexter for this treatment?"

"I told you. Dexter is the candidate whom I consider most suitable. He is suffering from tertiary neurosyphilis, he shows increased symptoms and there seems little to be lost."

"And when will you start?"

"We will start next week," Doctor Phillips said. "I am making arrangements for the delivery of malarial blood from New York. All should be in hand very soon."

Then he wished me a good night, and a pleasant weekend.

Sunday, April 10

I WANTED TO WARN DEXTER ABOUT WHAT DOCTOR Phillips had in store for him. I spent all morning hunting for him. He had been allowed out to walk freely, the first time in two weeks.

I combed the grounds of Orient Point, as far as the shore, through the ornamental and vegetable gardens, through the workshops and outhouses of the asylum. I asked everyone I knew, and finally, it was the patient, Jonathan, who found him for me. Jonathan was nervously weeding a flower bed. I know he speaks to Dexter sometimes and thinks highly of him, and when I asked if he knew where he was, he sheepishly stabbed his trowel in the direction of the crematorium.

Spring has come to Long Island. The grounds are looking verdant and green, and today was warm, so I found it strange that Dexter had chosen to go inside.

The door of the crematorium was open, and I walked in to find it empty. It is a small place with enough room to seat no more than twenty mourners. There is the door to the furnace, and some apparatus for that business in front of it. But, of Dexter, I could see no sign. I noticed a metal door leading to a set of steps, which headed down to the basement, I guessed, and that was where I found him.

He turned away from a set of shelves as he heard me come into the dark basement room. It is without skylight or ventilations of any kind, and all four walls are covered with shelves from floor to ceiling. Every inch of the shelf space, the entire room, is taken up with identical metal canisters, copper canisters, each about five inches high and four in diameter. I noticed that there is a label on each, with some printed sections and handwritten additions.

"What are they?"

Dexter gave me the saddest of the many smiles he's given me in our time together.

"This is the library of dust," he said.

Upstairs I had seen the cremation equipment, down here . . .

"Yes," he said. "You're right. These are the ashes of the dead. Each in their own little tin, with a label. Their name, the date. Their age. That's all. And one by one, they're eating up the shelves."

"Why don't the relatives take them?"

"You should know as well as me that asylums are full of people who no longer have anyone they can call a relative."

He was right and I felt foolish for even asking the question. Yes, even somewhere as progressive as Orient Point had its share of people that society just wanted forgotten. And here they were, lining the shelves of the basement. Forgotten.

"Except by me," Dexter said.

"Excuse me?"

"You were thinking about these people. All forgotten, yes? Except by me. And now you."

That was not the first time that Dexter had somehow seen my thoughts. It continues to disturb me how he knows things he should not know. I did not want to give him a chance to disturb me the more.

I came to tell him that Doctor Phillips was going to try a procedure on him that sounded experimental, at best, and yet then, standing in the library of dust, I thought better of it.

Perhaps Doctor Phillips is right. If the treatment is as effective as he claims, then maybe Dexter can be cured, and there is no doubt he needs help. His speech is becoming increasingly slurred, he stammers often and the shake of his hands is now impossible for him to hide. If the cure does not go ahead, perhaps Dexter will soon be joining those he mourns in the library of dust. Very soon.

It's something I hate to think about, and so I decided not to tell him of the treatment.

A week has passed since I read his strange dark poem and since I had my nightmare of the sea, and of Caroline. I was feeling stronger this morning, and I wanted still to know what it is about spirals that so alarms Dexter.

When I tried to question him on the subject, he grew evasive.

"Do you know what Edgar Allan Poe's first published book was?" he asked me instead. "It is also," he added, "perhaps the book that earned him the most money of anything he ever put his name to."

I played along.

"I'm not sure," I said. "*Murders in the Rue Morgue*? *Arthur Gordon Pym of Nantucket*? I'm sorry, I'm not as much of a reader as you."

"Don't worry. It's a question most people would get wrong. Mr. Poe's first published volume was a short history of conchology."

"Of what?"

"Shells, Doctor James. In fact, Poe did not write the book, someone else did, but he edited it and put his name to it because, being a noted newspaper man, he thought it would sell better."

"What of it?"

"Why on earth do you think a man as distinguished as Edgar Poe would bother with such a thing? Shells, Doctor! *Spiral* shells.

Page after page of them. Poe wrote some fine horror stories in his lifetime, but no one realizes that the greatest horror of all was a book of nonfiction!"

I became enraged by hi▄ ▄elusions. I, who have dealt with some of the worst excesses in the minds of men, and I lost my temper at this most rational of lunatics. Because I care about him, too much.

"Spirals, Dexter? Are you not better than this? Have you nothing finer to report from your wanderings through the universe?"

Then he turned a cold stare on me, and I felt ashamed at my rage. But he wasn't done with me.

"My wanderings? Yes, I have learned a lot. And I can help you."

"Why would I need your help?" I asked.

"I can get rid of Caroline for you. She is haunting you, from the spiral depths of the Atlantic Ocean, and I can get rid of her. If you wish it."

Soon after that, I left Dexter in the basement, and I prayed that somehow the malarial blood soon to be coming this way in an icebox from New York would kill the disease in his mind, and leave his true self unharmed. Yet, as I went, I was troubled with the question of whether I, or anyone else for that matter, had ever told Dexter my dead wife's name.

Wednesday, April 13

TODAY I DISCOVERED THAT VERITY HAS NOT BEEN GOING to school.

At lunchtime, as I ate with the other doctors in the canteen on the east wing, one of the warders came over to me to say there was someone at the reception desk who wanted to speak with me.

I left my lunch, glad of the excuse to leave Delgado to his wit, but less glad when I saw a lady I did not recognize, but who soon introduced herself as the schoolmistress from Greenport.

"We do not care for truants at Greenport," was her summary of the situation.

"I'm sure not," I said, torn between defending myself and sticking up for Verity. "I will see to it that the situation changes."

"I would be glad of that," replied the schoolmistress.

"And perhaps in return, you can see that my daughter is not bullied?"

I did not smile at her.

"Is that a fair agreement?" I added, putting her in a corner from which she could not escape.

She slunk away, but as soon as she was gone I worried that I might have done Verity more harm than good.

This evening, however, I had to make Verity see that what she has been doing has been unwise, and placed us both in a difficult place.

"You have to try and fit in," I told her.

She stood by her window, the one overlooking the south.

"But they're so mean," she said, and years dropped away and I remembered my own schoolyard days. Not with any pleasure.

"That may be so. But you must endure it. You should tell yourself how stupid they are for teasing you, and just ignore them."

I remember my own father telling me the same thing. I also remember how little good it did me. Is there no escape from the circular prisons we make for ourselves?

"I've tried," Verity was saying. "I've really tried. But they never leave me alone."

"And where have you been spending your days?"

It seems that Verity has been absent all week.

"Walking home, and at the beach. There's an old mill by the shore. It's fun."

"Verity, it could be dangerous. You can't just go wandering around Orient Point. You might meet anyone!"

"I'd be happy to!" Verity said then. "At least that would give me someone to talk to. I haven't spoken to anyone since the day I arrived! At least Charles listened to me. He was kind! I could speak to him!"

"No!" I said, and I tried to quash my anger. "You are not to speak to him, or to anyone. You are to go to school each day and study and if you want to speak to anyone, you can speak to me!"

Verity looked at me, scornfully, and I died.

"You? Speak to you? We never speak! At least Charles listened to me!"

"Really, Verity! This must stop!"

And it did, because that seemed to silence her. Into the silence came a thought I could not detach.

"What did you and Mr. Dexter speak about? You told me it wasn't us, and it wasn't Caroline. So what was it?"

"Geese," said Verity, miserably.

"Geese?" I said. "You spoke about geese? Don't be ridiculous! Why would you want to talk about geese?"

"We just did," Verity said. "That's what people do. They just talk about things."

Then I told Verity she was going to bed without any supper, she told me she didn't care, and both of us will spend a miserable night, I'm sure.

I return to my diary making some hours after the previous words.

It was as I feared; I was unable to sleep.

Eventually I gave up the battle to find rest, swung my legs out of bed, and sat on its edge, in the strong moonlight that broke through the thin curtains of my room. I pulled a robe around me as I stared out of my window at the night-gray sea shimmering. The sound was calm, and the light of the moon glittered like jewels on a dark velvet bedspread. It was so beautiful, and yet my heart could not accept the beauty.

Caroline, I thought.

I pulled myself away and, leaving my room, stole along the corridor and stopped outside Verity's door, listening.

There was silence, total silence, and after a time had passed I began to grow worried. I was about to put my hand on the door when I heard a snuffle from her, as she turned in her sleep. The springs of the bed squeaked and I knew she was safe.

Still, I knew I could not sleep and, returning to my room, I found the key to the gate, and then let myself out into the hospital, locking the gate behind me as I went.

The hospital, late at night, is a strange beast, I think.

In darkness, the wards are as quiet as they ever get, which is not to say they are silent. I found myself walking without purpose or direction, down the turning spiral of the floors. As I did so, noises rolled out of the darkness toward me, a shout that broke the stillness of the night, a murmur. A cry, a sound of banging, or a wail of fear that chilled me.

What do we do with these, our insane? How shall we care for them, when there is no care to be given? Most of them will die here, despite Doctor Phillips' proud claims of restitution. Die, be burned, and have their ashes filed in a copper can in Dexter's library of dust. To be forgotten. And if we are forgotten, surely that is when we truly die?

To be remembered after our death, that at least would let us live on, in some way, in someone's heart, but if even that is denied to us, then it is as if we never lived at all.

I found myself on the ground floor, in the great entrance space, and just as I was heading for the door, a voice called across the darkness to me.

"Doctor?"

"Who's there?" I said. I turned but could see no one at first; then I saw the faint glow of a cigarette's tip.

Approaching, I found Delgado lounging on a wooden chair by the doors to the women's ward.

"It's you," said Delgado.

"Of course," I said, stiffly.

"Well, we can't have anyone wandering around here, now can we, Doc?"

I tried to attain the upper hand.

"Is everything in order tonight, Doctor Delgado? I couldn't sleep and thought it wouldn't hurt to take a turn of the wards."

"Take that rod out of your ass, Doc," he said, and I was so dumbfounded I had no reply. But Delgado wasn't done. "You don't need to keep up that act. Phillips is safe in bed, snoring."

"Doctor Delgado—" I began, but stopped dead as the door to the women's ward suddenly opened. A guard, whose name I don't yet know, stepped through, speaking as he came.

"Hey, you were right, she is one fine piece of . . ."

He trailed off as he saw me, and then shot a glance at Delgado.

"Forget it, Micky, the doctor is cool. Ain't you, Doc?"

The guard shut the door behind him, guilt written all over his face.

"I said, Doctor James is cool," repeated Delgado. "Maybe we can fix you up, too, huh? That why you came down here? A little fun?"

I understood then what was happening, but was so speechless at first that I could find no words.

"Beat it, Micky," Delgado said to the guard, "I'll deal with the good doctor. And tuck your goddamn shirt in. Don't make it too obvious, huh?"

The guard crept away into the night, and I pulled myself together.

"Delgado," I said. "If what I think is happening here, is indeed—"

"Shut up," snapped Delgado. "Don't you think you can scare me. Now listen, why not be reasonable? There's this great girl at the end of the ward. Just came in. Foreigner, but that don't matter. And she's all warmed up for you, that's the best part."

Even in the half-light I could see the leer on Delgado's face.

I stood, trembling with rage and confusion. Hoping the dark would hide my shaking hands, I did my best to keep my voice even.

"How dare you? How can you do such a thing? I will see Doctor Phillips knows about this!"

"Yeah? You don't want any? No, of course you don't. You got your own, doncha?"

Unable to stop myself from being drawn in, I spluttered.

"What? My wife is dead!"

"Not your wife. You got that pretty little girl, right? She keep you happy up there on the roof, does she?"

He stood, jutting his foul face into mine, and then I could stand it no more, and I swung my fist as hard as I could at his chin.

He went down, sprawling into the chair, which went clattering across the marble tiles.

Afraid I might leap on him and strangle him, I stepped away, but pointed at him on the floor.

"You will be leaving this place tomorrow, Delgado," I hissed. "I swear it."

Still, I couldn't seem to even unsettle him.

"Yeah?" he snarled. "You think you're gonna tell Phillips? Well I wouldn't, because then I might have to tell him that the girl ain't your daughter. And I wonder what else I could tell him? Like what you get up to with her."

It was all I could do to restrain myself from trying to kill him, then and there, and instead, I found myself backing away in horror as he began to laugh at me.

I fled upstairs, running all the way, to the safety of my room.

Friday, April 15

TWO DAYS HAVE PASSED, IN UNEASE.

I have come across Delgado in the course of my duties, and each time I have done so, he has leered at me in the most unsettling way. I need to do something about him, and soon. I need to speak to Doctor Phillips, but I need to be sure of my own position first. I will do it tomorrow, whatever. Delgado must be stopped, and whoever else is involved. I shudder to think of how Doctor Kirkbride would feel, knowing what abuses of trust are occurring in a hospital of his design.

Every time I think of what Delgado suggested about Verity and me, I go cold with rage. The very idea is appalling, and yet also laughable in a way, to me, who cannot even be sure if he should put his arms around his daughter, or not. And how he knows she is not my flesh and blood, I do not know. Dexter must have told him, but I cannot believe Dexter would have betrayed me so. At least, I do not want to believe that.

This evening, after supper, I told Verity she could go down to the respectable library that the asylum houses, on the sixth floor, and choose something to read. I let her out of the gate on the seventh floor.

"I'll join you very shortly, dear," I said, and she went straight off. I must trust her to do what I say. I cannot be there for her all the time; with only me to look after her, she needs to be able to look after herself.

She trotted down the stairs and I heard her cross the sixth-floor landing to the door to the library, which sits at the back of the building, equally placed between the male and female wings, another service for the more capable inmates to use. I heard the door close again, and only then did I go back to our rooms, wondering, not for the first time, if I should try and find a mother for Verity. A wife for me.

But there is Caroline, still.

Dexter's words came into my mind.

I can get rid of her.

But do I want that? It's true that she haunts me, but can I actually bear to get rid of her from my mind, and from my heart?

I fiddled and itched around my study for a while, trying to write my report for Doctor Phillips, but finding myself unable to concentrate, I set off for the library myself, to see what Verity had chosen.

It is true that there are no children's books in the asylum library and it has a limited choice of reading materials, but I thought Verity might like to flick through some illustrated encyclopaedia or set of maps. Perhaps there was a volume or two of fairy tales, the ones Dexter reads from.

"There's nothing to read in here," she said, when I approached.

She was sitting in front of an open book, so that didn't seem to be entirely true.

"What did you find?" I asked, coming round the table beside her.

"Only this. It's very sad."

Looking over her shoulder, I was reminded of leaning over Caroline's shoulder to read, in just the same way. It was as if she was that miniature version of my wife.

"It's sad," Verity said again, and I started to read.

It seemed to be an account of the trial of a witch, somewhere in England. There was a picture of a young woman hanging from the branch of a tree, one of those old-time woodcuts. They always give me the creeps for some reason, no matter what they're depicting. This was no exception, so clumsy in its execution, so casual about something absolutely horrific.

"You shouldn't be reading that," I said.

I reached down and looked at the cover of the book; it was called *Witchcraft in England*.

"Why not?" asked Verity, but, in all truth, I had no explanation for her.

So I opened the book again and read over her shoulder.

It seemed that the witch, or the woman accused of witchcraft at least, had been a young woman. She had become what her mother had been before her; that is to say, a cunning woman. She had been found guilty of various crimes: of causing demonic possession in her brother, of causing the sickness of a nobleman's son, of murdering a rival's baby. Of using her familiars to steal jewelery from a lady.

After the hanging of the young woman, it appears that a chain of executions occurred in the small community, including some of those who had first testified against her. A girl who had lost a baby in infancy. Her parents. Others. All this happened in a village called Welden, a name whose meaning the book took some pains to explain. That alone chilled me, and mystified me, until I looked at the picture again, and saw something curious; in the background, just a short way beyond the tree, there was some sort of carving in the landscape: a large spiral. People were dancing along it.

I read the caption under the illustration but there was no mention of the spiral, of what it was, or why people were dancing on it.

"Here," I said to Verity, "read this part. At least some good came of this."

I pointed at a section of the text further along, where the book explained how this trial, relatively late in the course of witch hunts in Europe, had been partly responsible for bringing an end to the whole business. Outrage at the actions of a certain infamous priest had led eventually to changes in the law. An Act of 1736 declared witchcraft impossible and, therefore, to accuse people of it became illegal. The priest in question was dead long before then; the book left one tantalizing line saying he *"became sorely vexed as a consequence of his actions, and died a madman in the York madhouse."*

"Time for bed," I said to Verity, "maybe we can find you something better to read tomorrow."

"This book is fine," she said. "Sad. But I like it."

Just as we were leaving the library, I noticed the periodicals displayed on a table by the door, and saw that a recent copy of the Journal of the AMA lay there. Among the crowded type on the cover, listing the contents of the week's papers, one word leaped out at me: *malarial.*

It was all I needed to make me grab the journal from the table.

Back in my study, I turned quickly to the paper on the malarial treatment of General Paralysis of the Insane.

I read about the procedure: approximately one fluid ounce of malarial blood is injected intravenously between the spine and shoulder blade.

Between four to twelve days later, the subject takes on a very high fever as a result of the malaria. The subject is treated with quinine to combat the malaria, and when the fever abates, the whole process is repeated. *Up to twelve times.*

The paper described a number of cases, including those where the outcome was not successful.

Case II:

Male aged 33, admitted July 24, 1925. Patient com-
plained of loss of memory. His wife stated that for the
last year he had been mentally confused and had an
attack, several months before admission, in which he
lost his speech for twenty minutes without loss of
consciousness.

On examination, the cardio-vascular, respiratory,
alimentary and genito-urinary systems appeared normal. The pupils were unequal and did not react to
light, but did on accommodation; pinprick was dimin-
ished generally; motor power good; knee-jerks absent.

Mentally he was very confused and childish; memory bad; emotionally very unstable. He gave a very poor
account of himself, and was a very poor witness.

On August 7, the patient was inoculated intravenously with benign tertian malaria. A fever developed
October 12. From this time the patient's mental condi-
tion deteriorated with each daily rise of temperature.
On October 18, an attempt was made to stop the malaria on account of the progressive prostration of the
patient, but the patient died October 21.

There were other, similar reports.

All in all, in a trial of twelve subjects, five had died as a result of this supposed cure.

Saturday, April 16

I WENT TO SEE DOCTOR PHILLIPS, STRAIGHT AWAY. First thing this morning, I knocked on his door and demanded to speak to him about the malarial treatment he had planned for Dexter.

I told him that, with mortality rates as high as the paper in the AMA Journal reported, what he was intending to do was at the very best highly questionable.

At this, Doctor Phillips grew angry.

"I don't like what you are insinuating," he said, and then all his game-playing and taunting and callousness must have got to me, because I was angry in return.

"Good," I declared. "I'm glad you don't like it, because you shouldn't. And I'm not insinuating. I am telling you plainly that inflicting this procedure on Dexter is too much of a gamble, and that if the outcome proves as disastrous for him as it did in forty-two percent of the London cases, then you ought to be account-able for manslaughter."

That was really going too far.

"The success rates have changed since the work in London," he said, and for a moment he threw me off my stride, until he added, "Mortality has fallen to thirty-five percent now."

"Thirty-five? Just thirty-five? My remark still stands. Have you ever operated under such extreme lethal conditions before? This must not be allowed to happen, you cannot sanction such a monstrous plan!"

"Monstrous?" cried Phillips. "Let's not lose our sense of the situation here. Dexter is close to losing all mental faculties worth calling that. We must cure him."

"Or kill him? Is that your intention?"

I glared at Phillips long and hard, staring him down, forcing him to look away, and finally he did, meekly pushing some papers into neater order on his desk.

"Furthermore," I said, "When did you last see Dexter? I have been speaking with him at length and I can report that his symptoms are lessening somewhat. All in all, he is more lucid than when I met him first."

"Nonsense," said Phillips.

"Not at all," I said, as calmly as I could. "It is clear to me that what he needs is more time and the chance to work on his writing."

"Writing? Don't be ridiculous, how could that ever help anyone?"

"Perhaps with Dexter it has. I tell you, he is getting better and to try this dangerous routine on him now could be a mistake, a fatal mistake."

"Getting better? What proof do you have of that?"

Now, I saw a glimmer of a final chance for Dexter.

"If I can prove it to you, will you agree to relent? Delay your procedure for the time being?"

Doctor Phillips raised his eyebrows a fraction, as he contemplated the sight of me begging for a patient's life. Or so I saw it.

"How could you?"

I made a wild statement, one that I hope I will not come to regret.

"Dexter's morbid phobias," I said. "There is one which drives all the others, does it not? His fear of spirals. The spiral staircase."

"What of it?"

"If Dexter can walk to the top of the staircase, given that two weeks ago he could not place his foot on the very first step, you would have to agree that his mental well-being is significantly improved, yes?"

Phillips waited a moment before replying.

"Yes," he said. "I would."

"Do you agree then? If he can visit you up here, you will delay your procedure?"

"Yes," said Phillips. He nodded. "I agree. Tomorrow evening, I will await Dexter in my office."

He smiled, and I shook his hand warmly.

"Thank you!" I said. "Thank you!"

I left him then, and headed back to my rooms, and it was only after I left that I thought to myself, *What have I done?*

Monday, April 18

I KNOW NOW WHAT I HAVE DONE, AND IT WILL NOT BE easy to bear.

After my interview with Doctor Phillips, I realized the stupidity of my bargain with him. There was no way Dexter would be able to climb the stair, and Doctor Phillips knew it. It would only serve to drive Dexter all the sooner to his doom, and undermine what little authority I have in the case, not that I cared about that much by that time. Now I care even less.

I clung to the idea, foolish perhaps, that though I could not cure Dexter overnight, I might be able to reason with him about spirals. If I could get to the bottom of that reaction of his, I thought, I might get him to the seventh floor and buy him a little time, and I had an idea of how to do that.

I needed facts, and so I found myself in the asylum library once more, hunting out what books I could find on archaeology. There were two volumes that helped me, books, which, along with a vast number of irrelevant stories about the past and our investigations into it, contained some images of spirals.

There were spirals all round the world it seemed, in all times, from all cultures. Dexter was right about that. I read feverishly, and gazed at various carvings, but I could find nothing that spoke of their *meaning*.

But, despite that, I myself could not believe that the spiral was a sinister design, and I was determined to convince Dexter.

I found him in his room, and told him plainly how I saw the matter.

"Look!" I said, and flourished the open pages of the archaeology books in front of him. It was pitiful to see how he shrank from even the sight of what was in the books. His eyes fell on a page where there was a photograph of marks on a cave wall. Next to it was another of a series of handprints, which seemed disturbing in some way I could not fathom. Then I realized they disturbed because they were made by hands with half fingers missing, stumps for one or more fingers, in some deliberate ritual mutilation. I withdrew the books from Dexter, not wanting to do him harm.

"I cannot believe the spiral means anything evil," I said. "And you are a logical man. I can see that in the conversations we've had. Consider the paintings on the walls of rocks in Australia, or the carvings of Newgrange in Ireland. They are both sublime. Beautiful. They must have held some spiritual meaning for these ancient people, but not a malevolent one. There is too much care, too much beauty, for them to be signs of evil."

Dexter did not answer. He had his eyes fixed on the books as if they might leap up and bite him.

"At least, consider nature. The natural world is full of spirals, from the shells of snails, to the heads of sunflowers. The curls of my daughter's hair! Elegant, and once again, beautiful. There are also whirlwinds and tornadoes, I grant you, but these things, while bad, are not evil. Nature does not know good and evil, it merely *is*. How can you consider this shape to be guilty of anything? It makes no sense."

Dexter sighed.

"What are you trying to do, Doctor?" he said.

"I'm trying to help you, I . . ."

"I appreciate that," he said. "I can see you have been trying to help me since you arrived at Orient Point. What I mean is, what's happening? Why have you come here on a Sunday morning to talk to me about spirals?"

I held his eye for a moment, then hung my head. Was it that obvious that something was happening? Either that, or I am very bad at lying. Time was against me. And so I felt it was worth trying to shock Dexter into action, to save himself. He reached a hand over his shoulder, furiously scratching his back for a moment, and I could see the terrible tremble in his hands, worse than ever. My mind was made up.

"I have to tell you something," I said, and so I told him what Doctor Phillips had planned. I told him about the malarial treatment, and the survival rate. And then I told him about the deal I had struck with Doctor Phillips.

When I finished there was silence.

For a long time, there was silence. Dexter stood, then went to the barred window of his cell, staring out at the bright April morning sky over Long Island Sound. When he spoke, his voice was quiet, so quiet I could barely hear him.

"Have you ever suffered from a sickness of the mind?" he asked. He didn't turn round to hear my answer, and answer had I none. I think he knew that, and he went on speaking.

"What is the connection we have to the world, Doctor? Is it our hands? Our sense of touch? Our eyes and ears? Our sense of smell, perhaps all these things? Are these the connections we have to the world around us? No. They are not. The only true connection we have to the world is our minds. Yes, our senses can feed us information, but the information means nothing on its own. It is our minds that give things meaning. It is our minds that create the world for us. And minds can be mistaken. Minds can become confused. Damaged. What then of the world? How does it appear then? It, too, appears confused and damaged.

"When that starts happening," Dexter went on, "it is a frightening thing. A truly, deeply frightening thing. It is like running in circles, seeking answers that don't exist, only to come back to where you began, and no wiser than you were before. Like a mad dog in the sun, running in circles. And yet, with each completed circle, you do not come back to *exactly* the same place, because you have sunk a little further into madness. You are one level farther down on a spiral, and the spiral, unlike all other shapes you can draw, is infinite. It can never be depicted complete. You can draw a circle, or a square or a triangle. A star. You can draw it and it is done, but you can only ever show *part* of a spiral, you can only ever *hint* at it, because truly, it goes on forever. And when you feel your mind sliding down the spiral ramp to oblivion, to wild and dark and utterly terrifying oblivion, to an oblivion that you know full well to be endless, that you will suffer for all eternity as in some medieval hell of the mind; well, Doctor, it can be enough to destroy the strongest bravery."

He finished, and now I saw what it was that terrified him about the spiral; it was the endless slide into the void. The void of madness.

"Charles," I whispered. "What are we going to do?"

He turned away from the window then, and came and sat by me on the bed.

"Thank you, Doctor," he said.

"What for?"

"For using my name."

I remember blinking. Thinking.

I held out my hand.

"Perseverance," I said.

For perhaps the only time in our short friendship, I saw Dexter confused.

"Perseverance?" he asked.

I flushed, as I still always do when this comes up.

"It's my name," I said. I shrugged. "Parents with strange notions about the days of the Puritans."

He smiled.

"Perseverance," he said. He shook my hand. "This is what we're going to do. I'm going to climb to the top of that spiral stair. And then you have to promise to make me well again."

"Charles," I said, "I can't do that. But, I promise you, I will try."

He closed his eyes, and nodded.

Then his eyes slowly opened and he even winked at me.

"When am I to perform this miraculous feat?" he asked, and for the first time, I actually thought he might be able to do it.

"This evening. Doctor Phillips is expecting you at seven o'clock."

"Let's make it seven-thirty," he said, grinning. "Keep him waiting awhile, yes?"

I laughed.

"Good man," I said, and was about to leave him when he spoke again.

"Doctor? Those ancient carvings, of spirals? You think they are harmless relics of the early world. But take an atlas of the world, one evening, when this is all over, and plot their locations on the map. Then join the dots, as a child would . . . See what you find."

I said nothing. He was insinuating strange powers to these devices, and I refused to play along.

Once again I was about to leave when he spoke.

"Doctor?"

"Yes?"

"If I fail to climb the stair . . ."

His words trailed away. We both knew that his outcomes were bleak, whatever happened to him, but he saw it in more dramatic terms than me.

"If I fail," he said. "If I fail, Hell is waiting for me."

His eyes were hollow pools of fear and misery and I knew not what to say, until from somewhere in that strange Puritan upbringing I had, some words from a poem came back to me.

"Then in that case," I said. "Unto you I shall allow the easiest room in Hell."

Dexter smiled. Closed his eyes.

"Thank you, Doctor."

At seven o'clock, I left Verity in our rooms, unlocked the gate on the seventh floor, and went to wait at the door to the first-floor men's wing.

Dexter did not appear, so I went to his room and found Solway standing in the open door. True to his word, Dexter refused to come out of his room for half an hour, though Solway shouted at him, and insulted him, and jeered at him.

Then, on the stroke of half past, Dexter stood up, with Solway in midsentence, his mouth gawping, and set off down the corridor.

I followed a few paces distant, and the collective mind of the asylum was all alive around me. Somehow it appeared that every patient in the place knew what was happening, from the sanest individuals of the sixth floor, down to the truly disturbed minds of the first.

As Dexter walked along the corridor, the inmates banged on their doors and let out shrieks and cries of pain. It occurred to me then what phase of the month it was. Like an omen.

Solway walked behind Dexter, abusing him still, but Dexter showed no sign of concern at all until he came to the foot of the stair. Then he stopped, and my heart began to sink.

He could not do it. What had I been thinking? I looked up and saw Doctor Phillips at the balcony of the seventh floor, just as before.

He saw me and smiled. I looked away, noticing that once again, there was a jostling crowd of onlookers who'd come to witness Dexter's failure.

Then, just as I was berating myself for my idiocy, Dexter put his right foot on the first step.

It was as if the whole asylum held its breath. I glanced from Dexter to Phillips and back again; the Doctor was still smiling, confident no doubt that Dexter would be unable to make the second floor, never mind the seventh. That seemed likely. Dexter lifted his other foot and made the second step, and the third, but it was causing him immense strain to do it, that we could all see.

His fingers were clenched into tight balls, sweat was running down his forehead, and his mouth was set in a thin line. He was halfway up the first flight of stairs now, and his legs were shaking badly, but by God, he was still going.

I began to follow him. I kept my distance because I wanted Dexter to do it by himself, and for himself, something that I knew was important. He needed to beat Phillips, and beat him on his own terms.

When he made the second-floor landing, there was a banging on the glass and some patients who'd gathered behind the doors there were laughing, clapping their hands.

Dexter paused momentarily, then walked across the landing to where the flight to the third floor is, and placed his foot on the first stair.

A loud howl came from behind the glass as he did so, but Dexter showed no sign of noticing. He just kept going and going, and he reached the third floor in half the time of the second.

Again he crossed the floor and again he kept going, up and up, and I began to think he could really do it. Still Doctor Phillips was smiling down, serene, almost happy, and I saw the better side of him, that he actually wanted Dexter to prove him wrong.

At the landing of the fifth floor, the doors to the wards were open. A few warders hung about in the halls beyond, and came out onto the landing itself, some patients with them, but all kept their distance from Dexter, as he kept on, up and up, foot by foot, step after step, his eyes screwed tight.

I followed, closer now, and wanted to call to Dexter to

encourage him, to keep him on, but I dared not for fear that Phillips would accuse me of interfering, but it hurt me to keep quiet as I could see that Dexter was in trouble.

He'd reached the landing of the sixth floor and started on the last one, to the seventh, but it was costing him great pain. His legs were shaking, and his arms, as he clung to the bannister desperately for support, needing its help every step of the way now, and those steps were coming very hard indeed.

He had slowed to a crawl. After each step, he'd have to wait while he summoned enough energy to go on, and only when he could control the terrible tremors in his legs did he manage to take another step up.

But he kept on, slowly, so slowly, and then, he was within three steps of the top, then two, and then in a rush he hurried onto the landing. He fell to his hands and knees in front of Phillips, while the great crowd of patients who'd seen him make it, and followed him up, gave an almighty cheer.

I was one of those, yet I cheered silently, as I hurried after Dexter where he was still on hands and knees in front of Phillips. The Doctor was smiling still, smiling down at Dexter, who got to his feet, uncertainly.

"I did it!" he cried, in triumph. His eyes were wild. He looked terrible. He was running with sweat and his arms and legs continued to shake, but he lifted a finger toward Phillips and pointed.

"I did it," he said, his voice broken with high emotion. "I win the wager, Doctor. So you can call off your scientists. Doctor James told me what you're planning for me. But I won!"

Doctor Phillips' smile didn't falter, it seemed fixed on his face. He looked at me.

"Doctor James told you?" he asked. "That's interesting. Unfortunately, it's too late."

Dexter's smile faltered.

"What do you mean?" he stammered.

"It is too late. We have already begun the procedure. Last night you were given a sedative in your food, and in the night we injected you with the dose of malarial blood."

I stared at Phillips in horror. He was smiling as he told Dexter, "You might start to feel feverish soon. It seems as if you already might be."

Dexter rubbed the spot over his shoulder that had been troubling him earlier on, and my head swam as I realized Phillips was telling the truth. The whole thing was a game, and it didn't matter if Dexter won or lost. It never had.

There was a terrible cry.

It came from Dexter, but those words cannot fully elaborate my meaning. I mean to try to say that the cry came from within him, from *deep* within him. I, who have heard the shouts of the insane countless times. I, who have learned to block them from entering me; I, the calm and rational doctor; I trembled with terror at the sound of that scream. It was the sound of deep, primal terror, it was the sound that lies far inside us all, the fear of the horror of being born into a universe that has neither meaning nor purpose and which can offer us no comfort. It was the cry of the soul that is truly alone, abandoned and without hope, and I swear that everyone in that great, aching hall, everyone who heard that single note of pain, will never, ever be the same again.

All that in the smallest division of a moment of time, and then, as I lifted my head, I only had time to see Dexter rush forward at Phillips. He bowled into him and I thought he meant merely to attack him, but before anyone else could react, Dexter had charged into the Doctor, and hurtled with him toward the balcony. With an almighty push, Dexter lifted Phillips off the ground and tipped him over, roaring as he did so.

The Doctor's scream was the only sound as he fell the six floors to the marble hall below.

There was a moment of nothing, just stunned silence, and then pandemonium broke loose.

Solway and another warder rushed at Dexter, but it was as if this single murderous act was a trigger, because instantly those other, usually docile patients who had been watching Dexter's climb sprang upon the staff.

Uproar burst out on all floors of the hallway, and as more warders started to arrive at the sound of trouble, the patients who were free began to fight back. I tried to reach Dexter, but was detained in assisting Solway to wrestle another inmate to the ground.

By the time that was done, chaos was everywhere.

Someone had opened the doors to the wards of the second and even the first floors. A riot was in full spate.

It took a long time to quell the trouble. The inmates were aroused by the sight of Phillips' blood, which pooled out from his head and around his body, and it took every warder and doctor present, myself included, to restore order to the asylum.

When we had, Dexter had vanished.

I sought him.

I had ended up struggling with some patients on the third floor, and I ran back up to the seventh floor, expecting to find Dexter, but he was gone. Then, horrified, I saw that the gate to Doctor Phillips' and our apartments stood open, and in the back of my mind I knew that Phillips had left it open when he'd come out to watch Dexter climb the stair.

I ran through the gate, looking for Dexter, and with mounting terror, began calling Verity's name, loud at first, and louder still. I looked in every room, but there was no sign of her.

I knew who she was with.

Monday, April 18—continued

THE MANHUNT BEGAN AT ONCE, FIRST IN THE ASYLUM and, when that proved fruitless, outside. Dusk had fallen as Dexter made his climb and now darkness had come, so the entire staff of the asylum gathered on the gravel in front of the building with what torches and flares could be found.

There was no time to be lost. I rapidly gave orders to various groups as to which pieces of ground should be covered. Everyone looked to me. In a moment, I had been placed in charge, by Dexter's murderous hand. And even in that terrible moment I made some decisions. As soon as we had found Verity, and Dexter, that very minute, I would start to run the hospital my way. Delgado and the others would be gone, and I would do my utmost to disgrace them, too.

I made that promise to the poor women of the lower wards, unable even to voice what was being done to them.

For now, I only wanted to find Verity.

I barked my orders, taking it on myself to search certain outbuildings, beginning with the crematorium, for I felt certain that Dexter would be there. Upon searching the place, however, we found he was not there, and I began to doubt the equal certainty that I felt that Dexter and my daughter were together. I had left Verity in her room before coming down to witness Dexter's climbing of the stairs. There was no other way she could have left the seventh floor; unless there was still that possibility that she'd lied to me about the dumb waiter.

After the crematorium I searched the wood and metal shops, the barns, the garden tool sheds. I could hear the cries of other searchers and, once or twice, I bumped into people.

"Anything?" I cried.

"No."

"Nothing."

I hurried on, into the night.

Fear rose up and threatened to overwhelm me. I fought to ignore it, to focus on the task, and yet, as the first hour passed, and another, I could fight the fear no more.

Someone had ridden to Greenport to call out the sheriff, and some of his men began to re-cover the ground we had already

searched, which angered me. But I was powerless, as the manhunt for a murderer and my daughter swept on around me.

It was the head gardener who found Verity.

It was around dawn and I was on the steps of the asylum, trying to think what to do, exhausted in body and mind, summon-
ing energy for another effort. I was thinking about Caroline. I
was thinking that I could not bear to lose another loved one. First
my wife, now my daughter. It was too much, too much for me
to bear, and Caroline was still haunting me.

Then I saw the gardener running across the grass to me.

"She's here!" he cried as soon as I was in earshot, and waved
at me, beckoning me to follow.

I ran after him, through the gate of the asylum cemetery, toward the shore that lay just beyond it, through the gravestones,
remembering Dexter's poem, in which every grave was the black
rough fingernail of the monster that lay far beneath the human
world. I pushed those thoughts from me, thinking only of Verity, and pounded after the gardener. A few feet from the final
grave, he stopped dead, and stepped back, inviting me to go on,
as if he dared go no closer.

I came around the grave, my heart in my mouth, and saw Verity sitting against the headstone. She was staring out to sea, tears
running down her face. As I came into view, she saw me, and
broke out into wild sobs.

"Daddy!" she cried, and I ran to her and held her, as tight as
I could.

She did not stop crying for an age, and I wanted so much to

know where she'd been, yet all that truly mattered was that she was unharmed.

"Are you well?" I asked her.

She shook her head.

"You're hurt?"

She shook her head.

"No," she said. "But he's gone."

"Who? Charles?"

She nodded.

"Where? Where has he gone?"

She couldn't tell me. It was too much. But she lifted her arm and pointed at a gate set into the low hedge at the far end of the cemetery. Beyond it lay the waters of the sound.

"You're sure?"

"He told me he was going. We walked around all night, and I was so cross with you, and I didn't want to be found, and he said it was a good game. And then we came here, and he saw this . . ."

She stopped. Leaned forward, away from the headstone, which in the dawn light I could see had a pattern carved into it. The name on the grave meant nothing to me, but whoever it was had the same obsession as Dexter, for there, carved into its stone face, was a beautiful spiral.

"When he saw that," Verity said, "he said he was going to find out what lies beyond the gate."

"That's what he said?"

Verity nodded.

"Did he say anything else?"

"Only to remind you about the geese."

"The geese?"

I remembered Verity telling me that's what they'd spoken about. That first day.

"Remind me about the geese?" I repeated.

Verity nodded.

"Yes, remind you. But you never let me tell you in the first place."

She began to cry again.

I stared at Verity, and then I pulled her tight to me once more.

"Please," I said. "Will you tell me about the geese now?"

She did.

She told me about the geese who fly down the coast and who nest on the island. She told me what Dexter had told her, how the geese come here to mate, and how as part of their mating, they sing bird songs. But the male and the female don't sing the same song. They each sing one half of a song. Two parts that make a whole.

Then she told me that Dexter had told her that the geese mate for life. The same pair, each singing its own part of their own, unique song. And if one of them dies, then the other goose is left alone. If that happens, the bird that's left behind starts to sing both parts of their song. It sings for *both of them.*

That's what Dexter told my daughter. And that's what he told her to tell me.

"He said to tell you," Verity said, "that you have to sing both parts of the song now. Both parts. What does that mean?"

I held Verity for a long time, a very long time, unable to speak without tears coming to my eyes.

Finally, I managed to whisper.

"It means that I'm ready," I said.

"Ready for what?"

To find peace, I thought, but it was a while before I could say that out loud.

But I am ready now.

To let Caroline go, to have her find peace at the bottom of the sea, just as Dexter has done.

QUARTER FOUR

THE SONG OF DESTINY

1

EVERY NIGHT HE DREAMS OF THINGS FOR WHICH
there are no words.

The dreams are strange and last all night.

Each night is ten years long.

His days, by comparison, are but a blink in time. Twelve hours is all he is allowed, twelve hours for waking, to do whatever work must be done, twelve hours every ten years. He has been woken twice so far; when he is woken for the third time, *Sentinel Bowman* is 425 trillion kilometers from home.

Twelve hours is more than enough, he decided, the first time he was awake. Without the need to eat, and with a ship that runs itself, there is in truth little to do but read the reports of the five sentinels who were awake before him, one per year, each for their own twelve hours. Once he's done that, he writes his own report as Sentinel Six, adds it to the log of the others, and posts all of them for the four sentinels who will wake after him to read, each in turn, a year apart.

Outside the twelve-hour slots during which the sentinels are awake, for the rest of each year the *Song of Destiny* ghosts on through space, carrying its cargo of five hundred who float somewhere between life and death, in Longsleep.

"Yes," Bowman said aloud, to no one, the first time he woke. He wanted to see if his voice still worked after ten years in Sentinel Sleep, a gentler but vastly more expensive technique than that applied to the five hundred pods; hence the allowance of only ten sentinels to each wake, alone, for routine maintenance and surveillance of the cargo and other of the ship's systems. Just twelve hours every year.

When the five hundred reach their destination, to wake from Longsleep will be a slow and laborious process. The bodies slowly raised from sub-zero temperatures; the oxygenated preservation fluid drained from lungs and airways; the sustaining gel pumped from their digestive system, and so on and so on. The whole method will take a day or more, the waker only fully recovering consciousness some hours after that. Despite the ship's gravity system and constant bone/muscle stimulation on the sleepers, it will take weeks of recuperation before they can be said to be close to functioning normally.

The trials back on Earth for Longsleep were messy and dangerous. Only after decades of research into each individual obstacle posed by trying to shut down aging to an absolute minimum was the technique declared ready for purpose.

Sentinel Sleep, a rival system developed during the same period, is another matter; it is an almost prohibitively expensive technology aboard a ship where every single thing is unimaginably expensive. But waking takes only half an hour or so, during which Bowman tries to hold on to the dreams that slip through his mind, teasing and taunting his memory like sand running through his fingers.

Once the waking process is over, the lid to Sentinel Bowman's pod beeps twice as it glides open. Then there is only the need to remove the feeding and excretion tubes from his body before he climbs out.

Now, waking for the third time, he stands on the gently curving deck, testing his legs against the force of gravity. Even though he designed several of the ship's systems himself, he still marvels at the elegant simplicity of the gravity system; artificial gravity created by the application of basic physics.

The ship is a Toroid Class IV; essentially a giant ring, two kilometers wide, spinning; spinning perpendicular to its direction of travel. The *Song of Destiny,* like all the Toroid IVs, spins at just the right velocity to create a continuous outward momentum almost equal to the force of gravity on Earth.

It is this ring that forms the living space of the ship, if living is the word that can be applied to the five hundred Longsleep pods and ten sentinel pods that line its walls. On deck, the gravitational effect is almost indistinguishable from Earth. There are a couple of telltale signs that things are different: the gentle concave curve of the floor, and the fact that on the ship, gravity has a *supplementary direction.* Yes, the ship spins at its constant speed, so gravity pulls down just as it would on Earth, but then there is the rotation to consider; which means that walking one way round the ring of the ship's deck is more like walking uphill, and walking the other, something like walking down.

Even though, for the majority of the time, everyone on board the *Song* is sleeping, gravity is a necessary part of the fight against the long-term effects of space travel. And when the ship finally arrives at its destination and goes into orbit, then, of course, it will truly come into its own. For now, it merely makes the sentinel's work sessions that much easier than they would be in zero g.

The ship is completed by the five Bases spaced out equally around the rim, like five stones spread around an eternity ring. Each is a replica of the other: inside are computer terminals where the sentinels work, chlorophyll banks, water recirculation systems, nutrient facilities, control systems for the ship's motor, and a planet-to-planet ship, or PTP.

"Yes," says Bowman, as he wakes for the third time and climbs from his pod. He slides open the drawer from underneath the pod and pulls on his sentinel's uniform; dark gray, orange trim. Though he is effectively alone on the ship, it wouldn't seem right to go to work naked. Besides, there are CCTV cameras in various key places on deck, and he knows that some of the other sentinels are women.

"Yes," he says, "twelve hours are more than enough."

He gazes down the length of the deck, as far as he can see until it curves upward out of sight. Every ten meters is a Longsleep pod. After fifty Longsleep pods, there's the pod of Sentinel Seven; fifty pods the other way would take him to Sentinel Five. Whenever he passes one of his colleagues, he waves a hand in greeting. He's never met any of them, and never will, not till the journey is over. He saw a couple of them briefly on Venture Day, as they were installed in their pods for real, all practice done, a day or so before the ship left Earth orbit. He doesn't know them, but they are just like him, he supposes; each chosen for their special skills and aptitude, to be the guardians of five hundred souls through space for a hundred years.

There is not the slightest sound and not the slightest movement anywhere. Inside each pod rests a just-living human being, each of them invisible.

Since the ship has a radius of a kilometer it's over 1,200 meters from one Base to the next; Bowman's pod is 400 meters from where he has spent twenty-four hours in the last twenty-six years: Base Four.

The lights are dim but grow brighter as he walks toward the Base. He catches sight of his reflection in one of the small ports in the wall of the ring. It faces forward, in the direction they're flying, but there is no sense of movement at all; the stars are too far away for them to change position as they travel. It's hard to be sure in this light, but there is his face, looking back at him; not a day older than when he first climbed into the sentinel pod, twenty-six years ago.

It doesn't seem possible, but it is. Yet it is only possible because his waking hours are so limited. There is no option. In eleven-and-a-half hours, he must be refitting himself in his pod, waiting to be taken into Sentinel Sleep again. If he misses just one deadline with the pod, his life expectancy will drop, vastly. The chances are he will not make it to their destination a young man, if alive at all.

That's when it occurs to him, staring through the narrow porthole, he, like all the others on board the *Song of Destiny,* is not traveling through space in a straight line. The ship itself is traveling in a straight line, but the ship is spinning; so everyone on board is rotating as they move forward at something close to nine-tenths light speed.

He is traveling in a spiral, a helix through space.

He ambles into Base Four, shutting the door to the ring, only vaguely wondering why he is bothering to shut the door when there is no operational need to do so. If he'd stopped to think, he might have realized that the sight of pod after pod stretching away round the curve of the ring unnerves him slightly, as if he's flying a mortuary through space. He knows none of these people—none of them. That's why he was chosen for his job as a sentinel, in part at least. Along with the other sentinels, it is his job simply to see them, and the ship, safely through space.

He flops down into the chair in front of Terminal Base Four, and that's when he sees the series of red lights blinking on the screen in front of him.

Six of the five hundred are dead.

1 ───────────────────────────────────────

OF ALL THE PROBLEMS THAT FACED THE WORLD,
there was one that nothing could be done about, because it was
caused by the success of eradicating all the other threats to
human life: overpopulation.

It took centuries longer for the world to civilize than anyone
ever anticipated. But eventually it did. As artificially grown meat
solved the food crises; as the threat of climate change stabilized
with the disappearance of fossil fuels and their replacement with
renewable power; as even the poorest countries in the world became rich enough to be well off as the driving forces for wars
dissipated; as finally people everywhere became comfortable
enough that their need for religion waned and dwindled, a truly
united world Global-Government faced the last remaining issue:
there was no longer enough room for the billions of people living in the thin film of habitable space wrapped around the planet.
Deserts had been hydrated, floating cities spawned, even the Ant-
arctic colonized, and yet still the birth rate shot ever-upward.

As the memory of times of war and conflict began to raise
itself in countries' collective minds, the world clamored for a
solution to the problem. In response, birth limits were introduced, and so the population began to slowly level off, but, by
now, the question of the long-term prospects for the human race

was high in people's minds. It was, many people felt, in man's nature to explore, to expand, in short: to live. The desire to survive and prosper, it was argued, is the very meaning of life itself. It must go on, forever, without limit, and to deny that would be to deny life. Mankind should not live with birth quotas and assent forms and enforced sterilisation.

Billions of dollars were spent merely researching potential solutions, but they all revolved around the same idea: a new Earth must be found, or made.

As attempts to seed an atmosphere on Mars repeatedly failed, a new strand of thought emerged, so very unthinkable until all other possibilities had been exhausted: we must move to some distant, and already Earth-like, planet.

The problems facing such an endeavor were plentiful, but the biggest was also the simplest: the nearest habitable world known was very far away. So far that it would take light around one hundred and seventy years to reach it.

The planet, orbiting a star in the constellation of Lyca, had been dubbed New Earth centuries before anyone ever thought of going there; all the analysis showed this distant world was as close a cousin to our own as could ever be found anywhere, an Eden, waiting to be colonized. But, ever adaptable, the people of the world began to change their viewpoint. This was a journey of a previously unimaginable kind, and yet there was nothing in theory to prevent it. Each obstacle in the way of such a mission was attacked ruthlessly. Trillions were spent researching matters from zero-waste nutrients to chorophyll-based oxygen generators to the issues of the deleterious effects of space travel on the human body; from muscle and bone wastage issues, to electromagnetic shielding against interstellar radiation. The question of how to achieve near-speed-of-light travel was resolved after thirty years of development on the Clarke Drive, a radiation pressure engine that steadily imparted impulse to the mass of the ship.

Eventually, each and every problem was defeated.

Finally, there only remained the question of who would dare to venture on such a journey. People reminded each other of previous epic journeys made by mankind. History books told of the voyage of the *Mayflower*, but the comparison was weak. These would not be a hundred souls on board a ship crossing the ocean in a couple of months to colonize another continent; a continent much like the one they'd left, with other ships soon to follow.

Though New Earth was one hundred and seventy light-years away, the *Song*'s journey would take only around a hundred years of ship time to complete, one of the advantages of traveling close to light speed being that time dilation would make clocks on board run slower. With its passengers effectively frozen in time until they reached New Earth, and the ten sentinels to each wake just ten times for half a day to monitor the ship's progress.

These people would never come back. News of them would never come back.

Who would go on such a mission?

The answer, we should not have been surprised, was *millions* of people. As five Toroid ships were prepared by the Global-Government, one for each continent, the number of people not only willing but desperate to be part of the first wave of colonization grew. Debates raged endlessly; even those who had no interest in going had strong views on who should be allowed to.

Scientists would be needed, that much everyone agreed. Technicians of all kinds. Doctors. Engineers. But what of the other areas of human life? Should artists be included, and musicians? Wouldn't a life without such things be pointless to the human animal?

The arguments continued, but when it was announced that each of the five ships would hold just five hundred passengers. The arguments erupted into disbelief. Of the 45 billion people on the planet, how could just 2,500 be chosen? And what of these guardians, the sentinels? How could there be just ten per ship, fifty in all? Who would ever dare to make such choices? What calculations or formulas could scientists ever derive to neatly give such answers?

There was one calculation that was indisputable: the minimum number of people per ship should be at least five hundred. Below that number, there would not be a sufficiently diverse gene pool to support the healthy rebirth of the human species on New Earth. Below that number, the possibility of the Founder Effect was too great: the genes of one person could start to dominate the population with, theoretically at least, disastrous results.

But who would be the five hundred? And who would be the ten?

Keir Bowman knew he would be among them.

Yes, he'd worked on the Americas Continent Toroid, developing software for control systems. Yes, he'd been trained as an astronaut. Yes, he had no family ties: no wife, child, or parents living. His psychometric testing had shown him to be a near-perfect candidate for a sentinel. Early experiments in space travel within the Solar System had quickly demonstrated that no matter how high a compatibility score a group of astronauts might achieve, given the timescales involved, factions and politics and even fights would develop eventually in the close confines of the ship. The answer was the loner. The individual who preferred no other company than this own thoughts. Of course, the danger was that such individuals often displayed borderline psychopathic traits. The key was to find just the right person: calm, contained, at peace with their true nature, able to go for long periods in isolation.

Bowman knew he would be one of them. Partly because he was the near-perfect candidate anyway, and partly because he'd hacked the computers of the Americas' Selection Committee in order to erase the report of obsessional tendencies in his psychometric test results.

2

"NEVER LOOK BACK," WAS SOMETHING BOWMAN remembered his father telling him. It was about the only thing Bowman could remember of him, a man who'd died when his son was a young man. It was certainly the thing that he'd taken most to heart as a boy.

Bowman had never looked back in his whole life. Not once. Even before he left Earth on the shuttle to the *Song of Destiny*, he had been floating free. Floating away from people, away from his family, away from his last lover, to whom he had formed only the weakest attachment. He was always looking ahead, desperate to be somewhere else, though he never knew what it was that he wanted.

So now, staring at a computer screen that tells him that just over 1 percent of the population have died, for reasons unknown, he does not for one minute question his choice to become a sentinel, or regret coming aboard the *Song of Destiny*.

The fact that six people have died since the Sentinel Five was on duty a year ago was worrying enough, but there are further complications. Why didn't the computer wake him earlier, when the first death happened? The ship is programmed to wake the next sentinel in line for duty in the case of any untoward emergency, anything that it cannot sort itself. The fact that it allowed the deaths to continue is strange in itself. Maybe all six had died at once, but then comes the next problem: How did they die?

He glances at the large bio-clock above Terminal Base Four; the readout of his status displayed for him to see at all times. He has eleven and a quarter hours in which to find the cause of the deaths, work out how to prevent any more from occurring, and reboot the automatic alert systems.

He begins tapping away at the smooth black keypad. It seems so old-fashioned to interact with the computer in this way when Earth is full of gestural readers and brainwave-synced devices, but the designers of the Toroid ships wanted no room for the errors those devices still sometimes create. With a keypad, if you touch the glass then you touch the glass, and the extra time and physical movement it takes to do that gives everything a much more mechanical certainty. Bowman doesn't mind, and his fingers are fast.

He starts to run reports on the six dead pods, and that's when he starts to feel uneasy, because nothing is wrong. Since the medical history of all 510 people on the ship is recorded constantly while in their pod, any change in health whatsoever should show on the reports.

He feeds the reports through a medical analyzer, just to be sure he isn't missing anything, but the result is just as he'd first thought. Nothing was wrong with the people who'd died, until the moment of death, when their miniscule brain function flat-lined.

The obvious conclusion; there's something faulty with the pods themselves. Bowman runs tech read-outs for the six pods, all of which are stationed a way away from him; between Bases

One and Two. Over two kilometers away. The results are the same as with the people themselves. There is nothing apparently wrong with the pods either, and yet something is wrong somewhere; and something must be wrong with the alert system itself for the ship not to have woken him.

He is alone.

There is no one to help him solve this puzzle, but that's the way he likes it. He sits back and takes a precious two minutes of his waking time trying to decide what to do.

First, he reads the last report from Sentinel Five for signs of any issues, anything that might indicate problems were forthcoming. Sentinel Five's report is so routine as to be boring; everything was fine a year ago, and yet, somewhere in the time that followed, six pods went offline.

He is alone.

The ship's computers can only help him as far as he directs them to. The network of these computers is vast and unbelievably complex, but it is still only a computer network. Long ago it was decided that artificial intelligence systems posed just as great a risk to ultra-long space flight as teams of astronauts do. Suzuki's Law; that the closer a computer interface gets to seeming truly human, the more humans find it disturbing, holds true in space just as it did on Earth. In fact, given the isolation, having an artificial intelligence, a computer-generated voice, a hologram or other user interface to interact with, slowly eats away at us for some reason; unnerving us, unsettling us, until we feel that we are talking to a ghost, or some spectral god.

Bowman, therefore, is alone, but that is why he was chosen

for the mission; because he is fast, decisive, and doesn't need support from anyone else to make those decisions.

Even he, however, realizes it would be good to start recording a log for Sentinel Seven, should he not solve everything during this waking. So he sets up a recording, linked to his profile.

"Six failures are showing. No cause of death obvious in any case. No faults logged with the pods of the six. Alert systems did not operate. Proceeding to investigate."

He sits back, and thinks a little, knowing the recording will deactivate until he starts speaking again.

"There is another possibility, of course. Perhaps the alert system did not operate because the six occupants are not actually dead; maybe the fault is with the reporting of the pod status."

He sits up again, because he knows there is only one way to be sure. Since the computer is adamant that there is nothing wrong with the pods, he will have to go and look at each one and see for sure whether the occupant inside is alive or dead.

He checks the screens. The closest inoperative pod is almost three kilometers away. There is nothing for it but to walk.

"Proceeding to visual check of negative pods," he says, and without further hesitation, he opens the door to the deck and sets out for pod 89.

He's walking "uphill," against the direction of rotation of the *Song*. The rotation of the ship is a constant, and given its vast size, just under one rpm is enough to equate to one g. The effect of walking against the motion of spin is very slight, but noticeable, and Bowman begins to think it would have been faster to walk to the second-closest faulty pod, 4, even though it is actually farther away.

As he reaches pod 89, he checks the time on the clock on the wrist of his suit. He has ten hours left in which to work.

Longsleep pods look different from sentinel pods. Whereas his own is a long, blue, swollen cigar set against the wall of the deck, pod 89, like all the Longsleep pods, is white and much thinner. It is featureless on the outside; only the seal, closed now for twenty-six years, is just discernable, otherwise there is nothing to be gained by staring at the number etched in black on its white surface. It does not even bear the name of the person inside.

Underneath it are two drawers; the first contains the few personal effects that each occupant has been allowed to bring on the mission. On his previous, uneventful, wakings, Bowman has often thought about what strange things lie in these 510 drawers. He knows what is in his own, of course; not much. A book of poetry and some clothes that he really likes. But what weird things have the others chosen to bring to New Earth? He suspects there are lots of books; real paper books; such a status symbol these days, a mark of refinement and intellect. There will be photographs of loved ones, never to be seen again. Are there weirder things? Pointless things? Things of superstition?

The answer to whether to allow artists to be selected was, in the end, to choose people with multiple skills: the dentist who paints, the architectural technician who writes stories, the component manufacturer who makes short films in his spare time. In some of the drawers, therefore, there may be unusual things, but of genuine treasure, there will be none. No money. The entire system of work, payment and government will have no meaning where they are going. They will start again, according to laws drawn up by the Global-Government Special Committee created just for that purpose, a compact to which all 510 people on the ship have agreed, in writing.

Bowman's hand rests on the button to open the personal effects drawer of pod 89, but only on a whim. It will not open for him anyway as each responds only to its occupant's bio-print.

Instead, his hand slips down to the drawer underneath, again an almost featureless white surface into which are recessed two buttons, upon which he places the first two fingertips of his right hand.

The maintenance drawer beeps twice, and starts to slide open slowly. As it does, Bowman realizes he is staring at the fingerprints on his right hand, to which the maintenance drawer just responded. In the bright light of Deck One, it's easy to see the spiral patterns on the pads of his fingers, and then a question so stupid enters his head that he is shocked.

Who put those there?

Unhappy with himself, he turns back to the work in hand, and starts to inspect the readouts.

Inside the pod was a living being. Breathing had ceased and been replaced by a system of oxygenated fluid that fills the lungs. Brain function was reduced to a state little more active than a coma. But, it was still a person inside, and now, according to the pod, even those minute vital signs have gone, and that person is dead.

Either side of him, Deck One runs away out of sight to become Deck Two in the direction of spin, and Deck Five in the other.

The pods sit, apparently lifeless. One after another, after another.

The only sound is his breathing as he tries to make the pod tell him what went wrong.

The ship spins on through space.

Then, in the corner of his eye, he sees something move far away, at the horizon caused by the curve of the deck.

His head jerks toward the movement, and startled, he falls back, catching his heels on the floor of the deck, banging the back of his head, just under the skull, against the lip of the open maintenance drawer.

He feels nausea swim up into him instantly and knows he is fainting, but, as he does, he still has endless milliseconds in which to realize that he cannot have seen what he thought he saw, because what he thought he saw, crouching over a Longsleep pod, was a human figure.

3

WHEN HE COMES TO, HE HAS NO IDEA HOW LONG HAS passed.

He is immediately terrified, by two thoughts. The first is the idea that someone else is awake with him, on the ship. That cannot happen, the ship would not cause it to happen.

The second, which is now more pressing, is the fact that unless he returns to his sentinel pod before it enters the sleep cycle again, he will almost certainly die.

He checks the clock on his suit. With a shock he sees that he has been out for hours; his waking cycle is due to finish in forty-five minutes.

He forces himself to be calm, and work out what to do, in what order, and how to do it all in the most time-efficient way he can.

The back of his head is bleeding a little, or has been while he slept. He feels angry with himself for wasting even a second of his waking cycle on sleep, never mind many hours, but he pushes those thoughts down into the depths of his mind, and runs more checks on the pod, according to which, the occupant is truly dead.

If that's the case, he thinks, no harm can come of an actual, visual check on the occupant. In Longsleep, it's almost impossible to tell the difference between life and death states anyway, but there is one sure-fire method: pupil dilation. Even in the Longsleep state, pupils will constrict when exposed to bright light if the sleeper is still alive.

He begins to quickly tap away at the controls of the maintenance drawer, entering a series of codes known only to the sentinels to permit the lid of the pod to be opened in emergency situations.

It takes five and a half minutes to complete the protocols required, and as he finishes, the pod begins to give a series of low warning beeps.

The faint seal around its perimeter glows white and then the lid lifts, revealing the occupant inside.

It is a woman.

Bowman guesses she is around twenty-eight years old. She is beautiful, one of the most beautiful women he has ever seen, and he wonders whether all the occupants were chosen for their looks, as well as their intellect, skills, and personality traits. Have they chosen a perfect five hundred people from which to make a new world? Of the millions of people who applied for the mission, the numbers must have rapidly fallen away as the selection process weeded out any who didn't come up to the mark. Even this beautiful woman, who must have a CBC of at least 256, who no doubt has skills vital to the new colony and who probably plays a variety of musical instruments, even she might not have been selected, but for the fact that her age gives her at least forty years of childbearing ahead of her, for what is a new colony without babies?

His hand hovers over her, his fingers hesitating to touch her, as if she might be ill, or carry some contagion, though he knows there are no pathogens on board the ship.

His spiral-tipped fingers move to her right eyelid, to open it, but as he touches her skin, her entire body, now exposed to the air of the open deck, crumbles before his eyes, collapsing in on itself in a pile of dust and the strange fluids that had kept her half alive for so long.

His heart begins to pound.

He thinks he hears a sound behind him, and spins round, eyes wide.

Nothing.

He checks his suit clock. Thirty-five minutes.

He runs, downhill, back to Terminal Base Four, where he is unable to speak for a few minutes, since the run has left him short of breath. Sentinel Sleep might keep his body alive and not wasting away, but it does no more than that. He is badly out of shape.

Unable to speak his log, he begins to type a report for Sentinel Seven to read, and hurriedly performs three of the thirty-seven systems checks that he would really like to make.

He checks his watch.

He now has five minutes to reach his pod before it will close without him and leave him stranded, awake for ten years unless he can find a way to override the system, and it is not one of the systems that he himself developed.

He wonders how he lost track of time so badly—another half hour just to type a report?

He hurries as fast as he can back toward his pod, which is

already making warning noises when he reaches it, and as he climbs into it, he can no longer suppress the fears that are calling out from inside him.

Did he really see someone else awake on the ship?

Why didn't they come to him? Why didn't they make themselves known to him unless they meant some harm?

He pulls his clothes off, sitting up in the pod, and throws them on the floor, just as the lid starts to close on him for another ten years, and as he sinks away into the breathless dreaming of Sentinel Sleep, his last conscious thoughts are these:

Is there someone on board, tampering with the systems?

Is there a killer on the ship with me?

And will I ever wake again?

5

HE DREAMS FOR TEN YEARS.

During which he is not murdered, not for real, though in his dreams he dies a thousand times and then a thousand times more. The endless ways in which his unconscious mind seems to be able to horrify him means that no two of these deaths are the same. Not all his dreams are so horrific, however, but still, there are no words for some of the things he sees. What do dreams mean? And why are they there? What happens to the mind when they can go on, and on, and on, almost forever it seems?

He's tumbling down a spiral staircase, head over heels, infinitely, as the *Song* spirals through space, weaving 504 helical dream-threads through the galaxy as the ship heads for Lyca, still so very, very far away.

If there was a being, a being with no physical body, but one which grew and sustained itself purely on the traces of emotion, it would be able to drift through the stars after the *Song*, drinking in this trail of floating dreams.

Bowman is not killed, and as he wakes, he's dreaming about something he has not seen in a very long time—wet grass.

It fills his nose and covers his palms, but as the lid to his pod slips open for the fourth time, the grass vanishes like smoke. He was about to make the connection to the rest of the dream: a distant memory. He grew up in a rural part of the country, something more distant than a suburb, closer to the city than a backwater. His parents were successful people, but his father was rarely home. He remembers the house and garden better than his parents. There was the house itself, a fine and elegant old building with a hundred rooms to hide in, if only he'd had someone to play hide-and-seek with. He liked the summer best, because that was when he could live outside from dawn till dusk, pushing open the gate to the measureless gardens when he was young, sitting in an ancient apple tree in one corner, desperate to be old enough to be allowed beyond these confines, to see the world. As soon as he could, he didn't wait, and was gone into the woods and valleys below the hamlet, but those early days remain the strongest in his mind, and wet grass means one thing to him, which is the sensation of falling from a low branch of the tree, and putting his palms out to meet the ground. And then . . . But no, it's gone.

He sits up.

"Yes," he says, and then catches himself, and laughs. It is a nervous laugh, because though it has been ten years, to his conscious mind it seems only a moment since he climbed into the pod, wondering if someone malevolent was on board with him.

His first thought is that he should complete one circuit of the deck, from Base Four back to Base Four again, to see if anyone is there. Perhaps he imagined the whole thing, after all. Some trick of the light? And he did hit his head on the maintenance drawer . . . Maybe that made him hallucinate something.

Wait, he thinks, *that's wrong. I fell* after *I saw the figure. That was why I fell. That can't be what made me see something.*

Still, he is alive, and his first responsibility is to the voyage of the *Song of Destiny*.

He climbs from the pod again, pulls on his gray suit, and sets off for Base Four.

If there were someone on board . . . he thinks. *Well, there is nowhere to hide on the decks.* But each of the bases has many rooms, halls, hangars, and labs. It would take him hours to search just one of them, there's no way he can manage all five in this waking. But how could someone be on board anyway? They would have to have somehow accessed the food stores in one of the PTP ships, as well as overridden the oxygen lowering that occurs in the ten years when a sentinel is not active. That alone would have placed a huge drain on the output of the chlorophyll tanks. The *Song* is designed to carry sleeping, barely-respiring passengers, not fully breathing ones.

None of it makes sense.

He makes some quick mental calculations as he walks.

The radiation pressure engine is a slow but steady beast. It collects solar radiation channeled through the spiraling ring of the *Song* and uses the reaction it makes against a virtual sail to cause an impulse to the ship. The impulse is tiny, but it is constant, allowing the ship to accelerate at one meter per second.

When the *Song* left Earth's orbit, it was towed away from the effect of Earth's gravity by five tug ships. Left to its own devices, the ship has been accelerating only at one meter per second it's true, but for thirty-six years. The beauty of the radiation pressure engine is that the speed just keeps on building, until, after seven years, it reached its maximum velocity at around 260,000 kilometers a second. And so the distance to Lyca will be gobbled up in a mere one hundred years or so.

Bowman estimates that he is now 589 trillion kilometers from home.

He reaches Terminal Base Four.

Another Longsleep pod is dead.

8

BOWMAN CLOSES THE DOOR FROM DECK THREE TO
Terminal Base Four, then he locks it so it can be opened only
from inside. He also locks the door that leads through the Base to
the operational centers, and the one that leads to Deck Four,
with Base Five beyond it.

He returns to the console and slumps into the chair in front
of the bank of screens.

He needs to think, but it's so hard to think clearly when you've
just woken from Sentinel Sleep. He tries to remember how he
felt when he woke last time, but he can't seem to get that straight
in his head, either.

More than ever before, he needs to think logically, and use
his time well, but he's finding it hard to get rid of the dreams of
the last ten years, snatches of which keep flashing into his mind
even as he tries to concentrate on the status of the ship. The things
he sees are broken and distorted, but it doesn't take him long to
see that the theme of spirals runs through them all. He starts to
apply his mind to the question of why he is dreaming about spirals, he tries to understand what that might mean, and then, suddenly, he lifts his head, checks the clock, and sees he has wasted
a whole hour in this waking dream.

He looks at the medical pack fixed to the wall of Terminal

Base Four and wonders if he should give himself a shot of something to help him concentrate, but decides against it. He wants to know that his thoughts are his own and not chemically altered ones. With a great effort of will, he turns his eyes back to the console, and his mind to the problem.

Another ten years have passed. There has been one more death.

The first thing to do is to read the nine reports between the one he hurriedly filed and now.

While he's doing that, he has the ship run a scan of bio-forms on board.

It confirms what he feels he already knew: there are exactly five hundred and three people on the *Song of Destiny*. Given that there have been seven deaths, that makes five hundred and ten, the full original complement of the ship.

Something else is immediately obvious: if he really did see someone on his last waking cycle, they *must* be a sentinel. The process of emerging from Longsleep is slow, awkward and requires outside assistance. Only a sentinel could wake.

Which means that as he reads the reports of the other nine, he is looking for a sign of deception on the part of one of them. For some reason, no one else has left a voice log. Each sentinel has left written records of their time awake and while each of them expresses concern at the deaths, no one has been able to shed any light on the matter, and no one has any solution to the obvious technical problems that this shows the computer must be displaying.

He rereads the reports, looking more closely at the language used. He nearly gets lost in a reverie again as Sentinel Three uses the expression "spirals out of control," but then he gets a grip, and keeps on reading.

The obvious candidate is Sentinel Five. It was between Sentinel Five's waking and his own that the first deaths occurred.

He checks to see when this new, single death occurred, and is surprised when it falls not during Sentinel Five's last waking cycle, but somewhere between that of Sentinels Two and Three.

Does that mean that more than one of them is involved? Does it mean that someone is tampering with the records? Perhaps Sentinel Three, or Four . . . ?

He stops.

He has no evidence that anyone, never mind a sentinel, is intentionally committing murders of the Longsleepers. It's much more likely that there is some mechanical fault in the Longsleep system, and should he really be so sure that he did see a dark figure slip across the edge of his field of vision? Wasn't he warned about possible visual disturbances during his training? He can't remember.

It's so hard to think now, so hard to remember back past all those years of dreaming that seem to cloud his waking thoughts. Maybe he dreamed the whole thing. He feels the back of his head and can find no sign of a cut. It's not tender, but then, he's been asleep long enough for a hundred broken bones to heal.

There's one way to be sure: the ship's CCTV banks.

Every second they have recorded is stored in the ship's memory. The cameras are motion activated. They should therefore only be recording at all during the twelve hours of a sentinel's waking cycle. Anything outside those times would indicate something highly irregular occurring, and sure enough, as he performs a search on the years between all Sentinel Sleeps, he finds nothing.

Instead, he searches for the video from his last waking. He'd been working on pod 89. The beautiful woman, now so much dust recycled back into the ship's nutrient systems. He seems to be able to remember the time he was there, and sure enough, he is soon watching the playback of himself entering Deck One from the door at Base Two. The cameras are few, just enough to cover all habitable areas of the ship. Due to the concave curve of the deck, any one camera can only cover around a hundred meters or so before the floor of the deck slides up out of view of this inverted "horizon." So that's how far apart the cameras are spaced, and he finds that he has a pretty clear view of himself arriving to work at pod 89.

He sees himself reach the pod, and wonders why his hand hovers over the personal effects drawer for a moment. He doesn't remember that, or why he would have thought of opening it when he would not be able to anyway.

He watches as he opens the maintenance drawer, and then, his heart pounding, he sees his head flick around as he sees something, trips backward, and cracks his head on the drawer.

He can see no sign of any figure, and begins to doubt himself further.

He glances at the doors to the Terminal and checks that the red "lock" lights are still glowing. They are, but somehow it doesn't make him feel much safer.

What is going on? he thinks. *Was it all my imagination?*

And why would anyone want to murder the Longsleepers anyway?

Then, with a spring of insight, he realizes that where the camera is mounted, on the ceiling, gives it a slightly reduced view of what he'd have been able to see crouching by the pod. But maybe the next camera along can help him.

He searches for the file, forward to the right time code, and then is almost immediately sick as he sees exactly what he thought he'd seen.

The picture is small and the quality poor, but even so he sees quite clearly as a figure emerges from behind a Longsleep pod, flits across the deck, and hurries away out of sight, up the curve of Deck One. At no point can he see above the figure's shoulder height. All he sees are the torso, arms, and legs.

By rights he should be able to pick up the figure on the next camera, so he fumbles hurriedly to load the right file, but when he plays it, there is nothing there. The figure simply disappears between one camera and the next.

Dumbfounded, he sets the portion of video that contains the moving figure to loop, and he watches it, again and again. Round and round the clip plays, like a snake swallowing its own tail.

It's fuzzy, but he can see two things. Whoever it is, they are male. And from their dark gray suit with orange trim, he is a sentinel. A sentinel who seems to vanish into thin air right before the eyes of the camera.

* * *

Bowman doesn't believe in supernatural entities; no one does anymore. Not God, nor gods, nor ghosts of any kind, yet from some ultimate depth of the most primitive part of his mind, the ancient concept of one of these things begins to crawl upward.

13

IT SEEMS AN INESCAPABLE CONCLUSION, TO BOWMAN, that whichever sentinel was awake when he shouldn't have been is also somehow responsible for the deaths of seven Long-sleepers. This means that they have somehow managed to program the ship to wake them when it should not be waking them, and furthermore, have also managed to conceal their tracks within the computer system, which should be impossible, since every keystroke is logged. Impossible? Bowman thinks he might just be able to do it, given enough time, but he is rightly arrogant about his computer skills and doubts that the other sentinel he saw slipping out of the video frame could match him.

But it's a place to start, and he begins to hack into the computer, beyond where he is allowed access, in order to view the personnel files of his nine colleagues.

The files are only loosely encrypted and it doesn't take Bowman long to find the files of not only the nine sentinels, but also his own, and those of the five hundred passengers on the *Song of Destiny*; the ones who would populate New Earth.

All of the sentinels are, of course, highly intelligent. All of them match the ideal of a sentinel's personality profile. Some have more experience as astronauts than others, but they all have a minimum of three years' flying time. Like Bowman, two or three have experience on the creation of the Toroid ship venture, but only one of these is a man. Bowman doesn't even pause to read his name, but sees that he has been assigned as Sentinel Eight.

Bowman sits up.

He had hoped it would be Five, as his first intuition had told him. Still nothing is making any sense.

His mind starts to drift again. Without realizing he is doing it, he begins to flick through the profiles of the five hundred. He notes that the Selection Committee was assiduous in its accuracy to the profile of the Earth. At a rough glance it seems that all racial types are represented. There are exactly two hundred and fifty men and two hundred and fifty women, though whether they have been matched as monogamous couples, these simple lists do not indicate. Bowman smiles; even if they were, twenty minutes after landing he suspected they'd be making their own arrangements. He begins to picture inside the minds of the Selection Committee. Watching the files flick through underneath his fingertips, he learns the way they were thinking as they made their choices. Something begins to bother him, but he can't work out what it is.

Of course, he realizes, they would have chosen only physically healthy specimens of the human form. Perfect, if such a thing were possible. He himself is tall and strong, and he's never stopped to ask whether he is attractive or not. So the Selection Committee had chosen tall, strong people, from healthy genetic backgrounds, with no physical weaknesses of any kind.

"Playing God," he whispers, staring at the screen, but he asks himself if he would have done anything differently. Why introduce illness to the new world when it can be eliminated before they've even landed? Cancer is now a thing of the past; each of these five hundred comes from families where no cases have ever been reported.

And they've chosen two hundred and fifty of each sex, but did they stop to consider those who might feel differently? Were homosexuals chosen? Why wouldn't they be? Why *would* they be, when it would be vital to the survival of the new colony that they reproduced like rabbits in the spring? And in that case, wouldn't it have made more sense to have populated the ship with four hundred and ninety fertile women and ten, soon to be somewhat exhausted, men? Maybe the women would mostly be younger, to give them as long a reproductive life as possible.

Are they teenagers? It has long been recognized, Bowman knows, that the teenage mind played a large role in the explosion of humankind: the young adult mind, with its love of risk-taking and experimentation. Of freedom and exploration, of pushing the limits. In the aeons when life expectancy reached barely twenty years, when we clung to the fireside and when we drew magic on the walls of dark caves, those were things that set our entire species ahead of the competition, those were the characteristics that gave us an evolutionary edge. Perhaps, in this moment of desperate need, it was foreseen that we should turn to this youthful version of our mind, once more.

He, at last, understands the pitiless task that the Selection

Committee faced, and maybe, in the end, they left some of these things to chance. But he doubts that thought as soon as it enters his head.

Bowman sits in the chair at the console.

He ought to be reprogramming the alert systems, so that he, or one of the other sentinels, will be woken if further deaths occur. But he doesn't. He sits, flicking through the files of the five hundred, until he finds that he has brought up the file on pod 89.

Her name was Allandra Li. His guess was close; she was twenty-seven at the start of the voyage. She had trained as a dancer in Reykjavík until she moved to California at sixteen and changed the course of her career, enrolling with the Axe Apollo Space Academy. She excelled in her doctoral work as a geneticist, but just when she could have developed a highly paid career, she opted to work with underprivileged children in China, until she applied for selection to the New Earth voyage. She was kind. She was beautiful. She was intelligent. And now, Bowman thinks, she is dead. He flicks to the end of her file, where he finds that there are images of each pod occupant. One of these images shows the face in close-up. Two of these images show the whole body of the occupant, naked, from the front and back. Bowman finds himself desiring a woman who died before he even met her, and then he notices something: a mark between her shoulder blades.

He zooms into the image and sees it is a tattoo. That alone is odd, such primitive body markings would undoubtedly have lost her a few points during her selection assessment.

But he doesn't care about that. What obsesses him for the next two hours is that the symbol she chose to have placed on her back is the one that has been haunting him for the past thirty-six years of sleep: a spiral.

21

IT'S INCREDIBLE, THE THINGS THAT MANKIND HAS LEARNED how to do. The things that we have discovered. For example, it has been determined, by the interference of the planet now known as New Earth on light traveling toward us from stars even farther away, that the composition of this new world is 97.8 percent like that of Earth itself. That the planet is around a billion years younger than our own. That it is rich in plant life. That there is no advanced species there, no technology like our own. We can know all that from one hundred and seventy light years away.

So why is it, thinks Bowman, when we can know all that, that we cannot design an alert system on board a spaceship that works the damn way it's supposed to?

He tries to get the ship to analyze all the systems involved, and a prompt loads telling him it will take an hour and a half to complete the task.

He checks his clock. When that analysis has run, he will have five hours left before sleep.

What should he do in the meantime?

He thinks about writing his log for the other sentinels, but he hesitates. He wants to tell them he knows that one of them is a killer, but in order to do that, he would have to tell the killer, too. Better to hold his fire. He's working on the assumption that there is no reason for the deaths to stop, even though it was only one the last time, and six the first.

For some reason, the deaths are not being inflicted upon the sentinels. At least not yet. Maybe that's just random, or maybe the rogue sentinel has developed some weird grudge against the five hundred, against the mission itself?

That's a thought worth pursuing, Bowman thinks, but, in the meantime, he reallocates memory to the CCTV cameras on all five decks. The images are fuzzy not because the lenses on the cameras are poor, but because they have been given a limited amount of file space in which to store their images. By reallocating more memory to the next of his sleep phases, any images recorded will be of much better quality.

He wonders about the sentinels, starts trying to plan what voice log he could leave that would help him flush out the culprit. Is there some logical game he can play, perhaps using something that only the murderer would know? Can he set some kind of trap to be tripped over the course of the next ten years, while he sleeps?

It worries him. Better to play dumb. If he arouses the suspicions of the killer, he might never wake up again.

Then he's thinking about the woman again. Allandra.

He shuts his eyes and all he can see is the spiral between her shoulder blades. He can almost taste her skin, imagines he can lick the ink out of her tattoo.

His eyes snap open, and he begins to cruise through the ship's copy of the Earthnet. Everything that was recorded publicly across the entire world was archived onto the ship's network the day before the mission began. It is the encyclopaedia of everything ever known since the Internet was created.

Performing an entirely random image search floods the screens in front of him with beautiful images, and he asks himself yet again why it is that the spiral is so beautiful. What is it about this shape that sets it apart? What does it mean?

This time, he doesn't even stop to criticize himself for asking why a shape has to have a meaning. Of course it has a *meaning*, he thinks. Of course it does. Nothing is without meaning. The ancients knew that. People like Jung and Da Vinci.

He stops to browse on images that delight him particularly and he finds a series of sites with many artists he's never heard of—men from long ago who put spirals in their art—a man called William Blake created a piece called *Jacob's Ladder*. An even stranger piece by Hieronymus Bosch: the *Ascent of the Blessed*. The troubled night sky of Van Gogh. The crisp peculiarity of Escher. The fluid dusk of Rembrandt. He comes closer to his own time: *The Spiral Jetty* of Smithson, and *Final Words* by Rijndael.

The images go on and on, and he devours them, just as they devour him. He finds even older images of the spiral, carved triple spirals on some sort of Celtic tomb, spirals on an island he's never heard of, home to a religious order known as druids. And then older, and even older images—vast spiral lines carved into the deserts of South America, rocks in Australia, caves in France, caves in Borneo. No matter how far back he searches, the spiral is there, waiting patiently to be found, to be understood.

That's it, he thinks. It needs to be *understood*. And once again, he doesn't even notice that he is asking himself to understand an inanimate shape, an abstract design, and it is only when suddenly he feels a terrible pain in his shoulders that he realizes that he's been hunched over the console for a very long time without moving.

The analysis of the alert systems finished running hours before. A light winks at him from the screen, but he hasn't seen it. There is a beeping sound, and with shock he sees that there are just five minutes left on his waking cycle.

He throws himself from Terminal Base Four and runs toward his pod, but is forced to slow to a walk as breath abandons him once again. Staggering, he hauls his clothes from his body and tumbles into the pod, fitting his tubes with fumbling hands even as the lid starts to descend on him.

As he goes under this time, he is not worried about being murdered in his sleep. He is worried that he will never understand the spiral, that is what seems most important to him.

If it were not important, he thinks, why would it be there? At every level of existence. He is tumbling through space in a spiral fashion, and even the galaxy itself, which the *Song* is crossing one tiny corner of over the next hundred or so years, is a spiral. Spiral rotation of galaxies is what causes stars, planets to form. He knows that. And whatever level of life he thinks about, the spiral is there—from the hurricane eye of Jupiter, to the motion of the Earth, to the prints on his fingers, to the DNA inside him, even down to the spiral trails of particles flashing through a bubble chamber.

As long ago as the twentieth century, it was understood that radiation itself propagates through space not in straight lines, but spirally, something that accounted for the discovery that the speed of light is not constant, as once thought. Supporting this notion, it was soon found that light in some way *magnetizes* matter so that while some barely perceptible particles spiral *away* from a light source, others, such as chlorophyll, gyrate toward it.

The spiral is there, underneath it all.

Bowman is gone again. Gone into the sleep so close to death, slowing his aging down to almost nothing, so that his body is living in slow motion.

His mind, however, is not, and he knows his dreams will be wilder than ever.

He has always moved forward, always searching, always wanting, without knowing what it is that he wants. Ever since he was a boy, that's the way he's been, and finally, he feels he might be getting close to understanding what it is that he wants. Even in Sentinel Sleep, he knows his unconscious mind will keep working on the problem. Maybe, when he wakes, he will have the solution presented to him like a neatly wrapped birthday present.

As the lid closes, a figure in dark gray appears as if from nowhere, and stands beside the pod, briefly, before moving on to what it has come to do.

FOR MANY YEARS, THE SEARCH FOR HABITABLE planets was accompanied by a related search: the search for exo-intelligence; the signs of intelligent life other than that on Earth. Any species developed enough to have discovered radio waves ought to be making enough noise to be heard, eventually, across the other side of the galaxy. The Drake Equation was used to estimate the number of habitable planets in the galaxy, though the answers varied wildly as no one could ever agree on the value of the many components in the equation. By any measure, however, it seemed reasonable to assume that the galaxy should be full of noise—radio waves broadcast by our cousins scattered around the distant planets—and yet there was nothing. Total silence seemed to reign in the universe, aside from the one small ball of rock we know as our home planet. Somehow, the origin of intelligent life on Earth seemed to be a one-off event; the only such case, and given the vast size of the galaxy, this felt wrong. In fact, it seemed *impossible* that this was the case, and yet it seemed to be true. The conclusion: we are alone.

Searches were based on many concepts, the most common being that if an exo-species was trying to discover our existence, they would do just what we would do; namely broadcast a radio wave that could not be generated naturally. The idea: to broadcast something with meaning, something that displays a universal truth, such as the value of π, or a rising sequence denoting the atomic numbers of the halogens, or the universal sequence that creates itself from itself, the Fibonacci sequence—1, 1, 2, 3, 5, 8, 13 . . . Computers were set in vast arrays to listen to the universe, hunting out such regular patterns as these and many more, but still, the result was total silence.

Bowman sleeps. In his dreams he sees himself spiralling through space, alone, without a space ship—just his body floating free and flying fast across the galaxy. He has enough self-awareness in his dream to tell himself that he does not believe in the supernatural. The truth is maybe a little different now, and Bowman's mind starts to send him immense and disturbing images of the universe. What really lies out here? All man's efforts with space travel to date have seen ships footle around the Solar System; like the mission Bowman took to Jupiter and back. Compared with his forty years of flying, that was a stroll in the backyard. And the backyard is safe; there are no monsters there. But what about now? What lies waiting to be found in the very farthest darkest depths of the heavens? Do the normalities of space and time even hold good across the universe? What if they don't?

Bowman's dreams tear at him as if he's on a torture rack, opening his mind, pulling his brain apart, exposing everything *he is* to everything in the universe, and he begins to feel the presence of another intelligence, which he is approaching, rapidly. There are voices, though he cannot understand their words, only feel them. There are spirits all around him, and finally he knows for certain that the universe is not empty.

There are ghosts up there—the ghosts of Heaven—and they are calling to him, urging him to come and understand, and be damned.

So Bowman dreams as he sleeps, but this time he does not sleep for ten years.

He sleeps for just four, and then, the alert system, which he believes is totally unreliable, kicks into action and starts his waking cycle six years ahead of schedule.

It does this because it has registered the number one item on the priority list of emergency reasons to wake a sentinel. It has detected an ultra-low-frequency broadcast at around 1.618 Hz.

It has detected intelligent life.

55

BOWMAN KNOWS IMMEDIATELY THAT SOMETHING IS unusual. As he pulls his suit on, he sees the clock on his sleeve is flashing a priority alert code at him, and he knows exactly what it means: ETI. The signal denoting extraterrestrial intelligence has been detected.

He staggers toward Base Four and climbs into his chair at the Terminal, half his mind on this incredible event, half on something that was in his dreams as he woke, and that even now is slipping away.

"Yes," he says. Then, "Let's see you."

He pulls up the report of the signal, and cannot find fault with the ship's analysis of the situation.

At first sight, the broadcast might seem unremarkable. It is just a carrier wave, with no information in it; what is remarkable is simply the frequency of the wave; at an ultra-low level, just 1.618 Hz.

This level, 1.618, is in fact an approximation of the frequency that the ship has found. To be sure, Bowman focuses in on the wave and has it rescanned. To ten decimal places it reads 1.6180339887, and then he stares at the screen as a chill slides its way up his neck.

Bowman knows all about this number. Any scientist does.

The number is known as phi, and along with π it is the single best known and most important irrational number that the universe created. It is a number also known as the golden mean or golden ratio. It has been known for thousands of years, and what it denotes is the state of perfection. It appears in the natural world, in mathematics, in architecture, in the ideal proportions of the human figure or the most beautiful face, even in such mundane places as the performance of financial markets. In short, it underpins the universe itself. The number itself is a ratio. It describes the ratio of two lengths, where the ratio of the shorter length to the longer one is the same as that of the ratio of the longer one to the total of both lengths. Put like that it sounds meaningless, dull, pointless, and confusing, and yet here, there, out in the world, in the universe, this ratio is not only the one which we humans find most pleasing, it is the one which in some way the universe *itself* seems to find most pleasing.

For a radio wave to be broadcast at that frequency is the clearest possible indication that the source of the wave is an intelligence similar to, or greater than, our own. Billions of dollars, millions of computer hours have been spent on searching for such a thing, and now the *Song* has ventured into space and stumbled across one all by itself.

Bowman stares at the screen, because he, the man who moves forward, the man who does not hesitate, the man who always knows how to act, no longer knows what to do.

According to those mighty powers who created the *Song* and the other Toroid Class ships, the mission to New Earth, constellation Lyca, can be diverted for one reason and one reason only, and that reason has just popped up on the console screens, flashing in pale green, calmly, waiting for Bowman to acknowledge its existence. So now, there is just one question that rises above all others.

Should they alter the mission? More to the point, should *he* alone decide the fate of the five hundred and three people on board, and alter the trajectory of the *Song* toward the source of the wave?

It is a decision he does not want to take by himself. He finds himself wanting to consult others—the other sentinels. Theoretically, he could ask them. It would take ten years to get all their replies, but somehow he feels that the decision ought to be unanimous; they should all agree on this. The trace of the radio wave will still be there in ten years. The ship has logged the source now; diverting is such a long and awkward process that ten years either way is not ultimately going to make much difference. The key thing is to make the right choice, and there is so little information on which to base the decision.

The ship has woken only him; despite the potential magnitude of the finding, it cannot afford to wake all ten sentinels on a potentially false alarm. Doing so would only waste the waking life of the sentinels. Instead, the ship has woken the next sentinel due to come on duty, and so it is up to Bowman to verify the signal. But in exceptional circumstances, he can, if he decides it is absolutely necessary, wake his nine colleagues . . .

Should he instigate a vote?

As soon as that thought is in him; he feels odd. He has had, what is, for him, an uncommon reaction. He sees that he is regretting something. He curses his luck that the broadcast came about when he was the next sentinel up for duty . . .

Then he stops himself.

He *wasn't* the next. The ship should have woken Sentinel Ten. It has only been something under four years since he was awake last; why has it woken *him* instead?

Suddenly, problems seem to be mounting hard on each other; thinking about the sentinels, and why he was woken when he still had six years to sleep, he notices what he did not notice before.

He was so busy with the priority alert about the ETI signal that he has not seen the status alert about the Longsleepers.

Another screen is flashing a pale green alert at him; with a series of red lights glowing on the schematic of the ring of the *Song.*

Eight more pods have gone offline. Eight more people are dead.

He is dumbfounded. Adrift, he feels a powerful sense of terror rising inside him, not terror of the murderer who is aboard the ship with him, but the terror of not knowing what to do. It is something he has rarely experienced, and when he has, it has come close to paralyzing him with fear.

Trying to think of something to do, to kid himself that he is in control of the situation, he decides to read the reports of Sentinels Seven, Eight, and Nine, who have all been on duty since he last woke.

Again, they have left only written reports, and something about their tone troubles him. They sound concerned, they have performed what duties and investigations they can, but when he goes to check on the computer what those investigations were, he finds that nothing has been done that *the ship itself* could not have done.

Uneasy, he finds some of the words in the reports are bothering him. It's so hard to be sure, because he finds remembering anything at the moment is very hard, but he seems to find them very familiar. He hunts back to the previous reports from Sentinels Seven, Eight and Nine, and then he knows what it is that worries him. They use the same phrases. They repeat themselves. They use different combinations of key phrases, but the phrases are there nonetheless. Of course, people repeat themselves, but they do so in a loose way, not a perfect one.

He forgets everything else. For the time being, he wants to know something, because an awful idea has just crept into his head and he cannot focus on anything else until he has that idea disproven. At least, he very much hopes it will be disproven.

He knows that the entire mission files are on the ship. Most of them are open access to a sentinel. Some are classified, such as the personnel files that he hacked before. And then there are a series of files that are only to be actioned upon arrival at New Earth. These are files that contain information about landing procedures, sequences, settlement plans, security measures, and so on. He knows these are important because he has glimpsed them, hidden behind firewalls that it would take him years to crack, unless he happened to have the right access codes.

He digs down into the network until he's faced with the screen demanding the sixteen-digit access code to the mission files.

He stares at the screen and, as he does so, he remembers something else about the number phi—the number being broadcast through space. Phi also underpins something else, one of the most beautiful of shapes: a special kind of spiral known as the Golden or Fibonacci Spiral, one found again, and again and again in nature; in the shells of sea creatures, in the heads of sunflowers, in the branching of plants.

Bowman leans forward and, holding his breath, he types, without even thinking why he knows he has the correct code.

1 6 1 8 0 3 3 9 8 8 7 4 9 8 9 4

The screen turns green for an instant, and a whole new user interface that he has never seen before opens up before him.

And that's when it all unravels. The whole thing: the mission, the sentinels, and his place among them.

89

BOWMAN IS WRONG ABOUT ONE THING.

He had feared that he was the only sentinel. That what appeared to be the other sentinels was in fact just the ship, generated by the computer, to mimic the actions of his colleagues. He knows that Sentinel Sleep was unbelievably costly to introduce into the mission; maybe they only had the cash for one per ship. Maybe he is the only sentinel aboard the *Song*, that's what he's thinking.

But he's wrong. There are indeed nine other living sentinels on the ship. It's just that he's the only one who's been woken so far. In all of this last forty years, he is the only one, and now he knows why.

They lied about the distance to New Earth. It is not in the constellation of Lyca at all, but much farther away—around ten times farther, to put a number to it.

They have lied about the aging process too. Bowman is aging much faster than he was led to believe. If he had looked more closely at his face during any of his waking cycles, he would have seen lines appearing around his eyes, more gray hairs than his actual years ought to have given him.

As he reads on, Bowman learns the bald truth of his situation. He will never make it to New Earth. In fact, once he has worked his shift of a hundred years or so, he will die. Only then will Sentinel Seven be activated. Bowman was designated number Six so as not to arouse any notions of being the first in a chain, as the name One might have suggested to him. When he dies, Sentinel Seven will take over for a thousand years of duties, and then Eight, and so on.

They lied about other things, too.

He, like everyone else, had been told there were five Toroid Class IV ships leaving for New Earth, but that too was a lie, told in order to make the members of the *Song* feel less isolated, less alone, because it is well known that such thoughts can seriously undermine confidence and performance in the long run.

The *Song of Destiny* is alone—here will be no other voyages. It is simply too expensive.

They lied when they said New Earth was 98.7 percent like home. He reads now that there is a 65 percent chance it is as close to Earth as they hoped. The chances are high that the planet is something less than perfect for man to colonize. Even on which to survive.

Bowman sits at the console, staring into the nothingness with which he has just been crucified. They lied to him; they lied to everyone. He has a bitter picture in his head of the riots that took place around the launch base on Venture Day. People fighting to be allowed on board, even though they had never come close in the selection procedure. People died in that riot, and all over a lie. If only they'd known the truth, would anyone have signed up at all?

All his life Bowman has wanted to head forward, never looking back, searching for something that always eludes him. Now he knows what it is; he has lied to himself. His whole life, he has lied. Because he *does* want to look back. He wants to be a boy again. He wants his father to be alive, and his mother, but they are dead forever. He wants to fall from the apple tree and land in the wet grass at the end of the sloping lawn outside the house where he grew up, and have his father come and pick him up, as they both laugh about how silly life is.

He won't find that. He will never get back there, back to his childhood, or anything like it. He will die, in space, aboard a ship full of the victims of a terrible lie, approximately 16 thousand trillion kilometers from home.

He cries.

The hours tick away.

His tears have ended.

He stares at the information in front of him, wondering what else is untrue. For one thing, they must have programmed all the clocks and time codes aboard the ship to alter themselves, or future sentinels would know that the mission had been running for far longer than it ought to have been. They must have tampered with telemetry and astro-sextancy. They must have falsified so much.

He needs time to read everything, and the first thing he decides is that if he is going to die in space, it might as well be sooner than later.

He can break into one of the PTPs and make use of the food and other provisions there; there is enough on board each landing ship to feed 102 people for two years, and they are now fifteen people lighter than when they left Earth. He can, likewise, override the oxygen controls to allow him to breath those fifteen people's quota of air.

Maybe after ten years awake, he can slide back into the pod, and let it keep him alive, sort of, dreaming, forever. He could hack into it and make it do that. In fact, he could probably make it do anything, like take him to sleep only when he tells it to, not just once every ten years, automatically.

He is God now, not the Selection Committee. He can do anything he wants.

He hangs his head, and he cries again for a short time.

There is still another matter that Bowman has forgotten. It is only when he finally stands, as his sentinel pod starts to send him warning beeps that it is time to return to sleep, that he remembers it.

Let the pod go to hell, he thinks. *I'm not sleeping anymore. Not now.*

He wants, if nothing else, to know what is happening to his passengers, for that is how he has started to think of them since he met Allandra. There is the question of which of the other sentinels has been waking. And waking, he now knows, *far* ahead of their expected schedule. Waking and killing.

He sits back down again, listening vaguely to the sound of his pod emitting a final series of warning beeps through the clock on the sleeve of his suit, before lapsing into silence.

"Maybe now I can get a little work done," he says, and starts to punch up the video files from the last four years.

If everything has gone according to plan, he should have better quality image files than before.

He checks the numbers of the eight newly failed pods; he is, for some reason, disturbed to learn that one of them is right next to his own sentinel pod.

He plays the files.

He watches a dark gray suit appear in the field of the camera. His back is toward the lens and Bowman cannot make out the face. The sentinel kneels beside pod 269, and dials out the maintenance drawer.

Bowman's hand moves to his mouth as the sentinel sets up the routine to open the lid.

A few minutes pass but Bowman does not fast-forward the video. He is transfixed, waiting to see what happens, and he wants to see every second. Finally the lid slides open, and he watches in horror as the sentinel pulls from his pocket a Lethno probe, used to test the charge of electromagnetic bolts on the PTPs, holds it against the temple of the man inside, and squeezes the switch.

The body shudders once inside the pod, and Bowman knows that all brain function would have terminated immediately.

The sentinel is already closing pod 269, the drawer sliding shut, and then, as the figure stands and makes ready to leave for his next killing, Bowman's heart falls apart at the sight of the most horrifying thing of all.

He can see the killer's face.

It is him.

144

I KILLED THEM, HE THINKS.

He is horrified and scared, in equal measure.

I killed them all. I killed Allandra.

He thought there was a ghost on the ship with him.

Then he dreamed that the ghosts of the universe, the ghosts of Heaven, were outside, waiting to be spoken with, waiting to communicate. But now he knows the truth; *he* was the one who was floating away, he was the one who was disappearing.

He is the ghost.

It doesn't make sense. He knows he is not a killer. He has no memory of these acts whatsoever. But then, as he knows all too well, it has been getting increasingly hard to remember things. Although he's only been awake for a little over a day and a half since he left Earth, he has slept for forty years. No one has ever studied the long-term effects that this could have on the mind— how could they have done? Who knows what he is now? The evidence is incontrovertible; he has seen himself on screen applying the discharge of a Lethno probe to a man's head. His mind must have separated into two parts.

Then, he thinks, two or *more.*

That would account for the time losses he's been experiencing. He thought he had drifted off at the console while studying spirals. What if he had merely left one part of his mind there while another part stalked through the ship doing unspeakable things?

Have I gone mad? he asks himself. *Am I really a killer?*

He could verify that if he dialed up the video of activity aboard Terminal Base Four during his last waking cycles, maybe see himself leave the Base when he believed he'd been sitting at the console for hours.

He cannot bring himself to see. He wants to watch the video again, but he cannot do that, either. He cannot bear to watch himself murdering the sleeping occupants of the *Song of Destiny,* one by one. Except, it was not one by one. It was six first, *then* one. And then eight.

Six. One. Eight.

0.618

Immediately, he makes the connection. Phi is a remarkable number.

Phi, or ϕ, is 1.618, to three places.

It's reciprocal, $1/\phi$, is 0.618.

Subtract 1 from ϕ and you also get 0.618, the reciprocal.

It is a sign; this number; the number of the broadcast; it is a message, or a challenge, and he will only know which if he follows it.

There and then, he makes up his mind. He knows what to do again; he knows how to act, and he doesn't need to ask anyone else.

*   *   *

He begins to call up the protocols that will enable him to divert the mission. He will take the *Song of Destiny* to the source of the spiral, and confront whatever lies waiting for him there—be it nothing, or ghosts, or God.

HE DOESN'T THINK TWICE.

There is no other option. He could fly on through space, continue the mission to New Earth, and slowly allow part of himself to kill the occupants as they sleep. He could fly on and let the other sentinels take over when he dies. He could tell them the truth about the mission, that it is almost certainly pointless.

Maybe he should program his pod to let him sleep forever, to protect the Longsleepers. He could put everything in his report for Sentinel Seven, let him or her decide what to do about the crazy murderer who went mad in Sentinel Sleep.

Perhaps, he thinks, *I should never have tampered with my psychometric test results . . .*

It is an uncommon moment of doubt for Bowman, and it soon passes, because his hands and his mind are busy. There is only one choice, in his mind, one option. He is going to take the ship to the source of the spiral.

He has the computer lock the source of the radio wave in its starfield. He gets the flight computer to calculate the change of direction that the ship will have to make. Wryly, he thinks the flight computer could at least thank him for something to do; it has been flying in a straight line for the last forty years, without even once encountering an incident such as an asteroid field to compute a trajectory around.

The ship is traveling very fast now. It is not a ship designed to turn corners. The best it can do is to offer gentle curves by a fractional displacement of the virtual sail that is emanated in the space of the ship's toroid.

The flight computer gives him the results; it will take eight years to make the turn, another three to reach the calculated source of the radio wave.

"What's eleven years," Bowman says, "to a man who sleeps for ten every night?"

It takes him the rest of the day to complete the protocols for the diversion of the mission. The ship will only allow it at all because it agrees with the assessment that intelligent life has been found.

The mere fact that it *will* allow this shows Bowman that he is right: the Global-Government lied about New Earth. There is a high chance that if and when the occupants of the *Song* eventually get there, it will be an uninhabitable ball of rock, choked by acids and gasses. The Government Council that created the mission knew that there was always another option: signs of intelligent life denote a habitable planet, and all the best astrobiologists agree on one thing; that life is such a precious and precarious thing, that the conditions on Earth were so specific in allowing its creation, that any intelligent life on *other* planets will almost certainly indicate that the life there arose in very similar circumstances to our own. That the planet, therefore, will be like Earth, or near enough. Such is the arrogance and self-centerdness of the human. And that belief, that other life will be humanoid, is why the *Song of Destiny* carries an armory of weapons on each PTP.

At moments when he has to wait for the ship to perform various calculations, he starts work on his sentinel pod. He has changed his mind about staying awake. He would rather dream his way to the rendezvous. He hacks into the system that controls sleep cycles, and sets his pod to wake him after eleven years. He also finally tests and reboots the alert systems, and finds traces that someone has indeed been tampering with it. He knows now that it was him who did that, an uncomfortable feeling, but as he reaches the end of his work, he realizes that he has been working constantly, without any losses of time. He can remember everything he has done, and that gives him hope. Maybe whatever happened to his mind has rectified itself and there is no more cause for alarm.

What happened to the fifteen pods is regrettable, of course. But now there is a bigger mission, something that outweighs everything, something to rewrite the pages of history, something that changes everything about human existence and belief, forever.

And he, Keir Bowman, will be the one to do it.

He will change the universe.

Without any hesitation whatsoever, he makes the final keystrokes, and fixing the initialization vector to zero, prepares to unlock the secrets of the ghosts.

The ship begins its infinitesimally shallow turn.

Bowman retires to his pod, and prepares to dream his way to immortality. Just before the pod lid closes, he leans down into his personal effects drawer and takes out his book of poetry. Something has touched inside him, a memory of a poem in the book.

There is no more time to read it now, but he holds the book to his chest as he goes under, intending to read it in his dreams.

────────────────────────────────

HOW ARROGANT IS MAN, BOWMAN HAS SOMETIMES
wondered, to think he can know everything about the universe
while stuck to the surface of a tiny planet in a remote region of the
galaxy? Yes, great things have been learned, but not everything.
There is always the unknown. No matter how high you climb on
the spiral staircase, there is always another turn of the stair, out of
view, and that's where the unknown lies.

We learned long ago about such things as black holes; when
certain stars die and collapse in on themselves, creating a gravitational effect so strong that not even light can escape its pull.
And their counterparts, the white holes, spewing matter out into
the universe, creating new galaxies, new stars, new planets. Are
these two things linked? Is there a tunnel between them, from
one place in the universe to another, or even from one universe
to a different one entirely? Perhaps that's where we began, spewed
out of a white hole as a star in another universe died.

At these physical limits, who knows what happens to the laws
of the universe? And who knows what other extraordinary things
have yet to be found, far from Earth?

The *Song of Destiny* hurtles onward at speeds once thought

impossible. Inside the ship, it is totally silent. It is near dark. Nothing moves, except the dreams of Sentinel Bowman.

His dreams have taken on a new character. They have opened out, they have calmed down; in his dreams, he dreams about dreams. He dreams about dreaming about dreaming, and for almost all the eleven years that he sleeps, a calm greater than anything he has ever known settles within him.

But space is not as well-studied as the scientists back on Earth liked to think, as the *Song of Destiny* is about to discover. Ahead of it, in the extraordinary cold emptiness, there is the thing that Bowman has dreamed of, so often; a thing for which words do not exist.

The *Song* glides onward, traveling so fast now as to impress itself on the universe around it; blundering blindly toward this volume of space that is torn, damaged.

At first, the ship detects nothing wrong, but then, physical transformations begin to occur, and it registers a breach in the hull, even though no such thing has yet occurred.

Detecting the breach, the ship triggers emergency responses and wakes Bowman.

He climbs out of the pod, forgetting that he had placed a book on his chest eleven years before. It tumbles to the floor of the deck.

He looks at it, then ignores it, and looks at the clock on the wall. He reaches for his suit and checks his bio-clock again.

The ship groans.

It actually makes a sound, giving a vast and deep moan. It is the first unexpected sound that he has heard in fifty-one years, and it terrifies him.

He runs to Base Four, and is soon out of breath, even worse than before. He can barely pull himself inside Terminal Base Four and collapse in the chair at the console, and when he does, he sees the reason why.

There is a breach to the Base Four chlorophyll bank; oxygen is at critically low levels, about half what it should be. Already he recognizes the signs of oxygen deficit. He has a terrible headache, he is finding it hard to think clearly and every action takes an enormous amount of effort, leaving him spent.

He starts to get the ship to report on the status of all systems, that way he can just sit back in the chair, and . . .

What? Isn't there something he's supposed to be doing?

There was something that had happened. He knows they're heading for New Earth, but it seems that has he been woken a year late. Eleven years of sleep, not the usual ten. Haven't the other sentinels noted anything strange? Slumped in his chair, he reads their reports, trying to figure out what it is that bothers him about their words. There was something about the other sentinels, wasn't there? And their words.

Their words . . .

Words . . .

Then the *Song* slams into the destroyed pocket of space, the unknown, broken gate.

Bowman stands, and staggers, just as space and time stagger around him.

He sees a spiral of cold blue fire rise from the floor of the Base and twine itself around him.

The spiral vanishes.
Then the words come:
Why have you come?
says a voice from the air,
and what was it that you expected to find?
You who have come to trouble the dead.
You whose voice was swallowed by dark
should know the path that was laid for you.

Yes! Bowman thinks. He has learned something, that the communication of the dead is tongued with fire beyond the language of the living. Bowman can still half see the console in front of him, but it is faint, mixed with other images now.

Words coil around him. The words are Allandra and the other dead of the *Song*. They speak to him with their dead mouths, trying to explain themselves; they want only to be understood.

. . . should know the path that was laid for you.
Bowman cries out.
"Path? What path?"
Through the gate, under the apple tree,
across the wet grass . . .

The ship begins to complain. Forces greater than anything it has known start to claw and tear at it from inside and out. It shudders, and the spasms of the ship send great thunders of sound rolling down the curved decks of the ring.

Bowman stares down at the console, through a series of

twisting ropes he can just make out the schematic of the pods, red lights flashing across his eyes.

There is a pool.

A pool of cold brown water, stained by the peat from the dales. He's in the water, swimming, unable to breathe. He sees a spiral carved into the underwater rock. Hands reach for him as he tries to reach for the keypad to see if the leak in the chlorophyll banks can be contained.

He swims to the surface, spluttering, and finds that the pool has gone.

Behind Bowman, a dark gray figure walks across the room, calmly yet curiously regarding him fighting with the computer that won't seem to wake him up. Bowman knows that he needs the computer to wake him, or he won't be able to be here to do the things he has to do so he programs it to wake him. Then, he waits to see himself come in through the door.

As Bowman turns to Deck Three, waiting to see himself, the dark figure walks out to Deck Four, a Lethno probe in its hand. In the same moment Bowman realizes that *he is on deck*, that he is already awake because the computer *has* woken him. He is able to do what he needs to do.

He shakes himself, but it's so hard to think. His headache is slicing.

The ship's systems are fighting, burning.

Bowman sees that the other four Bases report no sign of oxygen leakage, but he wonders how much longer the ship can hold together.

Here, now, standing beside him on the deck, is an American poet.

He drowned himself, pushed over the edge by a meaningless spiral left on some unknown other's grave, having just retold a little girl called Verity a beautiful thing about geese.

"Let me tell you a poem," he says to Bowman.

Bowman stares, but in his mind he says, *Yes*.

"It's not by me," the poet says. "Mine were dark things that no one wanted. But I did not mind. Let me tell you this poem, now."

Bowman nods, slowly, once.

> *And those who never smiled at the sun,*
> *and lay on thorns, watching the moon,*
> *the thirsty, the hungering, the hollow,*
> *the trodden-down.*
> *Those who watched the damaged stars,*
> *waiting for One who would never come*
> *while beyond the final, broken gate*
> *the voices of ghosts come out of the air.*
> *What was it that you expected to find?*
>
> *And what did you expect?*
> *Satisfaction, understanding?*
> *Salvation before the ending of the days?*
> *Yet, just around the turn of the stair,*
> *a glimmer of torchlight awaits your discovery.*

"What do you think?" asks the poet. "Those are just a few lines, of course, but I find it startling and powerful."

"I don't understand," says Bowman.

The poet smiles.

"Neither did I," he says. "But I do now."

The poet is gone. In his place, Bowman finds that he is standing in a workshop of some kind. Carpentry tools lie spread on
the bench beside him, curls of wood shavings lie in little spiral
forms all about him, on the bench, on the floor. He hears the
scrape of a spoke shave and turns to see a man working on a long
wooden box. The man is middle-aged, heavy, and his hands are
both powerful and delicate at the same time. He lifts his head
and looks at Bowman.

"You know they used to use nails," he says. "In the old days.
Poor folk still do. Not the best idea, a nail in a coffin."

Bowman says nothing, but in his mind, he asks, *Coffin?*

The man nods, smiling. He picks something up now, and
shows it to Bowman, for inspection. It is a long brass screw.

"That's better," he says. "Better than a nail. Notice anything
about it?"

Bowman shakes his head.

"The screw runs widdershins. Back to front. 'Gainst the clock.
All other screws in the world turn the other way to this one. But
coffin screws are different."

Bowman forms a word in his mind.

Why?

The coffin maker smiles.

"To stop them coming back, of course."

Bowman closes his mind for a moment and, with it, his eyes.
The dead never come back, do they? In his heart he feels the

pain of a doctor with a drowned wife. He feels a rope tightening around his neck and above him the oak tree and the sky above it seem to spin as he turns in the noose, even as he and the oak, and the world it's a part of, spiral through the universe. He pushes farther, into the deepest cave of the mind and there is a girl, making a mark on the wall in ochre and charcoal.

The *Song of Destiny* fights for its life, and the life of all those aboard.

Bowman stands under an apple tree in the cave of Terminal Base Four.

It is dark all around him but he doesn't need light to see.

There are red handprints on the wall, and there are spirals inside the handprints.

Then, without warning, the ship is silent.

It is stationary.

It has stopped.

Terminal Base Four looks just as it always has.

It is not possible that the ship can just stop.

It has to *slow down first*. It takes almost as long to slow down as it does to speed up; it *cannot* be stationary, but it is.

Bowman sinks into the seat at the console.

His mind seems to have loosened. He can almost physically feel that something is different with his brain, as if it were a muscle that he has relaxed. He feels connections forming in his mind that he's never felt before, was never aware of. The connections are like thoughts reaching twisting tendrils toward one another, their helixes slide together and the two become one, and all across his mind such new thoughts are being born, growing, affirming.

Yet the madness of the ripped part of space has gone. He is alone now, in the Terminal, and the deck is solid and the walls are solid, even if he, more than ever, is floating free.

He lifts his head, and sees that oxygen levels are being restored from the surpluses in Base Five and Three.

Everything is quiet, and Bowman knows that he has arrived at the source of the radio wave.

There is no real need to see in space. The ship is not designed with much in the way of viewing platforms and the few limited portholes on the decks account for most of the facility to look outside—the sentinels know where they are because the ship shows them on screen, but when Bowman looks at one particular screen and sees that the *Song of Destiny* believes it is in orbit around a planet, he needs to see for himself.

There are cameras on the outside of the ship. They are used in the extremely unlikely event of an EVA, to provide a visual check on the astronaut making the journey outside the *Song*.

Bowman turns on the cameras, and moves them until he sees that the computer is not lying to him. They are in orbit around a planet, something he cannot make himself believe, and then, twinkling like a small star in front of him, he sees something else.

There is another ship.

Just ahead, following the same orbit, there is another ship.

It is a Toroid Class IV.

Bowman cries out, an incoherent cry, as he zooms in on it.

The lie was a lie!

There are other ships, after all. The *Song* is not alone.

He fiddles with the camera zoom, but it's dark; the ship ahead is caught in the dark side of the planet's orbit, but Bowman can see that dawn is about to break. Both he and the other ship are about to move into the light of whatever star this planet revolves around.

The ship ahead reaches the light.

Bowman can read its name now, painted in vast letters around the outside of the spinning ring: The *Song of Destiny*.

610

BOWMAN REMEMBERS, FROM HIS TRAINING THAT NOW seems to be as faint as to be almost nothingness, that exposure to astral radiation has been known to cause hallucinations. He also remembers that the hallucinations in question are small things—random flashes of "light" seen by the brain and known as phosphenes that take the form of lines, dashes and, now he thinks about it some more, spirals. But not entire spaceships. What he sees before him now, he knows, is not a hallucination.

Just outside the airlock, Bowman prepares his EVA suit carefully.

The ship, the other *Song*, appears to be lifeless. He has tried to contact it, without success. He has tried to get his ship to network with this other version of itself, but it cannot. He has performed a lifescan of the ship, but it is too far away to yield any information. The only sign of life is that this second *Song* is the source of the phi radio wave. Apart from that, as far as he can tell, it is a ghost ship.

He has to know.

This is why he has come.

He prepares his EVA suit carefully, pulling on the pieces one by one, like a knight putting on his armor.

At each step, he checks and double-checks the integrity of the suit, until finally he is ready, fully dressed in the large and cumbersome unit, apart from the helmet which hangs ready for him to step up underneath, and seal.

He hesitates, and then, seeing a Lethno probe attached to the wall, slides it inside his suit. Just in case.

Before he puts his helmet on, he checks the keypad on the sleeve is responding to the ship's network; that he has full control of the *Song* from within the EVA suit, then he steps underneath the helmet, fixes it, and starts the breathing supply. Satisfied, he begins the sequence to open the inner door of the airlock, using only the controls on his keypad to do so; he wants to make sure they work.

The inner door opens, and he steps inside. He types a command on his sleeve; the door closes behind him.

Fixing a remote tether to the waist of his suit, he turns to the outer door, types another command, and the feeble bubble of atmosphere that was with him in the airlock is sucked away into the void.

He test fires his motors, just a gentle puff, but enough to send him out of the door. So close up, the *Song* seems enormous, and he focuses on that, rather than the infinity around him. He makes some corrections to his trajectory and, with little puffs, squirts his way over to the other *Song*.

He wonders at it, but there is no need for wonder. It is here, and he has come here to find it.

The other *Song* is close to four kilometers ahead of him, in exactly the same orbit. It's easy enough to pay out on the micro-fine tether attached to his waist, which can extend to seven if need be, as fine and strong in relative terms as spider's silk.

He approaches the ship.

Still it seems lifeless, but then, glancing at the readout on his sleeve, he sees that his suit has already automatically networked with this ghost *Song*.

There is an airlock. It looks like Base Two. He heads toward it, and types a command to open the outer door. For one moment, it seems as if nothing is happening, but then the door opens, and Bowman neatly glides inside. He closes the outer door, opens the inner one, and steps into the preparation room, identical to the one he has just left, glad to feel the return of gravity under his boots, artificial though it is.

It is impossible to walk more than a few steps in the EVA suit. He begins the painfully slow process of removing it, one eye on the door to the rest of Base Two as he does so.

It's done.

He opens the door, concealing the probe in his hand, and begins to explore.

The ship is quiet, the lights are dim, but there are functional levels of oxygen in the atmosphere, which almost certainly means that someone is awake.

He makes his way along Deck Two, past the row of pods curving up, away, in front of him, out of sight.

Terminal Base Three is deserted, but he knows where he is going, and he begins to hurry through Deck Three, passing his own pod, toward Base Four. The lid of his pod is open, and so, when he walks into Terminal Base Four, he knows who will be there.

"Yes," says his other, ghost self.

Bowman stares. It is unnerving, unnatural to see yourself. Even to see yourself on camera is not a natural thing, a thing no normal person is comfortable with; for it shows us as others see us, not as who we believe we really are. But to come face to face with his own self is almost more than Bowman can bear. He hesitates, then forces himself to take a step closer to his ghost, who swivels his chair round to face him.

"You dropped your book," says his ghost, holding out the book of poetry with which Bowman slept for eleven years.

Bowman doesn't reach out for it.

"Or is it my book?" the ghost says, pulling it back toward himself.

Bowman doesn't care about the poetry.

"You brought me here?"

"It was easy enough to rig the distress system," says his ghost. "You know that. To broadcast a signal. Funny, isn't it, how they actually put a functional distress system on a ship when there was never going to be anyone to broadcast to? All part of maintaining the deception, I suppose."

Bowman knows all this.

Somehow, he knows *all of this*, it's like miming along to a tape of yourself that you've heard a hundred times.

Bowman looks around the Terminal. He sees several things.

He can see the schematic of the pods. All he can see is red lights. Not one single green light. They are all dead.

He sees a video looping of him watching himself climb into his pod the last time.

And he sees his ghost's EVA helmet, sitting on the floor near his feet. There is something wrong with the helmet. Scratched into the supposedly unbreakable glass face, is a large and bold but madly executed spiral.

His ghost throws the book of poetry at him and it lands by his feet.

"Why don't you read it? You might understand."

"Understand?" asks Bowman.

"What the spiral means."

"What are you doing here?"

"I, or rather we, are here, to complete another turn in the sequence."

Bowman shakes his head.

The ghost him stands.

"I need you. Or rather, I need your ship. For mine, as you have seen, is dead."

"You killed them?"

"No, I didn't."

"But I saw you. On the video. You were on my ship . . ."

"Are you sure? Wasn't that you?"

Bowman fights to think clearly, but his ghost is speaking again already.

"You're right. I was on your ship."

"But how? There weren't two of us then. How can you have been on my ship? There can't have been another you, until we came through that . . ."

"That what?"

"*That*," says Bowman, waving a hand behind him, the only thing he can do to indicate the gate through which he has come, the ripped gut of space, through which they have both come.

"And having been through there, are you still so sure you want to hang on to ideas about time? And about the order of events? About what comes first and what comes second, about the meaning of how one thing causes another to happen? Did you hit your head on the maintenance drawer, and that made you see me? Or did you see me, which made you hit your head on the maintenance drawer?"

Bowman understands that much, at least—that these are things that cannot be understood.

"So you killed people on my ship? My *Song*?"

"I did," his ghost says, "but don't think too badly of me. I wanted their air, because the Ship's chlorophyll banks were damaged and, perhaps more important, I wanted to draw your attention to the number phi. They would have died in the end anyway. Look at my ship. Every one of them dead."

"But the damage to the oxygen happened *only because* we came here . . ."

"Are you sure you don't mean that the other way round?" says his ghost.

Bowman cannot think. He shakes his head in frustration.

"How?"

"How what?"

"How did they die?"

"The cargo? They died because they stopped living. No one has ever tried this before, to have people sleep for so long. No one knew what effect it would have on the mind, and the body is nothing without the mind, is it? As a great thinker once said: 'man cannot bear a meaningless life,' and what is more meaningless than floating through space to an ultimately futile goal? Of course, they didn't know it was futile, but the effect of all those years of sleep must have felt the same. Some lived longer than others. I have an idea that those who dreamed the most vividly were the ones who held out the longest."

Bowman knows he is talking about him. Both versions of him.

"So why do you need me?"

"I said: I need your ship."

"Why?"

"Because eleven years is a long time to think, and I have changed my mind."

"You were awake?" cries Bowman, disbelieving. "Through all that time? Through that *place*?"

Bowman looks at the scratched face of the EVA helmet, and wonders how much of the eleven years was spent making tiny marks in it that slowly built into the spiral.

"As I said, I have changed my mind. When I learned that the mission was a lie, I decided to try the other option, just as you have done."

"But that option was the radio wave. You made the radio wave. That can't have been there before."

"It was there. It was made by the version of me that came before us. Who would have followed a radio wave left by the version who came before him."

"But that's impossible!"

"I told you. You can no longer hold to ideas about the order of things. It appears that we have been here, forever, you and I, or two versions of ourselves, repeating this little conversation, forever. Just as the spiral goes on forever. It has no beginning and no end."

"So? What now?"

"As I said, I have changed my mind. Eleven years is a long time. I thought the mission was pointless, a terrible lie, but it is my destiny, just as it is will become your destiny, to try and fulfill that lie. I need a ship to head to New Earth, and it needs living pods to give me a reason to do it. We may even make it there if our dreams are strong."

Bowman's hands are trembling. He needs to sit down. He feels weak and he cannot think straight.

"You will never find it," his ghost says.

"What?"

"What you are looking for. You want to go back to the start. You want to go back to where you began. You want to find the happiness you once had. But you can never get there, because even if you somehow found it, you yourself would be different. You would have changed, from your journey alone, from the passing of time, if nothing else. You can never make it back to where you began, you can only ever climb another turn of the spiral stair. Forever."

Bowman sinks to the ground, his head hangs. In his mind is wet grass, and his father's face, smiling down at him. The apple tree above him.

His hands loosen, and the Lethno slips from his fingers, onto the floor.

"That was the other thing I wanted from you," his ghost says, and stepping forward, picks up the probe from the floor.

Bowman reacts, too slowly, and as he tries to rise, his ghost self sticks the probe into his chest, and pulls the switch.

Bowman flies back across the room, flung to the floor. He does not move.

"Are you still so sure about the order of things?" his ghost self says, and then vanishes.

987 ———————————

WHEN BOWMAN WAKES, HIS RIBS FEEL AS THOUGH he's been hit by a god's fist but at least, he realizes, he is alive.

His ghost has gone, and he knows that for sure when he brings up a scan of the space outside the ship, because his *Song*, the one still with over four hundred living occupants, is gone, too.

Bowman knows where he has gone. He has decided to reclaim the mission to New Earth anyway, despite the near certainty that it will fail.

Is it true? he wonders. Has this been happening forever? A ghost version of himself luring him to this rendezvous, to steal his living ship, leaving him behind on that floating mortuary he had always feared.

There can be no other answer, he thinks. It has to be true, or I wouldn't be here.

For the rest of the day, he explores the dead *Song*.

His ghost has done well to sabotage it. All the EVA suits have great slashes in them—beyond immediate repair. One of them has only a small puncture, which he might be able to mend with some materials from the PTP. The ghost returned to the living *Song* in the suit that Bowman came over in, leaving behind his spiral-scratched helmet.

So what does he do now?

He sees two options; the first is to go mad, and through his dreams, enter his own mind on the next version of the *Song*, perverting his thoughts with spirals and codes, and have him start murdering the occupants in the phi pattern of six, one, eight. Set up a distress code, and lure himself here to repeat the process all over again.

That is the first option, but Bowman, *this* Bowman, did not try and make the eleven-year journey awake. He slept, and while he might not be the sanest occupant on board the ship, he is still far from crazy.

Let the other infinite versions of Bowman sail on to their destiny at New Earth. He himself sees a second option. He himself has another intention.

There is a planet below him, around which the dead *Song* is orbiting. He will perform a scan on it to be sure, but somehow he already knows the results, as if he's run the scan a hundred times before.

It is a habitable planet. A little smaller than Earth maybe, but it looks promising, it looks very promising indeed. Why didn't his ghost just end the mission here? Is there something he knew about the planet that Bowman doesn't? Or was it just madness that pushed him away? Bowman brushes these thoughts aside, and gets to work.

* * *

While he makes a repair on the EVA suit, and gathers food from the other PTPs, and makes other preparations for the descent to the surface of the planet, he also spends idle minutes reading the book of poetry that his ghost threw at him.

Now that he reads it again, he finds that he knows it very well indeed, as if he's read it a thousand times, almost as if he wrote the poetry in the first place, and as he reads, those spiral forms in his mind finally raise themselves into his consciousness, and Bowman starts to learn.

As he reads the ancient poetry, he finds that he comes to a very different conclusion about the spiral than the miserable, pessimistic interpretation his ghost found.

The spiral, he decides, is the ultimate symbol of life. It is infinite. It copies itself and builds on itself, forever, like life. And life has patterns that repeat themselves, but they are never quite the same, for time, if nothing else, has moved on. On that point at least, he agrees with his ghost, but he finds it a positive thing, not a negative one, because it liberates him. It makes him free. No longer will he have to live trying to get back to something that has gone. No more chasing the past. Yes, his father is dead, but Bowman *remembers* him. Even if all he ever has is that one memory underneath the apple tree, he remembers him.

With that thought, he knows he was wrong to float free, to run away from people all this time. Rather than running from his fear of his inability to recreate the past, he should have been building a new future, finding someone to love, and be loved in return by them.

Now that Bowman knows he is unable to go back, he is free to move forward, ever higher on the spiral stair. There is always only the future, and though unknown, the spiral leads us all, ever higher and higher, toward the divine.

Toward the beautiful unknown.

As the PTP leaves the dead *Song* behind, and begins its descent to the surface of the planet, Bowman reads aloud from the book.

> *And what did you expect?*
> *Satisfaction, understanding?*
> *Salvation before the ending of the days?*
> *Yet, just around the turn of the stair,*
> *a glimmer of torchlight awaits your discovery.*
>
> *I renounce belief.*
> *I renounce belief in going home.*
> *And with that thought*
> *the chemical action of radiant energy*
> *strips us of delusions,*
> *destroys those thoughts that would hold us back,*
> *would have us turn back, forever.*
>
> *Thus, illuminated, we are free,*
> *and turning to your friend you say:*
> *It is enough to know that not to know is enough.*
> *It is enough not to know.*

And what you could not hope for, you found.
Wet grass under your hands and knees,
sunlight falling through the apple tree,
and protection.
And then, in the stillness
between breaths;
redemption, safety, and love.

1597

SHE IS THE ONE WHO GOES AHEAD,
when others stay behind.
She is the one who goes to the water's edge,
though the sky is dark and cut through with a falling star.

The others watch from the trees,
while she, the one who goes ahead,
the one who makes marks in the sand with sticks,
and who paints on walls
with the red stone and black charcoal,
watches the fall of a star.

The star shoots at the water,
pounding the great lake with a mighty fist,
so that the earth shakes
and a terrible wave washes over them all.

Yet still, clinging to the trees,
she stands, while the others run in fear.
She waits, watching the water,
which settles.

And then, the water starts to move again,
but gently this time,
as just a stone's throw away,
a monster appears.
It is vast and slow, and lumbers from the lake,
with a shining skin and a glistening face.

There is a mark on its face;
like the marks she makes in the caves,
like the turn of the snail, and the fall of the falcon,
but then,
the monster removes its skin,
and its shining head,
and out steps not a monster but a man.

The man steps forward.
In his mind is a gate,
an apple tree, and a thought:
to be remembered in the heart of a loved one is to live forever.
The man laughs at the wonder in the young woman's eyes.
Yes, he says.

1963cc06fa39536790fa5c57ee90fce129bb77d0b66fca785e01cb
7fc9e582185e9497fcc2b65eb9f83623b09d173f28670676c18ee
46128ee1d00b099c3a9f586087d32ad1547454e7f1edb7765a738
8324e600a2e1a5a74c3129533d10590c2fbcd7eb772b6031182bdb
66021a53bf13ebb3a51f26cd291eb9e0788067493b4ac0cab42f
569424906d7ac283586ecc74f35692f6ec235a7968d5567db6fa1f
3c89b9705e6890dd3a19b2b1ce2021298f7e33379bc4a753744d
729672a73d9f80367ddc6c23cd863ee9990f2e07852a3641493a
73d11c687708b62089c7e9b614151d2d739d52b988b87840614c
befc01f0cb28e31eaf47655348e824784b11ff41cda6be4a22b6b8
4af2a8649a81f1525ecdb9cb30e22e08bfcb307bbfbdd9029866
0753bdb1772f621e88b361241920c42445920e8bdec28b584b7
bb1c2c339383854d67ffd7360734ac8533b0f28ade1849c3d80bc
76459e50a373ee04439f5e7567c25e6ee05e00fbe3384470089d
531566396a9ca00456b5e1148597046f869d91a4d7e9045bc316
782052e66dabe55b49280b7f588df143c00fecb8de28e27c7e0c60
1eb89ada6f500b2f636b2c13d53edcf9baf4e0fc934d1c02fc12d
79074c2854da19dea1fe244b4f29d6c2aa853431c2e51a1611b01
109146307c50db51a6ec250d8f8508dbd56f45de1c5dccf0c2a57
4e887c26dbfee230621dc

GOFISH

MARCUS SEDGWICK

© Kate Christer

What did you want to be when you grew up?
I had no idea. I had vague ideas about being a cat burglar, but that didn't work out. It's just as well I realized about writing in the end, or I might be in jail now.

When did you realize you wanted to be a writer?
I was about twenty-something, I think, though I had always liked writing.

What's your first childhood memory?
Believe it or not, being pushed in a pushchair by our nanny through the graveyard in the village where I grew up . . .

What's your most embarrassing childhood memory?
There are simply too many, and they are too embarrassing to think of, let alone write down. . . .

As a young person, who did you look up to most?
My brother.

What was your worst subject in school?
Chemistry. I just did not get it, at all.

What was your best subject in school?
Mathematics. No, honestly.

What was your first job?
I taught English in Poland.

How did you celebrate publishing your first book?
I'm not sure I did. . . . Maybe it's time to put that right.

Where do you write your books?
I have a glorified shed in the garden, heated by a wood-burning stove. It's very cozy.

The four quarters of *The Ghosts of Heaven* can be read in any of twenty-four possible orders. Is the sequence in which they were published here significant to you? Are there any other sequences that you feel are particularly powerful?
There are two sequences that have the most to say, for me. One is the order in the printed book, which was also the order I wrote the stories in. But there is another order, one that alters the meaning of the book drastically. However, I am keeping that one to myself, since it offers an understanding that I am not so happy with.

How did you determine what points in time to set the four quarters of this book?
I knew I wanted to look at the moment in which writing was discovered. I knew I wanted to spread a net into the future and show how we, our species, will always continue to explore, as

far as we're able to. The dates in the middle I chose as places and times that I find interesting, and were meant to represent two looks at the modern period—one toward the beginning, one toward the end.

What inspired the spiral theme that connects the pieces of this book? Did the four-quarter format evolve from this theme, or did the theme evolve from the format?

Spirals are everything to this book. When I was about twenty or twenty-one I decided they had a significance, and was pleased in later life to see that they have had similar significance to many people and cultures. So the book grew out of this very long-standing fascination with their "meaning." The hard part was trying to work out, once I had become a writer, how to write a novel about spirals.

Do you have a favorite character or section within *The Ghosts of Heaven*? Did any one section present a particular challenge for you as you were writing?

I like all the sections or I wouldn't have written them! I liked the challenge of the blank verse in the prehistoric section, but I also found that the section set in the asylum on Long Island could have been a book in itself, and I had to work to stop myself from getting carried away there.

To which character here do you most relate, and why?

Rather as I said above, I relate to all the characters. Even the bad ones. They all came out of my head, after all. Perhaps the one I feel the most for is Dexter, in the asylum, I think because he seems so lacking in hope.

Can you offer any clues about the long numerical pattern on the past page of the book?
I can indeed. The best advice I have is to read this: http://marcussedgwick.blogspot.co.uk/2015/04/the-ghosts-of -heaven-numbers.html.

When you finish a book, who reads it first?
My editor. It's her opinion that matters the most.

Are you a morning person or a night owl?
More morning. That's when I write. Afternoons are for naps. Evenings are for fun.

What's your idea of the best meal ever?
That's hard. But any meal with a decent red wine is okay with me.

Which do you like better: cats or dogs?
Dogs. Sadly, I'm away too much to make it practical to have one.

What do you value most in your friends?
Kindness, trustworthiness, humor.

Where do you go for peace and quiet?
Home. I live in a tiny village, and it's always wonderful to get back to my little cottage and hide.

What makes you laugh out loud?
My daughter's bad jokes.

What's your favorite song?
That's too hard! I could do a top one hundred. Or maybe a top two hundred . . . I love all sorts of different types of music and always have music playing when I work.

Who is your favorite fictional character?
Mr. Flay from Mervyn Peake's Gormenghast trilogy.

What are you most afraid of?
Not wanting to write anymore.

What time of year do you like best?
Autumn. No, summer. No wait, spring. No . . . I've got it now!
Winter! Which is my way of saying I love all the seasons, and I
like that I live in a part of the world where you get to see all four.
I love cold countries though, and snow, so if I had to pick one . . .

What do you want readers to remember about your books?
The titles would be a good start! And after that, if they remembered what it felt like to read them, that would be good too.

What would you do if you ever stopped writing?
Be sad, bereft, beleaguered. And I'd try to make music instead.

KEEP READING FOR AN EXCERPT OF *SAINT DEATH*,
a propulsive, unsparing novel from Marcus Sedgwick
about the violent world of the human and
drug trade on the US-Mexico border.

SAINT
DEATH

ANAPRA

IT DOESN'T LOOK LIKE THE MOST DANGEROUS PLACE on Earth. It looks like somewhere half-made; it looks like an aborted thought. It looks like a three-year-old god threw together some cardboard boxes and empty coffee tins and Coke bottles in the sandpit of the Chihuahuan Desert, and then forgot it. Left it to its own vices. The god was forgetful and has not returned to care for his creation, but other gods, pitiless ones, are approaching even now, in a speeding pickup truck.

There's no more than a hurried moment to look around this careworn land. A dozen of the roads are paved, cracked concrete and full of holes; the rest are just rutted strips of dirt. Most of the houses aren't houses at all, but jacales—shacks made of packing crates and sheets of corrugated iron, of cardboard and of crap, with roofs of plastic sheeting or tar paper held down with old car tires. The best have cinder-block walls. The worst take more effort to imagine than is comfortable. Few have running water. One or two have stolen electricity using hookups from the power lines, a dangerous trick in a world made of sunbaked cardboard and wood.

The jacales are things that might, some distant day, be the ghostly ancestors of actual houses. When those houses are finally built, they will be built on lines of hope—the grid that's already been optimistically scratched out far into the desert in the belief that this place can become a thriving community. Already, there are attempts to make this a normal kind of place: whitewashed cinder-block houses with green tin roofs, the Pemex gas station, a primary school, a secondary school. There's even the new hospital, up the hill. The Del Rio store on the corner of Raya and Rancho Anapra, the main drag through the town. But these are exceptions, and all this, all of this, is founded on a belief that needs to ignore what is rapidly approaching in the truck.

This is the Colonia de Anapra, a little less than a shantytown, trying hard to be a little bit more than a slum, poorest of all the poor colonias of Juárez. And Juárez? Juárez is the beast, the fulminating feast of violence and of the vastly unequal wielding of power, where the only true currencies are drugs, guns, and violence. Juárez is a new monster in an old land: Juárez is the laboratory of our future.

Juárez, from where the pickup truck approaches at pace, lies down the hill. Anapra is just a small feeder fish, clinging to the belly of the whale, and while it doesn't look like the most dangerous place on Earth, it is here as much as anywhere else where drugs are run and bodies are hanged from telephone poles, where dogs bark at the sound of guns in the cold desert darkness, where people vanish in the night. And the nights are long. It's the end of October; the sun sets at six o'clock and will not rise again till seven the next morning. Thirteen hours of darkness in which all manner of evil can bloom, flowers that need no sun.

* * *

The night is yet to come.

It's still warm. The truck cannot yet be heard, and on the corner of Rancho Anapra and Tiburón, where the paving stops and the road runs off toward the north as dirt, kids are playing in the street. Here, far from the ocean, where water is so precious, nearly all the streets have the names of fish. On Tiburón, the shark, a little girl and her friends watch her big brother wheeling his bike around in circles by the hardware store, showing off. Another group hangs out by the twenty-four-hour automated water kiosk, hoping to beg a few pesos to buy some bottles. A gaggle of parents coming back from a workshop at Las Hormigas passes by, talking about what it means to be better mothers, better fathers.

Then there's Arturo. Almost invisible, he steers his way steadily along Rancho Anapra. He glances at the kids. So serious. So seriously they play, that as Arturo weaves among them, they have no idea he's even there. There's a smile inside him, a smile for their seriousness, and on another day he might have joked with them a little and made them laugh, but he's too tired for that today, way too tired. Some days he helps out in an auto shop, and this is one of those days. He's been lugging old tires around the yard all afternoon and his shoulders ache from the effort of that while his brain aches from the effort of listening to José, the owner, complaining.

Cars come and go down the road. A bus stops and a load of maquiladora workers climb out and stand around for a while, chatting. A patrol car crawls by, a rare enough sight in Anapra. The factory workers see the car and begin to disperse into the streets of fish, but they needn't worry; the cops are just thirsty.

One of the cops gets out and wanders over to the water shop. He buys a couple of bottles and heads back to the car, ruffling the hair of one of the boys. He doesn't give them any money. Handing one of the bottles to his colleague through the car window, he pulls the cap off his own. Then, as he tilts his head back to drink, the sound of the pickup comes down the street.

Trucks come and go all the time, but the people know what this is. It's moving fast; it has the growl of a powerful engine. It bowls into sight over the crest of the road and moves rapidly toward them. The people scatter. It might be nothing, but better to be sure. The truck gets closer: a flashy dark-red body, tinted windows. Two guys in the cab, another four clinging on in the bed.

As if trying not to disturb the air, the cop carefully gets back in his patrol car and nods to his colleague, just as the truck reaches them, slowing right up, dropping to a crawl as it passes. The six men all stare at the cops, who make very, very sure that they do not look back.

Everyone else has disappeared. The workers, the kids.

Arturo, too, looks for somewhere to vanish, and quickly backs into the shade of the doorway of a green house on the corner opposite—an unusual house, one of the very few with more than one floor. The four men climb down from the flatbed and, pulling out pistols, head into the hardware store. The policemen start their car and drive steadily away, back toward the city.

Arturo doesn't feel that frightened; this is, God knows, not something new, but suddenly he feels very visible. He makes himself small in the doorway, as small as he can, and stands very still.

The four men are dragging the owner of the shop into the street. The man is called Gabriel. Arturo doesn't really know him, nothing much beyond his name. The men are roughing him up, nothing too serious, but then, as Gabriel tries to fight back, one of them hits him on the back of his head with the heel of his pistol and he slumps to the dust, barely conscious. Arturo can see the blood even from across the street.

The men haul Gabriel into the bed of the pickup and climb back in, two of them clinging to the sides and two of them lounging in an old sofa that's been bolted to the floor. The truck makes a turn across the median, heading back to Juárez, and Arturo starts to relax, but as it passes him, the driver of the truck looks over and sees him. Their eyes meet. Their eyes meet, and as they do, Arturo feels something jolt, as if the world has shuddered underneath his feet.

The man's face is tattooed, more ink than skin, markings of a narco gang, but at this range it's hard to see which. His head is shaven; he's dressed, as are all the men, in a white T-shirt; tattoos snake all down the muscles of both arms. In slow time, the driver straightens his left arm out of the cab window and points at Arturo. He makes a pistol with his thumb and forefinger, cocking his thumb back, pointing the gun right at Arturo, who cannot look away as the man drops his thumb and mouths something, something Arturo cannot grasp.

The man's head tilts back, his mouth open as he laughs. He drops his foot to the floor, and the truck speeds away, back toward the city. The cops are long gone, and anyway, it's not the police these men are scared of; they're scared of the other pandillas, the other gangs, like the M-33, the gang whose turf this is, for now at least.

* * *

They're gone. They're gone, the tattooed narco is gone, but Arturo can still feel that finger pointing at him, right at his face, as if the fingertip is pressing into his forehead. It's so strong a feeling that Arturo reaches up and tries to rub it away.

* * *

Above him, unseen, something hovers. It is something with immense power. Pure bone, and charcoal eye. Ephemeral yet eternal: the White Girl. The Beautiful Sister. The Bony Lady. Santísima Muerte. Her shroud ripples in the breeze, white wings of death. She holds a set of scales in one hand; in the other, she holds the whole world. Her skull-gaze grinning, her stare unflinching. She looks down at Arturo; she looks down at everyone.

As the truck disappears from view, Gabriel's wife, whose name Arturo does not know, emerges into the street, screaming, her kids clinging to her legs, crying without really knowing why.

"Hijos de la chingada!"

She screams it over and over.

"Hijos de la chingada!"

It isn't clear if she means the men who have taken her husband, or herself, her family. One or two people emerge from hiding and rush to give her comfort when there is no comfort to be had.

Far, far away, on the other side of the street, Arturo looks down and sees what he has been standing on.

Here, outside the green house, is something strange—a stretch of concrete sidewalk, where everywhere else the sidewalks are dirt. There are marks on the concrete, marks of chalk. They are lines and curves; there are arrows, and small crosses and circles within the curving lines. One device, a pair of interlocking curving arrows, is intersected by seven more arrows that point into the house. So now Arturo realizes where he is, which doorway he has backed into.

Cautiously, he backs away, and looks up at Santa Muerte herself, Saint Death. La Flaquita, the Skinny Lady. She's printed on a plastic banner that's pinned to the wall of the house, right above the doorway. The plastic has been in the full sun for years now; her blacks have become grays, the green globe of the Earth is weakened and weary. Above her, in a semicircle, it's still just possible to make out some writing on the fading plastic: *no temas a donde vayas; que haz de morir donde debes.*

Don't worry where you're going; you will die where you have to.

CHILLING BRILLIANT
re   ISITE

DATE DUE

PRINTED IN U.S.A.

978-1-250-01029-2   978-1-59643-801-9

fiercereads.com